"I laughed and cried fr⟨
start reading, you don't stop.
Jerusalem Post
"...combines the whimsical enchantment of
Amelie with the boisterous, boundless joy of *Mad
Rabbi Jacob."*
Michael Heuser, Producer

Alternately hilarious and heart-rending, "Rabbi
Have I Got a Girl for You!" follows the earnest - if
occasionally misguided - exploits of young Rabbi Ben
Zelig as he valiantly tries to balance the often
bewildering and sometimes tragic demands of his
calling.

Real, surreal and super real, each of the six
stories takes a unique stylistic twist. One of the most
riveting episodes centers on the Rabbi's desperate
search to recapture his lost faith. His Walpurgisnacht
quest leads him into phantasmagorical situations
where he encounters outrageous Fellini-esque
characters who lead him on a bizarre adventure that
starts in the ivory tower of The Rabbinical Academy,
winds its way through Harlem strip clubs and ends in
the Garden of Eden

The author obviously has particular affection
for the clergy and in this book he brings the reader
into the inner lives of these dedicated souls, who guide
and sustain us during our most tragic hours - as well
as our happiest and most triumphant - but whom we
know so little about. Their days - and nights - are
spent with saints and sinners, the gracious and the
rude, the sick and the sickening, the good, the bad,
the ugly - and the beautiful.

These are their stories.

Book orders: <u>call toll free</u> 1(800) 247-6553

The Author's Sources

Where do these stories come from? They are the fruit of seeds planted by inspiring teachers and nurtured by supportive colleagues.

Far more people deserve to be mentioned than space allows, but several of these illustrious souls must be recalled. Professor Shalom Spiegel made the wailing voice of Jeremiah ring in my ears. Together, we wept for the suffering our people brought upon themselves through their arrogance and greed. Dr. Abraham Joshua Heschel ignited my inner fire with exuberant joy that enabled my soul to transcend doubt and cleave to the Enduring Spirit. Professor Hillel Bavli, poet and scholar, taught me to sing the songs of Zion. Colleagues: Drs. Yochanan Muffs, Shalom Paul and David Segal, whose passion and contagious enthusiasm breathe life into history. Rabbi Jerry Cutler, whose every waking hour is dedicated to easing the burdens of the afflicted and comforting the broken-hearted.

Whether or not the events in this book actually took place, the stories are all undeniably true.

H.F.

First printing: Fidlar Doubleday, 2005

ISBN: 0-976-04372-9

PCN: pfx44035

Cover design: Marion S. Freed   ©copyright, 2004

ATTENTION: GIFT SHOPS, SYNAGOGUES CHURCHES, WHOLESALERS, UNIVERSITIES, COLLEGES, CATALOGUES AND PROFESSIONAL ORGANIZATIONS: Quantity discounts are available on bulk purchases of this book for educational, gift purposes, or as premiums for increasing magazine subscriptions or renewals. Special books or book excerpts can also be created to fit specific needs.

For bulk orders, email us at order@bookmasters.com

Movies written and directed by Herb Freed

A.W.O.L.

Beyond Evil

Child2Man

Graduation Day

Haunts

Paradise Lost

Subterfuge

Tomboy

Valor

For Marion

Sine qua non

Rabbi, Have I Got a Girl for You!

By
Herb Freed

Stories

*A loose, reader-friendly translation of
Yiddish words and phrases, listed alphabetically*

The Fatal Flaw

The Fatal Flaw

I met Seymour Katz at Beth Olam Cemetery when he stuck a twenty dollar bill in my hand and told me to buy a hat. It was the end of my junior year at the American Rabbinical Academy and I had just performed my first funeral, badly.

The faculty had recently instituted an intern program as a way to introduce their young scholars to the largely unscholarly congregations of North America. Students in their junior and senior years were encouraged to perform funerals, Bar Mitzvahs, and other life cycle functions in communities where a Rabbi wasn't available. Sometimes the requests came from hospitals, funeral homes or prisons, but more often simply from Jews who weren't affiliated with a Synagogue. The Rabbis-to-be could interface with their future *baale-batim* and everybody would be better prepared for the culture clashes that were sure to come. I looked forward to participating in the program because I really believed I needed more input from the world outside the Rabbinical Academy. For the past seven years I enjoyed a course of study that was a thrilling blend of intellectual discovery and spiritual awakening. On the other hand, when I listened to Leonard Cohen sing *"...they were a'drinkin' and a'dancin' and the place was really happenin' and the Johnny Walker wisdom's runnin' high..."* I knew what I was lacking: A heavy dose of Johnny Walker wisdom. My personal life had become painfully insulated.

2

When the call came from the dean's office on a Friday morning telling me I had been assigned a funeral in the Bronx the following Sunday, I welcomed the challenge. I had never performed a funeral so I went to the library and made a thorough study of the laws dealing with burial, mourning, condolence for the bereaved, etc. On Saturday evening, I took three subways to visit the family of the deceased on the Grand Concourse. The Zimmelmans were warm and friendly, particularly one of the grand-daughters when she discovered that I was single. Unfortunately for me, she was seriously lacking in personality and charm *and* she was at least a hundred pounds overweight. She was not at all the girl of my dreams and I managed to move away. Call it shallow, call it hormonal, but the fact is that underneath the *yarmulka* and *tallit*, my restive sexuality raged and I wanted desperately to be in the company of smart-looking exuberant women, having more fun than I was having in my classes.

"You want stories about Irwin Zimmelman, Rabbi? I got tons of 'em." Harold somebody-or-other was the most forthcoming of the large extended family.

"He was written up in books. Everybody knew Irwin Zimmelman. Great man, great man." Heads nodded as Harold praised the deceased. "May he rest in peace," he said.

The entire crowd mumbled "...rest in peace...*omeyn*...poo-poo...*nisht du ge-dacht...le-hav-dil...*"

There must have been forty people crowded into the small living room with plastic covered mohair chairs, an oversized couch and folding chairs lining all the walls. There were brothers, sisters-in-law and an endless number of children, grand-children and cousins, all of whom were introduced to me by name, profession or business and relationship to the deceased. They told me where they lived, whose grandfather, mother or distant relative never ate a piece of *traif* and never missed a fast on Yom Kippur, and whose great-uncle was a famous Rabbi, "someplace-I-can't-remember-where." I think they were disappointed that I wasn't more enthusiastic about these revelations.

"I'm sorry I never met Irwin," I said. "I'd appreciate it if you could tell me about him."

They all had the most glowing things to say about Irwin Zimmelman, but Harold made sure his would be referred to in the eulogy. "A saint, that's what he was. The man was a saint, and you can quote me on that," he said, pointing to the yellow pad on my lap. I took voluminous notes as they talked. This was my first experience preparing a eulogy so I didn't know what might be important and what to leave out so I wrote down everything they said.

"Did I understand you to say that he was mentioned in some book?" I asked Harold.

"Some book? All over, I'm telling you! The man was written up in tons of books." Harold shrugged. "I can't think of the names off hand, but look it up, you'll find Irwin everywhere." He thought for a moment. "I wish I could remember. It's hard when you get old."

"...Okay," I said, not wanting to put Harold on the spot. "Can anybody tell me something *specific* about Irwin?"

4

Silence...then, "he saved rubber bands," one of his grandchildren remembered.

"And don't forget the plastic bags from the supermarket," the boy's mother reminded him. "He always kept a huge stack of them under the sink."

"Why did he do that?" I asked.

"For the garbage," another daughter replied. "He always wrapped his garbage in neat little plastic bags tied with rubber bands, so the rats wouldn't make a mess when they put out the big cans on Wednesdays for the sanitation department pickups."

I looked at my yellow pad. Why am I writing this stuff down? How the hell do I build a eulogy around rubber bands and garbage? Was that why he was "written up in tons of books"? I looked around at the well-meaning relatives. "Anything else...beside the rubber bands and the garbage?"

"Uncle Irwin never let anyone near the dishwasher," the seriously overweight granddaughter finally made a contribution.

Her mother was delighted. There was only one way to load a dishwasher, he always said..."

"The right way and the wrong way," several of the grandchildren chimed in unison.

Then the discussion shifted to how hard it is to find a place to park ever since the Bronx Council introduced new alternate side of the street restrictions. "They'll cite you for a little nothing because the damn cops got quotas they got to fill. I'm telling you..." and Irwin was all but forgotten during the venting about corruption in city politics.

That was followed by a brief silence. Then, came the jokes. "Did you hear the one about..."

Next morning. Beth Olam Funeral Parlor:

A plain wood coffin sat on a gurney on the raised platform bedecked with drapes and flowers. I sat on the high back chair next to the lectern. When the small crowd settled down, I rose to speak. I barely began to chant the twenty-third psalm when an old man with wild white hair entered the room through the glass doors at the far end, screaming.

"Oh, my God, my kid brother Solly is dead. Good natured Solly, sweet poor boy. Why, God? Why?"

A man in his seventies stood up in the front row. "Dave. I'm your brother Solly. I'm not dead. I'm fine."

Dave looked at him. "Oh thank God you're alive, Solly. I felt so terrible. Wait a minute. Then, who died?"

"Irwin."

"Oh God, no! My handsome brother Irving is dead. Why God, why?"

Another man in his seventies stood up next to Solly. "Hey Dave, I'm your brother Irving. I'm alive, see? I'm not handsome anymore but otherwise, I'm fine."

Dave looked puzzled. "Then, who died?"

"Our brother-in-law *Irwin*, Sarah's husband. He's the one who died."

"Irwin? That's all? Oh, thank God."

It went downhill from there.

I was following The Rabbi's Manual faithfully but when I looked up and saw that no one was paying attention, I decided to liven up the service. I remembered a story I had heard the previous night about how Irwin Zimmelman was the first Jew to move into a Gentile section of the Bronx. That was a courageous thing to do in the Forties and it paved the way for integration.

"There have always been pioneers among us," I said. I spoke of the *Halutzim*, the first wave of settlers from Europe who went to Palestine in the early years of the twentieth century. "They faced hostile enemies on all sides, but they fearlessly cleared the malaria-infested swamps to prepare a homeland for their brethren from the far corners of the earth." From there, I spoke of the Biblical patriarch, Abraham, who left the comforts of Mesopotamia to endure the hardships of the desert so that he could fulfill the covenant with God to create an eternal homeland for the Jewish people in the land of Canaan. I wasn't sure how far to take the analogy, so I cut it short and went straight to Irwin Zimmelman, "who displayed the pioneer spirit required to be the first Jew to settle in the upper Grand Concourse section of the Bronx."

"Where did you hear that crap?" A man, who couldn't be more than four feet tall, wearing a red flannel shirt under his green plaid sport jacket, stood up and screeched in a high pitched voice. "I was the first one to move up there with the *Goyim.*"

"Be quiet Izzy." Solly and Irving stood up and glared at Izzy, who sat down but continued to talk, only low enough so that we couldn't hear

7

what he was saying but loud enough to know he was still bitching.

"Go ahead, finish up, Rabbi," was Solly's way of apologizing for the interruption.

I had just begun to recite the *Kaddish* when a young girl of around nine or ten came to the podium and handed me a note from the family. I took it and read aloud.

"Solly's cousin Milton is 111." On my own, I added "Congratulations, Milton, on your one hundred and eleventh Birthday."

There was an awful commotion. Then, Solly stood up and waved both hands.

"Rabbi, Milton isn't one hundred and eleven. My note said my cousin Milton is ill. For two weeks now he's got laryngitis. You read the note wrong."

"Why did you interrupt me in the middle of the *Kaddish*?"

"My sister Pearl says to me, as long as we're all here, for the same money, why not throw in a prayer for Milton also?"

"The *Kaddish* is recited to honor the dead," I said. "If you go to any Synagogue on the Sabbath, I'm sure they'll be happy to recite a prayer for Milton."

I don't know how I got into an argument with Solly, a mourner I had briefly met the night before, in front of a casket, but we were into it and I didn't see any way out. Solly, on the other hand, seemed to enjoy the spotlight.

"Everybody's here now. Who knows what will be with Milton? Maybe he'll develop cancer of the throat."

A woman next to him let out a shriek.

"I'm not saying he's going to die. All I'm saying is why not make the most of the occasion? Irwin is already dead, so nothing will help him anymore, but Milton might get better tomorrow if we can stick in the right prayer, no? What can it hurt?"

I didn't know how to counter Solly's argument, so I ignored it and completed the service by quietly chanting the closing prayers, without any mention of names, neither the dead, nor the sick.

After the burial, I looked for the quickest way to the subway. I had made a mess of things and I felt like a terrible failure.

"Hey, Rabbi! Wait up," someone called to me as I walked down the narrow paved road towards the cemetery exit. A very large man wearing a black suit, black shirt, white tie and black snap-brim fedora with a red feather approached me.

"Hayadoin', Rabbi. My name is Seymour Katz," he shook my hand vigorously. "I've known the Zimmelmans for years."

Who the hell cares was what I wanted to say but I didn't dare. Instead, I said what I thought Rabbis were supposed to say. "How interesting."

"Yeah it is. Irwin was a client of mine. We done business for years."

I ran out of things Rabbis are supposed to say so I just looked at this very large, unattractive man and waited for him to stop engaging me. He didn't.

"I'll tell you something, Rabbi, you did a hell of a job considering you didn't know anybody and you're obviously still green around the edges."

Rabbis are definitely not supposed to tell *nudniks* to go to hell but I was getting ready to make an exception.

"Listen," gargantua continued. "I wonder if you would do me a favor. My mother is buried on the next hill. Maybe you could say a few words over her?"

"You mean, an *el maleh rachmim* prayer?"

"Yeah. Whatever."

A *mitzvah* is a *mitzvah* and even a *nudnik* can't be denied a prayer. We walked over several hills and Seymour stopped at a large tombstone.

"This is her" he said to me, out of breath after the climb, then kissed the headstone.

I opened my Rabbi's Manual and began to chant the traditional *El Moleh Rachim*. I stopped at the part that called for the name of the deceased.

"Her name?" I asked.

"Theda Katzenelenson," he said, "like it says on the tombstone." He shook his head as if to say: "Can't you read?"

"What's her *Hebrew* Name?" The stone bore only the English inscription.

"Her maiden name was Kugel. She's been dead for over for twenty years."

"Not her maiden name. What was her Hebrew name?"

"Theda, like the silent screen star, Theda Bara. Ah, you probably don't even know who she was. You're kind of young to be a Rabbi, aincha?"

He opened a persistent wound and I just couldn't retaliate. I was wearing my Homburg precisely because I was sensitive to jibes about my youth but it obviously didn't deflect this one. I can't tell you how many people made comments about my age during the past two years when I performed High Holiday services in Oil City, Pennsylvania and Starkweather, North Dakota and it always made me feel defensive, as though I were not ready for the prime time Rabbinate. That was what prompted me to buy the dull gray hat. I thought it might make me look older. It didn't. At first, I tried to counter comments about my age with jokes like "Old Rabbis got to start someplace," but nobody ever thought that was funny.

Right now I was just too worn out to defend myself for being younger than older Rabbis. I was determined to finish this day and go back to my apartment and watch a ball game on TV. It was obvious Seymour had no idea what his mother's Hebrew name was so I inserted the name Thea, which means resurrection in Hebrew. For her father's name, which he also didn't know, I skipped a few millennia and addressed her as the daughter of Abraham, our Patriarch. Seymour Katz stood silently, head bowed and hands behind his back. As I approached the end of the prayer, I told him it was customary to make a charitable contribution in the name of the deceased.

"Don't worry about it," he winked.

I completed the prayer, said Amen and closed my Manual. He thanked me and shook my hand. I started to say "it's nice to meet..." but stopped when I felt something crumbly in my hand. He had slipped a twenty-dollar bill into my palm.

"This is not what I meant by charity." I felt belittled.

"Buy   a   hat,"   he   winked   again.

I couldn't restrain myself. Everything I did today was wrong and I hated feeling like a total loser. Now this stranger was making me feel like a *shnorer*.

"I have a hat!" I felt foolish enough wearing this stupid Homburg and the last thing I needed just then was his snide disapproval. "Where do you get off telling me what to wear? You asked me to do you a favor, which I'm happy to do, and you repay me by insulting me? I can't take money for offering a prayer."

"Who's insulting? You never heard the expression, buy a hat? It's a New York thing. Where did you grow up, out west?"

"Ohio."

"Figures. Buy a hat is what you say when you want to give a guy a double sawbuck. You must have slang out in Oklahoma, right? I'm giving you a friendly touch, Rabbi. No reason to get all huffy."

"Take the money back," I glowered. "I'm not huffy, but I'll get angry as hell if you don't take it."

What kind of sellout did he think I was?

Seymour took the money and shrugged as if to say, "what a jerk."

I felt like a jerk.

"So where's your congregation?"

"I don't have one. I'm still a student. I don't graduate until next year. Do you know how I can get the subway to Broadway and a Hundred and Sixteenth?"

"Sure, come with me. I'm going as far as Fifty-Seventh Street. Follow the signs from there."

We were on the Lexington Avenue line heading into Manhattan for about twenty minutes before we said anything to one another. It's so loud on the trains that you really have to want to communicate to speak loudly enough to be heard and I had nothing to say.

Seymour Katz did.

"How old did you say you were?"

"What is this obsession with my age?"

"Why are you so defensive? I'm being friendly. So, are you single?"

"Yes."

"Why is that?"

"Because I'm not married."

"Are you interested in getting married?"

"Are you proposing?"

Seymour laughed. "For a Rabbi, you've got a hell of a sense of humor." After slapping his thigh a few times, he sized me up again. "The reason I'm asking is, I know a young girl, the daughter of a close friend of mine. She is absolutely gorgeous, smart, a college graduate and not just any college, but one of those fancy schools around Boston."

I said nothing, which he took as a sign that I was interested.

"Now here's the beauty part. Her father is a banker, money up the kazoo."

"Who do you want to fix me up with, the girl or her father?"

Seymour laughed out loud again. "I swear to God, for a hick, you got a real funny bone. So, you're interested or not?"

What could I say? If a friend offered to fix me up, I would ask a question or two and call the girl. But a guy I just met at a cemetery, who I already don't like? Jews always feel they have a right to dump girls no one wants to date on naive young Rabbis. I've already had to dodge a few, and I'm not even ordained yet. A smirk formed on my face but I couldn't think of a graceful way out.

"What are you thinking so hard? Like I asked you to smell a chicken to see if it's kosher, like my mother used to take to *her* Rabbi? This girl I'm talking about is stunning. She dresses classy and she's funny. You got something against beautiful young girls?"

"So what's wrong with her? Does she limp a little but you don't notice it when she sits?" I said, referring to the old joke.

"What limp? The girl's a dancer, studied with Martha Graham for years...performed with the chorus at the Met when she was twelve. Limp? Hell, a pair of gams she's got on her, you don't see everyday. If you want to know what the problem is, I'll tell you plain out. She don't know many Jewish boys and her father doesn't want her going out with *Goyim*, so everybody's unhappy. Why am I talking to you? Because you're a nice Jewish boy, plus I owe you one. So if it should happen to click, I'm doin' my friends a favor and you, since you won't accept my double sawbuck, I'm giving an opportunity to go out on a date with one of the sweetest young things you will ever meet. I figure that will even the score between us. Is that so terrible?"

"So...what's her fatal flaw?"

Now Seymour was offended. "I'm talking a perfect girl here. What are you looking for flaws?"

14

"Look, Mr. Katz..."

"Seymour."

"Seymour, I'm not *looking* for flaws, but every time somebody talks to me about 'a perfect girl' it always ends up being somebody with a whole series of flaws, at least one of which is fatal."

He smiled. "Not this one. I swear on the prayer you recited over my dead mother, rest her soul. This girl is closer to perfect than anybody you'll ever find if you live to be a hundred. Look, the worst that can happen is you call her up, take her to a movie or better yet, go dancing. She loves to dance. Oh, I guess being a Rabbi and all, you don't know much about dancing, but maybe she can teach you."

"Of course I dance. I've danced all my life. Most Rabbis I know dance." No matter what course the conversation took, this guy found a way to insult me.

"Oh, yeah? I didn't know that."

I wanted to tell him he didn't know shit, but I knew that wouldn't be appropriate.

"So, you gonna call her or what?"

"Who is this flawless girl, a relative of yours?"

"Her name is Cynthia and no, we're not related. She's my boss's daughter and I've known her most of her life. Come on Rabbi, you're not married. I never heard of a queer Rabbi, so what's the problem? Are you engaged?"

"No."

"A steady girl?"

I said nothing, but he knew I didn't have that either. He took out a small pad, wrote down a name and a number and gave it to me. I took it absent-mindedly and stuffed it into my jacket pocket.

"What's your number?" He held his pen at the ready.

"247-6000." I didn't know how not to give it to him.

"What's that, an office?"

"It's the switchboard in my apartment house. They'll ring me."

"Who do I ask for?"

"Ben Zelig...uh, Rabbi Ben Zelig." This guy doesn't even know my name and I'm going to let him fix me up?

As I left the train on the 116th Street station, I tossed the note he gave me into a trash bin.

The more I thought about Seymour Katz the more I steamed. The arrogance, the effrontery. There was nothing about him I liked. He was crass and uneducated. How could he possibly know the kind of girl I would want to meet? Over the next few days, my irritation increased, more with myself for not responding aggressively to this jerk, but as "The Rabbi" I had no idea how I was supposed to act when someone pisses me off. I compiled a list of barbed retorts to nail him the next time he called, but after two weeks passed and I didn't hear from him, my annoyance disappeared and in a perverse way, I actually missed Seymour.

A month later, I was in my room working on a class paper on the rites of Passage and the major life changes that accompany them. Now that I was approaching my senior year, this was obviously a subject that lay heavily on my mind. *One more year!* And then...*Rabbi* Ben Zelig? That's an awesome challenge, but I had been well trained at the Academy and with another year of practical experience in the intern program, I believed I would be up to the task. But I did have some serious reservations. One thing that troubled me was the perception of many people that a Rabbi should be aloof and just a little ethereal. I had already experienced some of that, and the thought of pretending to be an effete cherub was totally contrary to my nature. I had immersed myself in my studies in order to expand and grow intellectually and spiritually, not because I wanted to be thought of as an elitist. It's true that I had some lofty interests but I had plenty of baser ones too. How receptive would my congregants be to my attempts at integrating them? How would they like it if they knew their Rabbi regularly engages in – make that, pursues - pre-marital sex? Could they accept the fact that their Rabbi was turned on by Leonard Cohen's music? What would they think of his lyrics?

"*...the women rip their blouses off and the men, they dance on the polka dots and it's partner found and it's partner lost and it's hell to pay when the fiddler stops...*"

For me, Sex, Torah and Rock and Roll are entirely compatible, but clearly not everyone shares that view. Some months ago I wrote a tongue-in-cheek article for Rolling Stone Magazine on the subject, for which I received both praise and excoriation from several of my professors as well as a few death threats from more fundamentalist circles. I admit the article started out as a bet and I was only half-serious when I began to write it, but by the time it was finished I had convinced myself of the validity of the thesis - although I'm sure I could have presented it better.

Jewish Tradition views life as an excursion through time marked by significant milestones. At these crossroads, old gates close and a variety of new ones open, offering an array of new opportunities and challenges. But, in my article I ask, "how do we know which of the new gates that bid us enter are appropriate for *us* at a particular juncture?" I suggested that a different tune wafts through every gate and the best choice for each of us is to enter the one where the music captivates our souls, cancels all reason and sensibility and makes us want to dance.

The article went on to describe what it's like when the spirit takes over and pushes us far beyond our physical constraints. As when an old Hasidic *Rebbe* who is barely able to walk, suddenly leaps into the air, a heavy Torah in his arms, and dances before his God with the passion of a Pilgrim and the radiance of a saint. I also likened it to the rapturous coming together of pre-ordained lovers who discover their common soul as their bodies intertwine and they dance to cosmic rhythms.

That last part was roundly criticized by fundamentalists of all stripes. A member of the New York Catholic Diocese wrote a scathing critique. He started out by pointing to the fact that I was not yet a Rabbi, but merely a "seminarian" who is obviously having a problem balancing his spiritual yin with his physical yang. "There is nothing pre-ordained about pre-Rabbi Zelig" he wrote. "He would do well to pursue a totally different vocation, more suited to his licentious leanings, before he is licensed to inflict irreparable harm on the religious communities of America."

One of my Professors, from the more Orthodox branch of the Academy faculty, called the article "a farrago of undulating nonsense". On the other hand, not everyone panned me. My mentor, Professor Jacob Rothstein, a world renowned Philosopher and Talmudic scholar and easily the most charismatic man I ever met, called to tell me how happy he was with what I had written.

"Few people are fortunate enough to truly understand how music lifts and guides the spirit. Remember," he said, quoting Tagore, "God respects us when we work, but he loves us when we sing."

The Academy was the perfect gate to enter seven years ago. My life as a student has been a joyous one, but soon that gate will slam shut and I will have to enter a new one. Will I choose wisely? How can I be sure?

The Rabbis say that at critical junctures, God makes a "long distance call" to guide the perplexed.

Where is *my* call? Why isn't my inner phone ringing? If I should receive the call, am I prepared to accept the charges, no matter how steep they are? What if...?

Just then, a street repair crew started to drill outside my window. Before I could close it, the phone rang. I picked it up. It was hard to hear with all the noise from the street, but after a couple of seconds, I got it.

"Haya doin', Rabbi. Betcha thought I forgot about you."

"Who is this?" I asked, knowing full well that it was Seymour Katz, but I needed a moment. There's no doubt he's going to try to dump his friend's daughter on me again. What do I say? Am I still angry? Am I more irritated than I am lonely? Before I could decide, he hit me again.

"Boy, for a Rabbi, you're not the brightest star in the sky. How could you forget so soon? It's me, Seymour. Listen, you remember the girl I told you about?"

"How could I forget 'the perfect girl'? Father's a banker as I recall."

"Also from a long line of famous Jews, did I tell you that? Listen, I told my friend about you. He keeps his daughter pretty much housebound because he doesn't want her going out with just any *shmuck*, but when he heard you were a Rabbi, well almost a Rabbi, he's willing to make an exception. Her name is Cynthia, which you probably forgot since you obviously never got around to calling her. So listen, she has long black hair, an hourglass figure and the face of an angel. She'll pick you up on the South-west corner of 113th Street and West End Avenue in half an hour. Look for a gorgeous girl in a black Corvette."

"Whoa! I can't. I'm busy tonight and how do you know I live on 113th Street and..."

"Half an hour. On the corner. Black corvette...and Rabbi, don't wear that silly hat."

He hung up and I fumed for a moment. I felt violated. How does he know where I live? How dare he...? I thought about the long black hair, the hourglass figure, the face of...an angel? Did that mean round and plump?

I waited on the corner for over an hour. I was getting angrier by the minute for allowing myself to be sucked in again and I was about to go home when a black corvette convertible pulled up.

"You the Rabbi?" A girl's voice called from the driver's seat.

As I approached the car, I couldn't help noticing an incredibly attractive face.

"I'm Ben. Are you Cynthia?" I said cautiously. This had to be a dream. Up close, she was one of the most beautiful girls I had ever seen.

"Get in," a smile lit up her perfect face.

It took me a moment to catch my breath. I stumbled as I climbed into her car. I had never been in a Corvette so I was unprepared for the contortions required by the ultra low frame. She smiled as I clumsily struggled with the slung-back bucket seat. I was eager to know what she thought of me but I didn't dare ask. Was she disappointed?

"For a Rabbi, you're quite a hunk."

I blushed. She laughed, put the car in gear and gunned the motor.

I felt so many things at once, but most of all, I felt incredibly lucky to be with this stunning girl.

"I didn't mean to embarrass you. Sorry if I did, Rabbi."

"I'm not really a Rabbi. Not yet, that is."

"But you will be?"

"Not if it makes me less of a hunk."

She laughed again. "I like your priorities. You okay with the top down?"

"The only way to ride in a Corvette, provided it's a convertible."

Her warm, easy smile at my lame joke made me feel perfectly at home as we drove off.

"When do you become a real Rabbi?"

"I graduate next year, but I haven't decided whether I'm going to continue in the Rabbinate or not."

"What's the alternative?"

"I have no idea."

"Oh, that magic feeling, nowhere to go," she said, as though she were reminding herself.

"Abbey Road! That's one of my favorite lyrics!" It suddenly hit me. "That *magic* feeling - nowhere to go." That was better than anything I wrote in my article. What a smart girl. I'll have to remember to use that in my paper.

Cynthia talked more about Abbey Road, The Beatles, the sixties, music. Everything she said was spontaneous and brilliant! She had a unique take on the evolution of rock and roll and it was mind-blowing to listen to her.

"Am I boring you?" she asked innocently.

"Are you kidding?" I can't get enough of you, I said to myself. I would like to have said it to her, but I didn't have the guts. "Please continue," was the best I could do.

She was driving towards the Village but I didn't care if we actually went anywhere. I just wanted to be with her, look at her and listen to her. What did I ever do to deserve this treasure? What a face! I wouldn't call it angelic, but it was even more attractive. She had perfectly chiseled features and the sweetest smile. Flawless.

"Tell me about you," she turned to me. "How are you dealing with the existential angst?"

"Badly, I'm afraid."

"But if you're not going to be a Rabbi after all that schooling, what are you going to do with your life?"

"I didn't say I was not going into the Rabbinate. I said I don't know."

"You're obviously contemplating some pretty radical changes. That's a scary place to be, not to mention lonely."

This girl tuned into my wavelength like no one else ever had. She said it all. She couldn't have chosen two more appropriate words to sum up my dilemma, "scary and lonely".

"On the other hand," she said, "a *ngst* is a double-edged emotion: Making choices for the rest of your life is a heavy burden, but having the power to make those choices can give you that special exhilaration that only comes with the freedom to choose."

My God, she's quoting Kierkegaard! How many girls have I gone out with who even know who Kierkegaard was?

"Unless..." she was somewhere deep inside her own head. "...unless Kierkegaard lied about the special exhilaration and he only said that to make the burden more bearable."

"I hope that's not true. I'm badly in need of some exhilaration because for the most part I'm stuck between scary and lonely."

"You'll survive," she said sadly. "Everybody does. You're not alone, you know. Most people continue to make major changes throughout their lives. I certainly do."

"Amazing you should say that. Earlier this evening, I was reading a quote from the Talmud that said "change is the central ingredient of God's cosmic plan."

"Darwin wouldn't disagree."

I laughed out loud. It was a free, easy laugh that released more tension than I realized had been building up inside me. This blind date has turned into the most thrilling adventure I could imagine. I had to let her know how she made me feel.

"Is it too early to tell you how great I think you are?"

"Yes." Her tone was so solemn I knew I had better slow down.

We didn't talk for the next few blocks. Finally, I said "It was nice of Mr. Katz to fix us up."

"Who?"

"Seymour Katz?"

"Oh, Uncle See," she laughed.

"He's your uncle?"

"No, just an old friend, but I've known him since I was child. He's worked for my father for years."

"Seymour said your father was a banker."

"I guess you could say that. Dad's a loan shark. Uncle See used to be one of his enforcers."

I was bombarded by new sensations. Could I really get serious about the daughter of a gangster? Ah, so that's the flaw. Who cares? I won't be marrying the father, I reasoned. I was silent for a few minutes, sorting all this out as we drove through the Village.

"Are we going somewhere in particular? I heard you like to dance and I know a place near here I think you'd like."

"Is that so?" She wasn't at all interested in my suggestions but I didn't mind. I was flying on the wings of an angel.

This was a totally new experience for me. Whenever something seemed too good to be true, it always ended up being just that. But where was her fatal flaw? If her only drawback was her father, I could live with that.

She pulled up in front of a gaudily lit smarmy club on Greenwich Avenue called La Cucaracha and looked me over.

"You might want to take off your jacket and tie. This is a pretty casual place."

I took off my jacket and tie and looked for a place to put them.

"Toss them behind the seat," she said.

I didn't know there was an open space behind the tight fitting bucket seats.

"Maybe the shirt, too," she added.

I thought for a moment. Could I be sure I was wearing an undershirt that didn't have holes in it? Not worth the risk, I thought.

"I'm good," I said.

A Puerto Rican kid opened her door. I figured he was either a parking attendant or a thief. Either way, the only thing for me to do was get out. A Corvette isn't the easiest car to climb out of, but I pulled myself up and took a couple of moments to tuck the shirt-tails into my trousers. When I saw Cynthia's dazzling face come around the car, I took her extended hand.

In a shocking moment, the sunshine quickly dimmed. So there is a flaw, a real one. Three fingers were missing from her disfigured left hand. How could I not have noticed it?

"I guess Uncle See didn't tell you about my hand." There was no way for her not to see I was staring.

"Sure he did," I lied. Who was I fooling? "An accident, right?"

"Congenital. I've lived with it all my life so it's no big deal for me, but it is for some people. Look, you can leave now if you're uncomfortable." She pulled her hand away and walked towards the low-life bar.

I caught up with her before she reached the entrance. "Cynthia, I think you're perfect and I'm the luckiest guy in the world to be with you tonight."

She looked at me for a long moment then flashed the sweetest smile and touched my face with her good hand. It felt like velvet.

As soon as I walked through the door I was hit by a wave of brassy salsa music and momentarily blinded by a circling band of colors from a light wheel.

As I followed her through the crowd, I felt immensely satisfied with myself. I had discovered her flaw and it really didn't bother me.

The bar was filled with the dregs of humanity. I had never seen so many unattractive people making themselves more repulsive by sporting weird hairdos, gross tattoos and rhinestone studs sticking out of every visible part of their bodies. As we pushed our way across the dance floor, I tried not to look at the couples alternately leaping and swaying, particularly as

26

girls were humping girls and guys had their legs wrapped around other guys. This was my first experience in what looked like a gay bar and I tried to pretend I was cool.

A richly painted girl on stage had a microphone in her hand and goaded the audience between verses of a song that was as hot as the lyrics were unintelligible.

"Who got the better voice, *maricon*, Celine or Tina?" She taunted a heckler at the bar in a T-Shirt with writing on it that I couldn't read because a big white question mark was painted over it. Cynthia waved to the girl on stage whose accent was so thick, it was hard to tell where it came from. It could be Puerto Rico, Mexico, or a dozen backwater countries where people speak dialects that have no grammar, spelling or any specific pronunciation. She was obviously an entertainer of some kind. I didn't know if she sang or told jokes, but whatever she did she had the crowd in the palm of her hand.

When she saw Cynthia, she blew her a kiss and mouthed something I didn't get. I gather from the catcalls and hecklers that her name was "Magdalena". Her blouse was cut low highlighting her well-shaped breasts. When she sat on the stool in the center of the stage and crossed and uncrossed her shapely legs, the dark at the top of the stairs was definitely on view. As my eyes adjusted to the spinning light and the silent boxing match on the huge TV screen on one of the walls, I saw that the girl on stage was really a beauty.

The noise in this shit-kicker bar seemed to be a surreal extension of the racket outside my window earlier in the evening. Then, the strangest thing began to happen. Out of the din of this cacophonous weirdness, Leonard Cohen's soft clear voice emerged from some dark place in my brain and settled in my soul.

"*...there is a crack, a crack in everything. That's how the light comes in, that's how the light comes in.*"

My insecurity drifted away and I felt myself seeing, hearing, feeling more clearly than I had in years. I was suddenly at ease. Somehow, I was *led* to this place and I knew I was exactly where I should be at this moment.

"Celine, man. No contest." The Puerto Rican heckler of indeterminate age and sex turned to an equally unpleasant African-American boy (?) and they gave each other a high five.

"Tina ain't shit, man," the Puerto Rican kissed his ugly friend on the mouth.

Magdalena got up from her stool and gawked at the two hecklers.

"What is it wit youse two *maricons*? You on your honeymoon, or what? Go out to the parking lot fer chrissakes, or at least, the bathroom."

The music came up full again and the crowd howled as Magdalena began to move to the music with the intense frenzy of a dervish.

I had no idea what kind of test God was putting me to by bringing me to a place like this but I was confident that in time "*...all will be revealed.*"

The bar was steamy, smelly, boisterous and dark except for the brutal flashes of garish lights, but when I allowed myself to really listen to the music, it was intoxicating. Everyone in the bar seemed to be regulars: Blacks, Puerto Ricans and a variety of mongrel ethnicities. Each group might have shied away from contact with one another while they were in prison - their tattoos and hair nets identified their respective gang affiliations – but here they were each other's main men...and bitches.

"Who's the ho?" I didn't know the young man at the bar with a tattoo across his bald head was talking to me until he poked me and asked again. Then, I realized he was a she when she pointed a small finger at Cynthia.

"My wife." I don't know why I said that, but it felt good to hear myself say it.

Baldy turned to another gargoyle with the same tattoo on her shaved head. "*Maricon*", she pointed at me, "brings his wife to a shit hole like this. What an *esse*".

Now Magdalena started to sing again and she was fantastic. I didn't get the Spanish lyrics, but the rest of the bar did and they cheered her on. Her body jerked and swayed to the syncopated rhythm of the trumpets and her chesty voice filled every crevice of this rat infested place. I had never seen such erotic movements. There was a refrain that everyone seemed to know and they all joined in. Cynthia's face glowed as she sang along and I suddenly felt joyous and safe, protected by my deliciously beautiful Divinely sent guide. I found myself joining in and mouthing words that sounded right, at least in my head. When Magdalena finished the song, everyone was on their feet cheering, applauding, whistling and shouting words or parts of words I didn't understand, but apparently they did.

As soon as she finished, Magdalena made her way towards us.

I didn't know what to say. "You're unbelievably talented..." I started to tell her, but she paid no attention to me. The music had picked up again full blast. She smiled conspiratorially at Cynthia, then without a word, they joined arms and started to rock in perfect rhythm, locked in an exotic dance. They spun and twirled, their eyes riveted on one another like gypsies dancing flamenco. Then their bodies slowed and swayed in sensuous, rapturous rhythms. When the music stopped, they looked at each other for a long moment, then, kissed passionately. I was confused and excited. I wanted desperately to enter the erotic bubble that had engulfed the two of them, but I didn't know how.

After the long embrace, Magdalena looked at me "Who's the beard?" she asked.

Cynthia smiled sweetly at me and touched my face tenderly with her mangled hand.

"His name is Ben. He's a Rabbi."

"A Rabbi? No shit!" Magdalena looked slyly at Cynthia. "So that's how you got your old man to let you out." I still couldn't place her accent.

"Ben, this is Madge. They call her Magdalena here."

I didn't know what to say so I repeated "I think you're incredibly talented..." Suddenly, the tone in the bar changed. Everyone was looking at the open door.

An old Hasid with a long white beard, black coat and hat, slowly entered the bar. He became red, then blue, then yellow as he passed beneath the light wheel. The goons at the bar were raucously heckling this gefilte fish out of water.

The old man strained to see through the smoke filled bar, bombarded by flashes of violent lights. Knifelike scratches of salsa music pierced the ears. When he looked at us from afar, I panicked. He must be looking for me. Why else would an old Hasid come into a place like this? Who is he and how does he know me? This must be part of my cosmic test. The Hasid pushed through the gyrating forms on the dance floor. The denizens shoved and teased him. *"Hola esse!* Watch where you're goin...hey, check out this *maricon,* man."

"Which one of you *muthas* forgot to pay the rent?" One of the brothers on the dance floor called out and the crowd around him broke up. Amid the crescendo of catcalls, the bearded man finally reached us.

"I'd like to explain..." I began, but stopped when I saw that he had no interest in me. He stood before Magdalena and stared at her.

"Kum aheim, tay-ere." The man said in Yiddish.

"Go home, Papa." Magdalena said softly. Suddenly, her accent was gone and Magdalena became Madge or possibly Miryam.

"Ich gay nicht mit-on dir. Dine mama challisht avek," the old man said.

"Farshteys du noch nicht? I can't be in the same room with her." Madge tried to keep her voice down, but she was losing control.

"Your mother loves you, *tay-ere.*"

"She hates me, Papa. She's always hated me. I can't live with her another minute."

"So this is where you live now?" The old man looked around at the gaping faces. "With these animals?"

A small tattooed bull-dyke wearing a hair net grabbed the old man's collar. "Who you callin' animals, *maricon?*"

"Back off!" Madge screamed. The bull-dyke backed off immediately and the place became deathly still. The ground had shifted and no one was sure where they were.

Madge kissed Cynthia on the cheek. "I got to go, Cyn."

The old Hasid shifted his eyes to me. Was it because I was the only one without pink and green hair, no tattoos or metal sticking out of my flesh or was it something else?

"Who are you?" he asked softly.

"Ben," I said weakly.

He leaned forward, his intense sad eyes trying to understand. He cupped his ear with one hand. "You don't got a name?"

I don't know how it came out, but the words flowed from within me.

"I am Benjamin, son of Joshua, of the tribe of Levi," I said proudly.

Shocked, he stared at me for a moment. "You're a Jew?" He squinted as he studied my face.

"Yes." Was this an interrogation or an induction?

His look turned contemptuous. "What are you doing in this sewer? Get out of here! Recite Psalms. Go to a *mikveh.* Fast. Repent! I can't believe you are really a Jew."

"As a matter of fact, I'm going to become a Rabbi..."

His mouth dropped. He reached up and touched my head. I was not wearing a *yarmulka.*

His face twisted in anger as he pointed a shaking finger at me.

"No" he shrieked. "You must not do that. If you become a Rabbi, you will delay the coming of the Messiah for another thousand years."

Madge grabbed the old man's arm and led him away. The shocked spectators gave them a wide berth. When they reached the door, Madge turned back and waved to Cynthia. "Call me!"

I was bewildered. Who was this man and why did he say that to me?

Cynthia looked at me tenderly for a long moment. Much as I wanted to, I couldn't let myself engage her eyes. It's not that I *believed* I was personally responsible for delaying the coming of the Messiah - at least I hoped I wasn't – but the words hung in the air and reminded me that my soul was in transit. Cynthia slowly wrapped her arms around me.

It was like being anointed. Magically, in her embrace I felt the sludge that had begun to form around my brain, drain away. Cynthia had the power to lead me on the right path, I was convinced of it. In her arms I heard the music I needed desperately to hear.

We remained locked in that embrace. I needed to kiss her. I tried, but she turned away. I tried again...and again. Finally, she dropped her embrace...and the music died.

On the way home, we didn't say a word. I looked at Cynthia several times, but her eyes were glued to the road. When she stopped at the corner of 113th Street, I opened the door and got out but I couldn't leave. I just stood there next to the car, wanting so much to reach in and touch her, kiss her, tell her...ask her... plead with her to give me a chance. I could deal with anything if she'd just let me be with her.

"Can I call you?" was all I could say.

She looked at me and I saw a tear rolling down her cheek. She brushed it away with the thumb and only finger of her deformed hand.

"I think you'll be a fine Rabbi, Ben, if that's what you want," she said softly.

"What I really want is to see you again."

She sat for a moment and wiped away more tears. She said nothing and in an instant she was gone.

An intense sadness descended on me. A soft rain began to fall. As it increased, I felt I was Adam banished from the garden. I was Moses on the mountain overlooking the Promised Land without any hope of entering it, but most of all, I was Isaac. I had been brought to the sacrificial mount but God wasn't there to receive me.

The downpour became torrential and soon I was drenched. Just then, a truck drove by and hit a deep puddle, splashing muddy water all over me. I wanted to leave...to go somewhere...but where? I stood in the rain, rooted to the spot. My wet clothes felt warm and I was waiting to be born. More cars splashed me and people ran by bumping me with umbrellas, but I couldn't move. I stood there waiting for a sign. It never came. Finally the rain stopped and I began to feel chills through my whole body.

As I entered my apartment, dripping all over the Oriental rug my mother gave me when I entered the Rabbinical Academy, the phone was ringing. I stumbled to the table near my bed to answer it. My hand was shaking as I lifted the receiver. "Hello?"

Silence.

"Cynthia? Is that you?"

A male voice answered. "You wish."

"Who is this?"

"I'm sorry," a deep, resonant voice said. "I must have the wrong number."

"Is this my long distance call? I'm ready! Speak and I will listen."

The voice on the other end laughed and hung up.

I held onto the phone, trembling as I squeezed it, hoping that I might make it say what I wanted to hear. After a moment there was a click and a voice said "Your call cannot be completed at this time. Please hang up and try again later."

"When? In another thousand years?"

Silence. Another click and the recording started again. "Your call cannot..." I dropped the receiver and collapsed onto the bed. Now that the rain had stopped, Con Edison was back on the job and the noise from their pneumatic drills became unbearable. I wanted to close the window but I couldn't get up. My head felt light as air and my body was on fire. The room began to sway and a group of enthusiastic Hasidim appeared out of nowhere. They picked up my bed and carried me out into the street where the ConEd repair crew joined us and we danced down Broadway toward the Village singing, "We're off to the see the Messiah..."

And a Pair of Pants!

"From *all* my teachers have I gained
understanding."

Psalms 119:99

And a Pair of Pants!

A month prior to my Ordination, I broke out in hives. My life was about to undergo cataclysmic changes for which I was hopelessly unprepared. There would be no more casual afternoons visiting galleries or attending matinees. No more looking for girls on protest marches. No more evenings in the Village with kindred spirits, men with odd facial hair configurations and sexy girls in black leotards and matching eye shadow, drinking cheap wine and raging against globalism. Instead, I would be expected to assume the overwhelming burdens and obligations of a practicing Rabbi.

Am I ready to do that? Is that how I want to spend the rest of my life?

My hives began to itch like crazy.

What are my options?

I have no other skills!

Why didn't I acquire any?

Why did I wait so long to make the most critical decision of my life?

Time out!!! Who says I have to become a "professional" anything? I don't need much...I could...what? If I didn't assume a pulpit, what *would* I do? Am I prepared to walk away from eight years of training to ...do...what?

With each day that passed, the pressure mounted until finally, two weeks before Ordination ceremonies were to take place, the *kreplach* hit the fan. Uncle Joe, the only member of my family who was both a millionaire and illiterate, picked me up at the Youngstown airport. We were en route to my mother's house

37

where I would be spending the *Shavuot* holidays, when he mounted an all-out attack.

"What de hell's de mattah wit you Benny, you wanna woik in a shoe store, hold up a bank, maybe? You got yourself a respectable profession and you're aksally tinkin' about trowin' it away? Whatayou, *meshuggah* altogether? Dis ain't Europe. In de old country, a Rabbi didn't have a pot to piss in. It's different in America. Here, a Rabbi can make a damn good livin!"

I winced. I had spent my college and post-graduate years studying with some of the most erudite and saintly men in the world, many of whom were rescued from the camps and ovens of occupied Europe and brought to the Academy to ignite the spark of Jewish commitment. Through them, I discovered my place in a four thousand year old tradition dedicated to expanding the mind, sensitizing the soul and searching for ways to make this a better, more Godly world. The emblem over the entrance to the Academy bore the verse from Exodus. *And the bush was not consumed.* Every time I went through that gate I was filled with a sense of awe and pride.

"Those years at the Academy were dedicated to scholarship and the study of *Torah.* They were not spent acquiring a profession in which I could make 'a damn good livin."

"Eh!" was Uncle Joe's way of dismissing any argument that didn't have a cash equivalent. Then he cut loose. "What some people call a scholah, oddeh people call a *shnorer*, a bum. I don't onastan you, Benny. You supposed to be smart. Your muddah says you know de whole Torah by heart." He thought for minute. "What else is she gonna say, her son is an imbecile?

Please explain me, Mr. smart-feller-who-knows-de whole-Torah-by-heart, what's wrong practicing a profession where you can earn a dollah?"

I countered with a quote from the Talmud. "One should not use the study of God's word to enrich himself." I wrapped a protective shield of important sounding Rabbinic maxims around my arguments, but had I really been smart, I would have known that wouldn't work with Uncle Joe.

"Who's talkin' rich? I'm talkin' payin' your bills so you won't have to live like a dog in de street. Listen Benny, de reason I'm wasting my time talking to you is because I believe you are a smart boy and I hate to see you slide down de toilet. I'll tell you de true. You're a natural. You'll be a big hit as a Rabbi. I know. I heard plenty speakers in my time. Only a few of dem knew how to sell de goods. Most of dem was nuttin wit nuttin, a bunch of bums. Dey put you right to sleep. But you Benny, you!" He pointed at me and winked. "I heard you talk from de pulpit last Chanukah when de Rabbi invited you up. You're a natural born salesman. I never fell asleep on you once."

"I am not a salesman, Uncle Joe. I don't know a thing about selling and I don't want to know." I had gotten used to posturing to deflect arguments that were true but uncomfortable. The truth is, I enjoy preaching. Writing sermons for homiletics classes and delivering them in local Synagogues as part of the intern program was a source of considerable pleasure for me. I have to admit that few things thrilled me more than communicating ideas I felt strongly about to a responsive audience...and discovering that I was actually good at it!

"Let me explain you what it means to be a salesman," Uncle Joe beamed right in on my dilemma. "When somebody wants someting I got in one of my shops and I sell 'em, you tink dat makes me a salesman? NO! Any clerk can sell someting off de shelf. So, what's a salesman? Maybe somebody who sells you someting you don't want? NO! Lots of people can talk a fella into buying de next best ting. You want to know what's a salesman? I'll tell you what's a salesman. Det's de man who can sell you someting you don't want, det he don't even have!"

I didn't get it. How do you sell something you don't have? It sounded more complicated than calculus.

He flashed a triumphant smile. He knew precisely what he was talking about and he enjoyed the fact that someone with my education couldn't follow him.

"I'm not surprised you don't onastan. What I'm talking about isn't in any of your books."

This was a different Uncle Joe from the "ignoronimus" who was scorned by the more educated members of my family. He knew things they didn't and he was about to reveal them to me.

"Why does de man who sells you what you don't want, det he don't have, become a huge success? Because he is selling ideas, not moichendise. He onastans human nature. He knows what a poisun would really *like* to buy and det's what he sells him. He onstans det de *sale* is de ting, not de goods. Once you make de sale, it's no big deal to go out and find an acceptable product to delivah. De best salesman is not de one wit de big store. It's de man wit de big ideas."

Uncle Joe was a philosopher!

"Lookey, here," he went on. "I can't explain you in de Holy tongue what it is to be a good salesman because I neveh had de appatunity to learn much *Ivreh*. A couple of years of *cheder* is all I had, but I know what I know, so let me try to explain you anoder way."

He swept away some dust on his dashboard. Uncle Joe bought new Cadillacs every year but never washed them. He was semi-retired, but the car commanded respect in the squalid ghettos where he collected rent and from the small grocery store owners to whom he delivered the occasional salami in exchange for vegetables, a "nice piece fruit," or good conversation.

"What kind of place you live in at det college, a hotel, a house?"

"I share an apartment in a dilapidated six story walk-up on 111th street and Broadway with three other guys. One goes to Juilliard, that's a music school in the area, and the other two are grad students at Columbia."

"Ha many students dere is in all dem schools around dere?"

"I don't know. Between Union Theological, that's the largest Protestant Seminary in the country, The Rabbinical Academy, Juilliard, Barnard College and of course, Columbia, I would guess around thirty, forty thousand students a year, maybe more."

"Dey all got a place where to stay?"

"Affordable rooms are scarce. My apartment is a dump and I was lucky to find it. A lot of students have to live with relatives or find what they can up in the Bronx or downtown and

41

take the subway to school. I looked around for nearly six months before a place became available."

"Ha many rooms in dis dump where you live at?"

"Four bedrooms, kitchen and a bathroom."

"Rent is ha much?"

"Three hundred dollars a month, we all pay a quarter."

"Ha many apartments in det building?"

I told him.

He thought for a moment, then, made some scratches in the dust on his dashboard.

"Here's what you'll do. You'll buy de building and sub-divide. You'll rent out each one room apartment for twenty-five dollahs a week. Even students can affordeh twenty-five dollahs a week, no?"

I had the sense that I was being pulled down into the moral muck the mystics call the nether world, but I admit it was not without its own particular titillation. Before I ever entertained the idea of studying at the Academy, I was fascinated by stories of how some of my father's friends amassed fortunes after the war. Some developed tracts of one family houses, others built aluminum plants or acquired foreign car dealerships. I often wondered how I would have fared had I devoted my energies to commerce. But that was a long time ago. Now, the idea of spending my life in pursuit of money and "things" was too depressing to think about.

"You're missing the point, Uncle Joe. There is no way..."

"Please sharrup for one minute. I'm trying to teach you someting here, so listen wit your ears for a change and stop making wit de stupid interruptions. You're a smart boy, Benny, so just hear what I got to say. After det, if you got someting woit saying, you can talk. But listen foist, okay?"

"Okay." What else could I say?

"Now, all your tenants share one batroom and one kitchen, so you got no new plumbing expenses."

"Yes, but..."

"Again wit the mouth? I tought you was gonna listen wit the ears foist."

"Okay."

"Boy, it's hard to teach intallekshals tings that ain't in books." He shook his head, then went back to the scratchings in the dust of his dashboard. "So, you'll collect twenty-five dollahs for each room, det's a hundred dollahs a week, det gives you four hundred dollahs a month. Det's a tirty-tree and a tird, nearly tirty-four per cent increase over what de guy makes who owns de building now. Good, no?"

"Good," I said unenthusiastically. I didn't want to be told to "sharrup" and I certainly wasn't eager to be called stupid again.

"Now, you'll raise de rent say, tree, maybe five per cent a year. Dere is five floors wit two apartments on each floor. Det comes to..."

My head was swimming and I had a shooting pain in both temples. I didn't mind entrepreneurial discussions in the abstract, but the idea of renting apartments and painting toilet seats made me feel queasy.

"Where would I get the money to buy a building, even if I wanted to, which I don't?"

43

"Any bank would be happy to loan you money wit an idea like det. You can write your own ticket. You can get a tirty year mortgage wit low interest, I'll betcha."

I suddenly felt sullied. I thought of the evening so many years ago when I walked around the red light district in Amsterdam for hours, embarrassed that I was so attracted to the whores in the windows until I actually entered a stall and engaged one. The experience was thoroughly degrading and I felt I might be repeating it now by sinking into the abyss of borrowing, renovating, renting and selling.

"You think I want to spend the next thirty years of my life paying off a loan for a building I don't want?"

"No, of course not. You nevah pay back a loan. When de bank sees how good you're doin, dey'll give you anoder loan to buy anoder building, maybe two. You'll be making money hend over fist."

When he saw how gloomy all this was making me, he relented.

"Benny, do you onastan why I'm telling you dis? I'm not saying you should go into real estate. I know det's not for you. I'm only trying to explain you det success in life depends not on what you stock in your shop, but what you got in your noggin."

I remembered reading Eric Hoffer, the longshoreman who was a popular philosopher in the fifties. He was a strong socialist, but he couldn't mask his admiration for the genius of American businessmen. He believed they were poets and visionaries. "Everywhere else in the world, a man opens a store and remains there, selling his goods at a modest profit, day after day, for the rest of his life. His American counterpart doesn't open a store, he creates a chain of stores and ultimately goes public, creating wealth for others as well as himself."

"The trick," he goes on to say, "is not to copy other entrepreneurs, but to find that 'something' that you see more clearly than anyone else and can do better. That's not easy and not everyone has the gift, but for the lucky few who do, I say pursue it with all your energy, your talents, both instinctive and acquired, and most important of all, your passion."

Uncle Joe never learned English well enough to read Eric Hoffer, but he understood him perfectly.

"Here's de point I'm tryin' to make," Uncle Joe said as he drove down the center of the street. He never felt safe driving either on the left or the right. "I seen a picture a few years ago," he said, "maybe you seen it too. Some Dutch guy had an idea to paint a picture of an old pair of torn pants and *ba-kakte* wooden shoes. Now everybody sees bums in de street wit *drek* on dere cuffs everyday, but nobody knows what dey're lookin' at until dis one smart Dutchman paints det picture. When you see dem holes in de knees and de crusted cow-shit on de cuffs and de broken down shoes, you suddenly onastan how dis poor son of a bitch lived his whole life. I'm sure he sold it for a pretty penny, believe you me. You, Benny, you're like det painter. It took a lot of years and a lot of study, but you finally learned how to look at the same tings everybody else does, but you see de life lessons in everyday tings det odder people don't. Don't sell yourself short, *boychick*. Det's a real talent. When you pluck an idea out of de air and wrap it up in a good story – and believe me, you know how to tell a story – and along wit it you teach us sweet words from de Torah, you make us see everyting a little different and det fills up de heart. I'll tell you de true, you wasn't always like det. You was one wild animal when you was growin up. I used to tink dis kid got nuttin but *shmutz* in his head. But somehow det Rabbi Academy turned dose coals into diamonds. I see dem shine from you every time you speak in de *shul*. What you got in your noggin is more valuable den all de buildings and all de jewels. De only trouble wit you is you don't onastan how important it is to make a decent dollah. You got dis funny idea det maybe people will respect you more if you don't tink about money and live like a bum, but you got it *pink-farkert* (ass backwards). Dis is America. If you don't earn a decent dollah and live like a *mench*, people won't respect you and dey won't listen to what you have to say. What's woise, dey'll tink our *Torah* is also not woit respecting. Live like a *mench*, Bennie, you desoive it and so do we."

Mench

The image of my father in his last days came soaring back with blinding clarity. My mother and brother had gone out to talk to the surgeon and I remained opposite his bed reading from a small Bible as he slept. His body was ravaged with cancer and tubes ran from every orifice to machines and plastic bags. Suddenly, dad opened his eyes and saw me reading.

"Are you reciting Psalms," he asked softly.

"No dad, why would I do that?"

He smiled bitterly. "Because that's what religious Jews do in the presence of someone who's dying, isn't it?"

"You're not dying. You're going to be fine," I lied. I told him I had been reading the section of Genesis that deals with the sons of Isaac, Jacob and Esau.

"And what do you think about when you read that?" His voice was weak but his eyes locked onto mine.

"I think about Art and me. Art is so handy with mechanical things. He loves to go fishing and skiing and do all the athletic stuff, whereas I prefer to spend my days studying."

Dad smiled. "So you think Art is Esau, the savage brother who would sell his birthright for a bowl of soup."

What I was really thinking was that Isaac loved his firstborn, Esau, more than he did the younger son, even though Jacob was far more deserving and how unfair that was and how I wished to God dad loved me as much as he did my older brother.

Dad continued slowly. "And how do you explain why the saintly Jacob sold his hungry brother a bowl of soup? Why didn't he just give it to him?"

"Because he felt his father had been tricked into giving away the birthright that should have been his."

"Benny, Benny, don't make your brother out to be as bad as Esau. Arthur's not a scholar like you, but he's a fine young man and believe me, he's no savage. And you, my dear son, you have many wonderful qualities, but a saint you're not. But who says you should be? Just be a *mench*. That's not easy, son, but if you succeed, I'll be very proud."

I climbed up the brick steps to the porch of our old house on Prospect Street where I grew up and I thought about my birthright. Uncle Joe came with me to the door and looked on proudly as my mother joyfully embraced me as though I were Elijah the prophet. Without asking, my mother set out Joe's cup of tea on the kitchen table with a crystal container of small sugar cubes and a huge plate of her honey covered, nut *tegelach*, which he devoured in no time flat. For me, she set out a glass of milk as though I were still her little boy and a mound of pastries which Uncle Joe finished.

After he left, I went up to the bedroom I had shared with my brother all the years we were growing up. It felt claustrophobic. I didn't remember the room being so small. The intoxicating smells of mom's holiday cooking permeated the entire house. I could taste the different kinds of *koogles, latkes, blintzes*, the chicken soup, matzo balls, brisket, roast chicken and all the mouth watering desserts as I lay on my old bed, my feet now creeping over the edge of the mattress. I thought about Uncle Joe and how unfairly the relatives treated him. It didn't matter that he was the only millionaire in the family. Because he was uneducated in both Hebrew and English, he was relegated to the status of "ignoronomus". Uncle Ziggy was especially cruel.

"The man can't even *doven* right and he speaks Yiddish with that damned barbaric-sounding *Galiztianer* accent." He insisted that Joe sit in the kitchen with the women at the weekly family get-togethers. The men sat in the living room around Uncle Ziggy, who occupied the big red mohair chair. Ziggy owned The Reliable Clothing Company on East Federal Street. He sold exclusively to the *schvartzes*, but as he proudly boasted, "to the better class of *schvartzes*." It was acknowledged that he was the one responsible for bringing my father, and his five sisters to America. It was never quite clear how he did it and there were rumors that he simply put their names on a list sent to HIAS, the Hebrew Immigrant Aid Society, but he always took exclusive credit for saving the family from the Czar, the Bolsheviks and later, Hitler. Somehow, the family went along and gave Uncle Ziggy the place of honor at all family functions.

When Ziggy died, my father insisted that Uncle Joe join the men in the living room. That was a precious gift and he never forgot it. Each week Uncle Joe brought us long kosher salamis and cartons of Tam-Tams. After my father died, he became especially solicitous of me. After I entered the Academy, he would save a seat for me in the Synagogue on my visits to Youngstown so he could sit next to me.

My thoughts drifted back to my last trip home. After the Saturday morning service, the men who made up the *minyan*, or prayer caucus, assembled for a *kiddush*, at which the Temple provided several bottles of Seagram's Seven and

Four Roses, surrounded by plates of marinated herring and *kichelach*, hard crusted but hollow sugar coated cookies. All the men in the group were old but Old Man Kreutzer was the oldest. No one knew exactly how old he was and when I asked Uncle Joe, he simply said "plenty." He also explained that the secret of Kreutzer's longevity was the ten-ounce glass he brought with him to the Saturday morning *kiddush*, which he filled to the brim with whiskey.

My father had always liked Old man Kreutzer, so I went over to wish him a *guten shabbos*.

He focused his one good eye on me. "Do I know you?"

"Yes, Mr. Kreutzer. I'm Ben Zelig."

He thought for a minute. "Doesn't ring a bell."

"Ben Zelig, Sol Zelig's son. You used to play pinochle with my father in the back of Gus's delicatessen."

"Sol Zelig...Sol Zelig. I don't know any...wait a minute. Little Solly?"

My father wasn't tall, but he towered over Old Man Kreutzer who was somewhere in the four-foot range. Still, the taller men in the community called my dad Little Solly, so it stuck.

"A real *mench*...fine chap," he said, reaching back into his fading memory. "I loved your father. He was...wait a minute, I remember now. He had two sons."

"That's right, Art and me."

"That's right, he had two sons. One of them died...which one are you?"

"My brother Art is the one who died. He was the pilot."

"That's right. One of them died...and the other one was studying for Rabbi," he was navigating through the fog in his brain.

"That would be me."

He looked at me, trying hard to focus his good eye. He looked and looked, then smiled. His face lit up as he touched my arm, then put his hand to my face.

"You're the one with the smiley face. I remember like it was yesterday. Maybe not yesterday, but I remember. Oh yeah, sure. Little Solly. I never seen a man *shep* so much *nachas* from his boys, especially the one who was going for Rabbi. A prouder man, you never saw. You got no idea. You see, when we came to this country, everybody worked like a dog to make a living. Nobody had time for *Shabbos*, so we stopped going to *shul*. Then, we started to eat *traif*, like the *Goyim* because it was cheaper and little by little, we forgot what it was to be a Jew. It was depressing to think that nobody would ever study the holy books again. *Yiddishkeit*, everything we loved, the way we lived for thousands of years...all that looked like it was vanishing forever. We used to say it was a cryin' shame that in our great America, there's room for everything but *Yiddishkeit*. Our people lived through all kinds of expulsions and pogroms and everything else over the years, so you would think that when we finally came to the *Goldine Medina* (the golden land) where life is so good, we would return to our old ways. But we didn't."

He looked at me again and a small smile appeared on his face. "So what happened in the end? Did everything that kept us together all those centuries die out?" He refilled his glass with whiskey – to the brim - and took a deep draught. He gargled involuntarily, then swallowed. His eyes turned red, his voice got higher and his smile broadened. "No, we're still here and you want to know why? I'll tell you why. Because a double miracle happened. Israel became a state and finally the Jewish people could defend themselves. *Also*, little Solly's boy was going to become a Rabbi and bring a whole generation back to *Yiddishkeit*. Imagine that. How thrilled we all were. It gave us back our hope for the future. We won. Because of Israel and Solly's boy, we won. Everybody said the kid was so smart he coulda been a big doctor or maybe an important lawyer, but no, he went to become a Rabbi and save *Yiddishkeit*." He took another gulp, a bigger one this time. "You should only know what that meant to us. I'm not just talking about Solly, but all of us. The son...what's his name?"

"Ben," I said. It didn't register. "Ben Zelig."

"Of course, Zelig, like his father. Listen, if you ever run into that boy..."

I fell into a deep sleep and when I awoke, I was ravenous. My mother was delighted to feed me samples of all my favorite Holiday dishes. As soon as I finished, I called New York.

"I'd like to leave a message for Rabbi Joel Levin, the Rabbinical Placement Director. Please tell him Ben Zelig called. You can tell him I decided..."

After the holiday, I returned to the Academy and found a message from Rabbi Levin. There was an immediate availability in Lake

LaSalle, a suburban community about fifty miles north of Manhattan. He had arranged for me to preach there the first Friday after the Ordination ceremonies. I would spend the rest of the weekend getting to know the movers and shakers. They would give me an honorarium of five-hundred dollars plus bus fare, hotel and meals. If we liked one another, we could sign a contract.

Two weeks later, I was on the pulpit, looking out at a congregation of three to four hundred well dressed people in their forties and fifties, plus some old timers, a smattering of kids and a couple of Roman collars from the neighboring churches. I had made a decision to move into my *mench* phase and I was determined to succeed. I prepared as I never did before and loved every minute of it. Now as I was about to deliver the goods, I would see whether or not it all came together.

I had chosen a controversial topic and constructed it like a play. The movie *On the Beach* had just been reissued and given the geo-political situation, the threat of nuclear annihilation was on everybody's mind. There was hardly a TV or radio talk show that didn't discuss the movie and how much more dangerous the world has become since it was first released three decades ago.

I rose to speak but said nothing for a few moments. Then, I boomed out: "Once a jolly swagman camped by a billabong under the shade of a Coolibah tree..."

"Hey, Rabbi, speak into the microphone! We can't understand a damn word." The cries came up from some of the old *Machers* in the first row.

I continued to intone the arcane lyrics avoiding any mention of *On the beach.*

"...and he sang as he watched and waited till his billie boiled..."

Harry Zack, head of the Temple maintenance committee called out. "We spent nearly ten thousand dollars on that damn amplifying system and we still can't make out a word you're saying."

"It's okay," I smiled confidently. I had overcome my reluctance to become a *professional* preacher and now that I was here, I was going to give it everything I had. When the congregation settled down, I opened my arms wide and sang the first line of the theme song from the movie. "Waltzing Matilda, waltzing Matilda...who'll come a-waltzing Matilda with me?" The perplexed looks on the faces of the congregants confirmed to me that I was right on key. I had set the stage and now it was the time to raise the curtain. "We can no longer deny the obvious. We – all of us - are *On the Beach*....waiting...waiting." A sudden awareness came over them. I was talking about the unthinkable.

"How much longer can we dawdle, like the old Aussi in the movie, waiting for his teapot to boil, while the world around us hovers on the brink of nuclear annihilation? Have we all gone mad? Reason demands that we learn to live together on this increasingly crowded planet, but fear possesses us to compete with one another to acquire increasingly potent and ever more deadly weapons. Is there no way to halt the race towards Armageddon?"

I looked slowly around the packed Synagogue. "I believe there is. Come with me," I quietly urged, "on a journey through time," and with that I took them on a brief tour of Jewish history. I reminded them that the reason we were able to endure millennia of unspeakable hardship and suffering was because we never lost faith in God's promise of a better tomorrow. Yes, the world is badly damaged now but our history has proven that *we* possess the power to repair it. I led them through the allegories of the Bible and reminded them of our ongoing partnership with God that raises us above our beastly nature and of His covenants with Noah and Abraham that extend to every one of us. I recalled inspiring lessons I had learned at the Academy. I made sure to plant the seed of hope with the words of Theodore Herzl. "If you truly will it, it is not a dream." I ended on the last image in the movie that had set the stage for my sermon. It was a banner that read: "It's not too late." I had submerged myself so completely in the images I had created that I didn't even know I had concluded until I heard myself say "amen."

Well, the evening was - as Uncle Joe would say - a hit. The entire congregation lined up after the service to thank me for an inspiring sermon. I can't tell you how heady that is. Deep down, I know that's what everyone says to every Clergyman after every service, but this time they said it to me and I know it's not the kind of thing one should take personally, but I did.

I couldn't help noticing a few young women in high heels, attractive dresses and suits and looking great. Could I...should I...? How would I go about it? Well, if I don't get the job, I'll never see them again and if I do, dare I make a move on the daughters of my congregants? The next family in line was the Grossmans. The wife, Charmaine, was a knockout. Tall, slender, long dark hair and a tight fitting dress. The husband, Morris, was a tall pudgy man with kinky reddish-gray hair. He had a nervous twitch and he talked out of the side of his mouth. Heather, the teenage daughter had red curly hair and wore a short skirt and flat shoes. It was hard not to stare at Charmaine and she didn't make it any easier by staring at me. Heather had a distant look in her eye. Charmaine held my hand warmly and wore a perfume that was positively intoxicating. Morris broke the spell.

"I thought of becoming a Rabbi once."

"Really," I pretended to care.

"Yeah. My favorite story from the Torah was the one about Adam being created out of earth, which is why men don't stink. But Eve was created out of Adam's rib and we know what happens to meat when it gets old." He laughed and nudged his wife. Charmaine didn't even feign a smile. Heather started to giggle, but stopped when her father continued.

"Remember that part, Rabbi?"

"I can't say I do. It's in the Torah, you say? Where exactly?"

"Who knows? It's been thirty years since I opened a Jewish book, but gems like that you don't forget. Look it up, you'll find it."

For a brief moment, I wondered about the husband, but only for a brief moment. As I watched Charmaine walk away, I was totally entranced.

All weekend congregants called me at the hotel to tell me that they were spellbound by my message and hoped I would agree to become their Rabbi. So many people wanted to "get to know me".

"Would you honor us by coming to our house for a barbeque on Sunday, some tennis and waterskiing on the lake?"

"You must be our guest at the club for the dinner dance on Saturday night, etc."

I met some very lovely people over the weekend, but I couldn't get Charmaine out of my head and I was bewitched by the thought that I might run into her. But if I did, what would I say? I would never sleep with a married woman anymore than I would murder or steal. I might use the Name of the Lord in vain occasionally and even covet my neighbor's ass, but adultery? Never! But...what a beauty. She was a little older than I, but that didn't matter. She exuded femininity like no one I ever knew. Would I be happy just to have coffee with her and inhale her fragrance? Probably not, so the best thing that could happen was for her not to call me. Still, I made sure to keep the volume down on the TV so I would hear the phone if it rang. It did ring several times, but none of the calls were from Charmaine.

Late Sunday afternoon, I returned to my hotel, wearing shorts and a sweater. The Phillips, one of the wealthier families in the community, had invited me to play tennis at their private court. Al Phillips and his wife Lorrie are charming, intelligent, interesting people, not at all like the hippies I hung out with in Greenwich Village, but much more fun to be with.

"This is exactly where I should be at this stage of my life," I thought to myself. "Uncle Joe, how can I thank you for your ungracious but much needed Zen slap?"

When I entered the lobby, I was sweaty and tired, but when I saw Charmaine and her daughter standing at the front desk, my energy returned.

"It's so nice to see you, Mrs. Grossman, and you, Heather. What brings you to the hotel?"

"Look, mom, the Rabbi remembered our names. How do you do that? There must have been a thousand people in the Synagogue on Friday night." Heather had an open childish face.

"The truth is, I don't remember everybody's name. Only those..." where the hell was I going?

"Only those...?" Charmaine had the most delicious smile...fortified by that intoxicating perfume.

The answer was obvious but I couldn't muster anything more than an embarrassed blush. Not attractive for a spiritual leader I realized and I tried to smile through it.

"We were in the neighborhood and Heather thought it would be nice to stop in and say hello to the handsome young Rabbi."

"Well, hello," I blushed even more. "Would you like to join me for a soft drink?"

"We'd love to," Charmaine said.

I was heating up. "I have to take a quick shower. Al Phillips had me running all over the court. Why don't we meet in the coffee shop in about fifteen minutes."

Charmaine suddenly shifted gears. "I've got an engagement but Heather can stay, would that be alright?"

"Sure." I was confused.

"Heather, be on your best behavior. I'll be back around six, dear."

I watched as she walked her special walk through the revolving door and out into the parking lot. I forced a smile at Heather. She smiled back. I didn't know what to do so I said "I'll just go upstairs and change. It'll only take a few minutes and..."

"I don't want to sit in the coffee shop all by myself. I'll come with you."

Not knowing what to say, I mumbled something and walked to the bank of elevators.

"Mom was right." She was smiling now.

"About what?"

"You got a nice set of buns there, Rabbi." Without her parents around, Heather took on a totally different persona.

We didn't say anything all the way up to the fourth floor, down the long hall and into my room. I was worried that someone might see me and get the wrong idea. I was a Rabbi and Heather was a teenager, for God's sake. Once inside the room, I felt a little relieved.

"Want something to read while I shower?"

She picked up the hotel guide and flopped into a chair. "Do your thing," she said without looking at me.

When I came out of the shower wrapped in a towel, I walked toward the closet and saw that Heather was lying on the bed, wearing only a pink bra and matching bikini panties. Her clothes were draped neatly over the chair. I freaked. If anyone saw...what's going on? How do I...? Then, she removed her bra and her full, round breasts adorned by light pink nipples seemed to beckon and I felt a strong pull in my groin.

"Nice towel rack", she laughed.

My towel had dropped and was supported only by my sudden erection. My immediate impulse was to climb on the bed, devour those lovely breasts and...what the hell am I thinking? I felt like a cartoon character with the devil and an angel talking into each ear. I wrapped the towel as tightly as I could around my waist. It wasn't much good at concealing my protruding member, but it was a gesture.

"Look, Heather, you're a very attractive woman...uh, girl. Heather, how old are you?"

"Old enough."

"But you're under eighteen, aren't you?" I knew I would regret it if I let this go on much longer, but looking at her burgeoning breasts, I didn't want to just end it.

"I'm very mature, I promise you."

I was paralyzed. The devil was gaining influence. My erection was definitely calling the shots. "Look, even if I wanted to, which believe me, I would love to, despite the fact that I know I shouldn't, because of your age and it's wrong...and what if someone found out? It would ruin both of us. And besides, I don't have a condom."

"Don't worry about it. You don't need one."

I took one step toward her, then stopped dead in my tracks. *I don't need a condom?* The erection began to disappear as it dawned on me.

"Are you pregnant?"

"Only two months. Not a problem."

I called Uncle Joe as soon as I got Heather dressed and out of my room. Heather had been promiscuous since she was twelve. Now she was seventeen and pregnant.

"It's a goddam minefield out dere. You got to watch every step wit dose bestids."

"What was she thinking, that I would have sex, then agree to marry her and support her child? Did she think I was that naïve?"

"Probly. Dat's what people expect from Rabbis."

"I don't believe that. You should have seen the way I've been treated all weekend. I never got so much deference and respect in all my life."

"Of course dey give you difference. What does dat cost dem? *Bobkes.* Dey smile nice, but down deep dey know Rabbis are only good in de book learning department but pretty dumb everywhere else, so when dey got a problem and dey got to find a *shnook* to dump it on, you're a prime target. Enjoy de respect, Bennie, it's important but don't take it too serious. You did good getting de little *nafka* out of your room. You didn't touch her, did you?"

"I swear I didn't. I've been debating whether to call her parents. I think they should be aware of what their daughter is up to."

"Benny, Benny. You're smart and you're smart, but in some ways, you're pretty stupid. Who do you tink put her up to dis whole ting?"

"Her parents?"

"Soitenly her muddah, from what you tell me. She sees dis young wet-behind-de-ears Rabbi and she tinks to herself, dis guy is poifect. If a goil has a baby in seven months, it's a bastid, but if de faddeh is a Rabbi, it's a premie. Dis muddah is no dumbbell. Better watch out for her."

"This is a small town. What do I do if I run into her?"

"You smile and say have a nice day. Believe you me she won't be chasing you anymore. She tried to sell you damaged goods and you didn't buy, so why should she waste anodder minute on you? She got to find anodda customer who's even dumber dan you."

"That's so cynical."

"It's reality. How come dey don't teach you how to survive in de real world at det Rabbi Academy? Don't dey tell you det together wit all dose nice people who give you so much difference and respect, dere are also a few sharks? Everybody's fair game in America and a Rabbi's got to learn how to protect himself like everybody else. You see, Benny, in the old country it was different. De good people looked out for dere Rabbi so de bestids couldn't take advantage. In America, everybody looks out for deyself and nobody even tinks about protecting de Rabbi. So, wit nobody to look out for dem, American Rabbis end up getting screwed more den anybody because dey're so naive. They like to tink people is basically good. Of course dey're wrong but nobody wants to correct a Rabbi, dey'd rather give him difference and respect so dey can *kak* all over him if dey need to. In Europe, dey used to say a Rabbi could walk wit his head in de clouds because dere was always somebody to keep him from stepping in de dog shit and soiling his trousers. It's different in America. Here, Rabbis walk de same streets as everybody else and nobody gives a good goddamn, so you better watch where you're goin' *boychick* or your pants will get all *ba-kacked.*"

Uncle Joe's metaphors weren't the easiest to follow, but he understood the dark side of human nature better than most. Throughout my student years, when I pondered the moral imperatives, I thought of Uncle Joe as an aberration. Where was Aristotle? Kant? They were certainly nowhere to be found in his universe of discourse. What was so troubling now was that as I ventured forth from the ivory tower I could not deny that his view of our species was in some ways as accurate as those nobler ones I had previously chosen to espouse.

I left Lake LaSalle on Monday. Despite what happened with the Grossmans the day before, I was exhilarated by all the approbation, the smiles, the warm handshakes and the promise of what lay ahead. But as the bus entered Manhattan and we drove through the graffiti and detritus of Harlem, Uncle Joe's admonition came back strong and clear. I was walking the same streets as everybody else and I had better watch my step.

"They were very impressed," Rabbi Levin, placement director of the Academy, said. "The Chairman of the Board of Directors of Beth Israel called and said they'd like you to be their Rabbi." He congratulated me and said all that remained was for me to negotiate a contract.

Me, negotiate? How was I to do that? In all my classes no one ever taught us how to deal with practical issues unless they occurred sometime before the twelfth century.

I had no idea of what to do or how to do it so I thought it would be wise to consult Uncle Joe. I told him the going rate for a newly ordained Rabbi was forty-thousand dollars a year. "Everybody knows that, so what is there to negotiate?"

"Going rate, shmoing rate. Dey won't pay you a nickel more den dey have to, so you better learn how to negosherate, *boychick,* or dey'll eat you alive."

A week later, I was in the conference room of Temple Beth Israel sitting opposite six members of the Board of Directors. Uncle Joe assured me I was ready. He had called me every night during the past week at exactly one minute past nine, after the long distance rates dropped, and drilled me for an hour on the essentials of "negosherating".

The five men and one woman on the Board greeted me warmly. "Not to worry...relax...we have a deal," wink, wink, elbow nudge. "The only reason for the meeting is to work out a few details," they said and proceeded to offer me coffee, a soft drink and anything else that would make me feel more at home and "part of the family".

That's exactly what Uncle Joe said they would do. How did he know that?

Leonard David, known among trial lawyers as the velvet dragon, opened the interview. "The important thing for us, Rabbi, is we want to be fair."

My first reaction was to say, "Why go on? Since you're going to be fair, let's just..." But before I opened my mouth the word "fair" rang a familiar bell in my head.

"Whenever dey tell you dey want to be fair or 'dey're being generous,' you know dey're gettin' ready to cut off your shmekel."

Leonard looked warmly into my eyes as he continued. "Naturally, we wish we could be even more generous, but as you know, we're a small congregation and we don't have as much in our modest budget as we would like. Notwithstanding that unfortunate fact, we are prepared to offer you TWENTY THOUSAND DOLLARS for the first year." He smiled broadly and raised his eyebrows for emphasis as though he were conferring a magnanimous gift.

I was in shock. How could he offer me half of what the Rabbinical Academy Placement director said was the going rate?

I saw Leonard's mouth move but all I heard was Uncle Joe's voice. *"When a rich bastid cries poor, fold you legs quick before he shoves someting up you ass."*

Here I was, Daniel in the Lion's den with nothing to protect me but my illiterate Uncle Joe's coaching. In our intensive rehearsals, he forced me to concentrate on the numbers, how they were rendered and nothing else. So, when Leonard completed his remarks and looked to me for a *fair* response, I did exactly as I was prompted. I said nothing, but smiled back, first at Leonard, then slowly around the long oak table at each of the six members of the Board. I was amazed at how well that simple tactic worked. As the seconds ticked by and still I said nothing, I realized for the first time in my life, the power of silence. When you say nothing, they think you really know something.

Howard Gewirtz broke. "Let's not beat around the bush." He was chewing his unlit cigar faster and faster. "People who met you think the world of you. You know we want you to be our Rabbi, so what's to talk about? Name a figure."

"Just make it fair, that's all we ask." Leonard wasn't about to give up control.

Saliva was dribbling down Howard's cheek. He was a stock broker with a bleeding ulcer. He wasn't allowed to smoke but he couldn't kick the cigar habit, so the compromise was that he would chew unlit cigars until they got too slimy, then he would clip off the end with a small scissors and start again. Chew and clip, chew and clip. You could tell Howard was getting nervous, because he chewed faster and snipped more often. He started to cough and the dribble intensified.

"Howard, for God's sake." Mable Soretsky, the only woman on the Board, drew a small white tissue from her purse and tossed it across the table.

Howard wiped his mouth, but continued to cough as he clutched his unlit cigar.

By the time all eyes came back to me, I was ready. Uncle Joe had drilled me on every detail of the plan of attack. It was up to me now to execute it. *"De most important ting,"* he reminded me every night, *"is de pants. Det's absolutely non-negosherate-able. If dey tell you dey can't affordeh, tell dem to shove de whole deal up dey ass and det's all."*

This being my very first pulpit, I was totally ignorant of how Rabbis are supposed to conduct contract negotiations. I'm sure there were other strategies I might have considered, but I could never have come this far had it not been for Uncle Joe so I tried my best to strike a balance between his proposition and the English language.

Leonard exploded. "You want forty-five thousand dollars a year *plus* a pair of pants? This is Temple Beth Israel of Greater Lake LaSalle, for goodness sake. What do you think we are, a bunch of tailors?" All six members of the Board appeared to share his indignation.

A month ago, his withering look alone would have been enough to make me capitulate but now all I heard was *"whatever you ask for, dey gonna hit de roof. So, let dem blow off steam. If dey really can't affordeh, which I don't believe for a second, dey'll shake your hand and ask you to go home and tink about it."*

"Then what?"

"Den nuttin. We'll look around to see if dere's someting better. If not, you can always go back and accept dere offer, but I don't believe det's gonna happen. I heard enough Rabbis to know dey ain't lettin you go so easy."

I looked at the curious faces sitting opposite me and waited, silently. They didn't end the meeting and they didn't ask me to go home and think about their offer. Leonard leaned toward me, his hands spread and his mouth open. He didn't look so intimidating anymore.

"I'm sorry gentlemen...and lady," I smiled at Mabel. "That's what I require."

The atmosphere in the minimalist conference room suddenly became confused. The board members figured this would be a slam dunk. Where does a Rabbi get the chutzpah to haggle with Leonard David or any of the other millionaires on the board for that matter? The only thing that's supposed to count in our society is one's net worth. But how much is a Rabbi worth? They were stumped. Even Leonard didn't know the answer to that one.

"You've taken us completely by surprise, Rabbi, I can tell you that," he sounded angry and disappointed. I felt bad that I had upset him. He waved his hands, but said nothing. He waited for a moment in agonizing silence, then looked around the table and said "give us a few minutes, please."

"Of course." I walked to the door in silence, convinced I had blown it.

I called Uncle Joe from the phone booth downstairs. "I think I screwed up. They're mad as hell."

"Whatta you talkin'? In business, dere's no place for mad. You win *odder* you lose. Dey meeting wit you because dey want you should take de job. If dey get you, dey win. If dey don get you, dey lose. But dey don't want to just win, dey want to win big, dose bestids, det means dey got to get you for a little nuttin. Don't worry about making dem hangry. When you're negosherating you don't get hangry. You pretend hangry if it helps get the price down and you stop pretending when it don't woik."

"But maybe they don't have the kind of money I'm asking for in their budget."

"Dey don't have in de budget? Rich bestids can always find money to put into a budget, but det's not de issue here. If dose bestids see dey can *schnor* you down to a measly twenty tousand dollahs, dey will treat you like a *shmateh* and make from your life a misery. But if you stand up to dem, dey will respect you like crazy. Why? Because you kicked dey ass and in America de only ting people respect is somebody who kicked dey ass."

"Would you please come back in, Rabbi?" Mabel was the one they sent to find me.

Back in the conference room, Leonard looked at me with a half-chastising, half-sly look he had obviously mastered over the years in the conference rooms of the mighty.

"Well, Rabbi where do we go from here?" Leonard opened.

I said nothing, but smiled back.

"Is this some kind of ethical lesson you're teaching us through the allegory of a pair of pants?" Hoppy Halperin was the mattress magnate who greeted everyone with a big handshake and a warm smile, but now he wasn't smiling, he really wanted to know.

"Maybe not." Larry Owitz, the C.F.O. of Gimbel's, with the gold cufflinks and matching pocket watch, rang in. "The Rabbi says he wants a pair of pants, okay, I think I understand where he's coming from. I know it sounds peculiar, but this kind of stuff goes on with the clergy. I got a call a couple of weeks ago from Bishop O'Shay. When my secretary told me who was on the phone I didn't know how to talk to him. What the hell do you call a Bishop? I know the Pope is uh...your highness, but a Bishop? Anyway, I said Good Morning your Majesty and he seemed happy with that. I told him how honored I was by his call and everything. You know what he wanted? Two hundred yards of red satin curtains for the big cathedral, what the hell's the name of it, on Madison Avenue?"

"Saint Mary's?" Hoppy really wanted to make a contribution.

"I don't know. Anyway, that's when it hit me. Clergymen are strange about fabrics. Maybe that's why they're called men of the cloth. You know, *material* things, spiritual things. Could be, no?"

Morry, the stuttering C.P.A. shook his head. "Let's take...one step... back." It was agonizing to watch him twist to form the words. "Beside the ...pants, you named a... figure that seemed ...awfully..."

"Forty-five Thousand Dollars, *plus* the pants," I reminded him.

Morry twitched. His stutter became worse. "You know, your...uh...uh...your...predecessor was considerably...uh...more experienced...and we, uh...only paid...him..."

"What kind of car did he drive?" I asked, paraphrasing Uncle Joe.

Morry twitched again. "What does that... uh...have to do...with...uh...?"

"He drove an old Subaru, a dilapidated junker." Hoppy was back.

Howard snipped off another piece of saliva soaked cigar he had been chewing. "I can't tell you how embarrassed I was at the interfaith service at that new Catholic Church. You know the one on Mohawk Drive with all the glass and steel? We had to call the AAA to tow the Rabbi home. My Gentile neighbors wouldn't let up on me. 'You people are so rich', he says to me, 'why can't you buy your Rabbi a decent car? Our Priest drives a new Volvo.' I tell you I was never so humiliated. Listen, whatever we do, we got to insist the Rabbi drives a nice car. What kind of car you got, Rabbi?"

"An aging Ford, but I'm in the market for a replacement." I looked at Howard, who smiled at me approvingly.

Leonard resumed control. "Now, Rabbi, let me get this straight. We're not talking about an entire wardrobe here, are we?

"Just the pants." I looked around the conference room and realized that Uncle Joe, the "ignoronimus," had learned more about business from the school of hard knocks than any of these millionaires with degrees from top Ivy league colleges. They mastered economics. He understood human nature. Thanks to the scribbling on his dashboard, I, too, had learned a few things

"What kind of pants, *exactly*?" Leonard was determined to get to the bottom of this.

"Well, that's the thing," I said. "Not just any pants, that's for sure. They've got to be gray flannel, 100% Italian wool, with reinforced knees and you'll have to pay for alterations, of course. The cuff has to be above the shoe. I don't want my pants dragging in the street."

They looked to one another and finally to Raul Hollander, the only member of the Board who wore a *yarmulke* and whom I later discovered was the real power broker. As founder of Allied Radio, which became Radio Shack, he was also the richest member of the Temple. Leonard and the others had gone as far as they could go. Until this moment, Hollander had not uttered a word. Now it was time for him to take over.

"O.K., Rabbi, what's the bottom line here?" His raspy voice only added to his presumptive authority. The time for jockeying and metaphors was over and everybody, including me, knew it.

"Okay, Uncle Joe, here goes," I said to myself.

"Gentlemen...and lady," I lowered my voice and spoke softly to make sure they had to pay attention to hear. "You are all immensely successful businessmen – and women - and you can literally negotiate the pants off anybody, pun intended, so in that regard I'm obviously no match for you, but I would like you to understand my position. Sure, I could live on less than forty-five thousand dollars a year, but do *you* really want me to? If I can't afford decent furniture, should I keep my shades drawn so the neighbors won't see how shabbily I'm forced to live? Do you want me to spend my time scrounging for bargains in discount stores because I can't afford to buy a decent suit? Should I not have my lawn mowed because I don't have enough to pay the neighbor kid? Everyone in Lake LaSalle would have to conclude that the members of Temple Beth Israel don't feel their Rabbi deserves to live like a *mench*. Is that how you feel?"

It was obvious from the way they looked at one another that Uncle Joe's point had hit the desired nerve.

"Okay, let's go back to negotiating," I said. "No matter how much I ask for, we all know you won't be happy unless I give up something, so let's wrap this thing up. Bottom line? The forty-five thousand dollars is non-negotiable, but I am willing to give up the pants."

All eyes turned to Raul Hollander. He looked at me for a long moment, then smiled and said "You drive a hard bargain, Rabbi."

"But you got me to give up half of what of what I was asking for."

He took my hand and turned to the other members of the Board. "Congratulations, distinguished members of the Board, we have ourselves a Rabbi."

Everyone, with the single exception of Morry the C.P.A., broke out in spontaneous applause.

Howard triumphantly mashed his cigar butt in the ashtray. "No pants," he wagged a faux-threatening finger.

"No pants," I agreed.

"I got a condition for the Rabbi," Howard continued. "I insist he become a member of the country club. I'll pick up his tab, but I want our Gentile friends to see how we treat our Rabbi." He turned to me. "What do you say?"

"You win", I conceded.

On my next trip to Youngstown, Uncle Joe beamed with pride as he drove me around to visit all the relatives. He made me recite the story to him over and over again. After the first telling he knew every detail, but he loved hearing it again and again.

"Do you think I got their respect?"

He smiled. "You did good, Benny. Dose bestids will tink different about Rabbis from now on, I guarantee you."

"Should I have asked for more?"

Uncle Joe smiled. "Forty-five tousand dollahs is a fair amount of respect your first time out." He reached over and pinched my cheek. "Listen Benny, next year you'll negosherate again. And de year after det. You know you don't have to stay in det place, what de hell's de name, Lake Salami, all your life. Dere's de big towns: Cleveland, Pittsboig. I even called my bradehlawn in Chicageh yestiday. Big shul dere. Dey like dere Rabbi, but he's old. He'll die off in a couple years. Don't worry. I got it all figured out." Joe was positively triumphant.

I looked at the dashboard and saw a wide swath of fresh scratches in the dust. I couldn't make out the figures but I knew he could.

Incorpora Borealis

Incorpora Borealis

"How many angels can dance on the head of a pin?"

In the seven months I had been working with Brigham Horowitz to prepare him for his Bar Mitzvah, this is the closest he had ever come to making a philosophical or theological inquiry. Brigham was a sweet, fairly intelligent twelve year-old with an easy smile and lots of friends, but he had absolutely no interest in learning, neither at the Hebrew School where he doodled on his desk three afternoons a week nor at Public School where he cheerfully maintained a C-average.

"Why do you ask, Brigham?"

"I saw a preview for 'Annihilation of the Species 2' where this cool monster from hell, who can turn himself into a gigantic dinosaur, threatens to annihilate all the humans on earth unless someone can come up with the right answer."

"The answer to...how many angels can dance on the head of a pin?"

"Yeah. I'm pretty sure the monster turns out to be the Devil himself, but they don't tell you that in the previews, I'm just guessing. Anyway, there's this big promotion. Whoever sends in the right answer gets two free tickets to the opening. The only people who don't qualify are Priests and Rabbis and stuff, so I figure you guys must know. That's why I'm asking you."

"You want me to tell you what Jewish tradition has to say about angels?"

"Whatever it takes to get the right answer, but try to keep it short, Rabbi."

I had to think hard about how to discuss a complicated theological question with a pre-teen whose sole sources of information were movies and TV.

"Brigham, the Bible...you know about the Bible, right?"

"Uh-huh."

"The Bible talks about angels in a variety of ways. In the early books, certain emissaries, that is to say, certain *messengers* are referred to as angels. They're usually ordinary men or women who are called upon to perform specific tasks. Nobody knows they're angels and once they complete their mission, they disappear and we know nothing more about them except that something unexpectedly important happened because of them."

"What do you mean, nobody knows they're angels? What about the wings?"

"What wings?"

"You know, like John Travolta in that crappy movie where he drank beer all the time? Remember, he was an angel so he had to hide his wings under his coat whenever he went out."

"Brigham, *nobody* knows for certain what angels look like. They could even be purely spiritual like an insight or a premonition, in which case they have no physical form at all and, in answer to your question, an infinite number of them can dance on the head of a pin because they are not limited by time or space. But, if they have bodies and mass like people, with or without wings, there is a limited amount of room on the head of that pin, but the exact number of dancers depends not only on their size but also your understanding of their essence."

I saw the glaze spread over his eyes and I knew I had lost him. I had no idea what to say next, so I waited.

"So...," he was deep in thought. "What's the answer?"

"The answer to what?"

"How many angels dance on the head of a pin. Pay attention, there, Rabbi," he smiled and fake-punched me on the arm.

Great personality, nothing upstairs. I was in a quandary. What can a Rabbi say to a good-natured kid who wants nothing more out of life than two free tickets to a horror movie? I couldn't drop to his level. I just couldn't.

"There isn't any answer, Brigham."

"What! They shouldn't be asking trick questions on a national promotion. That sucks!"

"Sometimes you can learn more from analyzing a question than from getting an easy answer. All I'm saying is it has nothing to do with numbers. It's about substance. The fancy word for that is corporeal. The opposite is incorporeal."

"His eyes lit up. "Oh, I know about that."

"You do?"

"Yeah, I saw them in camp last summer."

"Angels?"

"Yeah, *incorpora borealis*. They were really neat, lit up the whole sky like fireworks."

I had no idea where to go from there.

"So now that we're talking the same language, you can tell me, right?"

"Tell you what?"

Brigham rolled his eyes as if to say "Rabbis have such a short attention span!"

"How many of them can dance on the head of a pin?"

Back in my study, I had the depressing feeling that I was not living in the same world as most other people. When I decided to become a Rabbi, I imagined I would lead and inspire my flock like the prophets of old. They were one with their people. They challenged them and forced them to confront their shortcomings. I can't seem to connect on any level. Is it because I've only been in the pulpit for ten months and I've got a lot of growing to do, or...what?

The phone rang for quite a long time before I could get myself to answer it. When I did, instead of the anticipated hello, a strident voice with an accent I can only describe as generic foreign demanded to know.

"What's your name, Zelig?"

"Ben Zelig...uh Rabbi Ben Zelig," I said.

"How come I never heard of you, whatta you, new?"

"I've been Rabbi of Temple Beth Israel for nearly a year, who's this?"

"Omar Hakim! From Crazy Omar's Royal Catering Hall in Canaan. Didn't your secretary tell you it was me on the line? I'd fire her if I was you. Listen, I'd love to chit-chat with you all day but I'm in a bind so let's cut to the chase. I got a Jewish wedding scheduled for Sunday and I'm short a Rabbi."

"That's the day after tomorrow!"

"No kiddin'. Anyway, here's the story. I'll be honest with you. I had a Rabbi all lined up, but it turns out he's in jail and every other Rabbi I know is unavailable so the job is yours if you want it, what do you say?"

I must admit I was curious to know which

Rabbi was in jail and why, but I didn't know how to pursue that. "Omar...Mr. Hakim, I can't perform a wedding for a couple I don't even know. Marriage is the most intimate of life cycle ..."

"You been a Rabbi for one lousy year in a little hick Temple nobody ever heard of and *you're* talking to *me* about life cycles? How many weddings do you do a year?"

I froze. I had never performed any. "That's not the point," I tap-danced.

"The point is," he cut right in. "Nobody knows more about the life cycle business than me. I know more than God, fer Chrissakes. I get five, six weddings a week, every denomination, Catholics, Protestants, Hindus; every race, Blacks, Spics, you name it. I get the Gays and the Lesbians, I even had a couple monkeys got married last year in my place. I was gonna do the famous pandas, but one of them died. Don't you watch television? I'm the wedding king! And not only weddings, I cover all the sacraments. I got baptisms and circumcisions up the kazoo. I get wakes, bar mitzvahs, confirmations, coming out parties - and not just the ones for fags, although I get plenty of those, too. Listen Rabbi, I don't have a lot of time to spend on you. You got a problem, talk to me. Normally, I pay three hundred for the clergy. You want a kicker, I'll throw in an extra fifty, any other problems?"

Yes, I've got lots of problems, I said to myself. I had seen his TV commercials on the local cable channel. "Crazy Omar, the most innovative caterer of religious *and* non-religious sacred events in the Tri-State area." His ads featured couples mud wrestling in their gowns and tuxedoes, food fights and even farting contests! I shuddered to think that my first wedding might be held in a sleazy circus like Crazy Omar's Royal Catering Hall. I had often thought about how I would conduct my first wedding. When that occasion presented itself, I wanted to be ready to perform it with elegance and sincerity. I would do my best to tailor the ceremony specifically to the bride and groom, so that it would stay with them for...

"Okay, I can tell you're holding out," Omar said. "You want to put a gun to my head, go ahead. Four hundred, but that's my absolute limit."

"You misunderstood me. I could never accept money for conducting a wedding. A Rabbi performs *mitzvot*..."

"I know all about *mitzvot*. You want to perform one, take the money and make a contribution someplace. You'll feel like a big shot." As an afterthought he added, "just make it in my name," he laughed. "I'm kidding."

This guy actually believes I'm for sale! I wanted to tell him to kiss my ass right then and there but I phrased it as I thought a Rabbi should.

"I'm sorry, Mr. Hakim, but I don't feel right..."

"You don't feel right?" He mimicked me. "Oh, that's too bad. Never mind, then. You were my last hope but if *you don't feel right*...whatever that means, don't do it. It's all the same to me. I can always call one of the internet certified non-denominational ministers. It's the kids and their families who will be disappointed as hell."

"Non-denominational ministers? Isn't the couple Jewish?"

"Of course, that's why I'm talking to you. Two nice Jewish kids can't find a Rabbi to marry them. Damn shame, I say. What does that mean, their kids won't be Jewish? I'm just asking. I'm not Jewish myself, but I'd like to know."

"As a matter of fact, according to Jewish law there are a whole string of complications that arise from improperly administered marriage vows." *Why did they only teach us about laws governing sacraments at the Academy and not how to deal with intimidating caterers?* "I wish you'd called me sooner," I said. "If I'd had a chance to meet the families we could have arranged to do the service here in the Temple..."

"Shoulda...woulda...coulda. The wedding's taking place here on Sunday with or without a Rabbi. I'm sorry but that's the way it is. I really feel bad for the kids. They had their heart set on a traditional wedding with the canopy, the blessings, breaking of the glass and all the rest of it but if you can't do it because *you don't feel right,* so be it. If you can live with that, I guess I can too."

My heart sank. How could I turn my back on a Jewish couple asking for a religious ceremony knowing that if I don't do it, they will be married by some internet certified non-denominational "minister"?

"Have a nice day, Rabbi."

"Mr. Hakim...Omar...don't hang up."

"So...what's it going to be?"

"I'll do it," I said sheepishly.

"You will? That's great. The honorarium is three hundred, payable after the reception. That okay with you?"

"Fine," I said.

"Be here Sunday afternoon at five-twenty sharp. You'll park in front, next to my Rolls, but be on time. The Wedding's got to be over and out by eight so we'll have time to bring in the corpse for a nine o'clock wake."

"When can I meet the bride and groom?"

"What am I, a social worker? The wedding's a day after tomorrow. Come five minutes early, you'll meet. You want to call them, be my guest."

"Can I have their numbers?"

"Hold on. Dorothy!" Canned music came up loud and for the next five minutes I listened to a bunch of violins playing in unison "I've got to be me" followed by more violins performing an endless version of Guantanamera. Finally, a hoarse woman's voice interrupted the muzak.

"Okay, Father Zeldon, Dorothy Gruber here. I got you the number for Sunday's bride and another one for the groom."

"It's Rabbi Zelig."

"What?"

"I'm Rabbi Zelig, not Father whatever-you-said."

Dorothy's voice turned brittle. "Okay, whoever-you-are, do you want the numbers or not?"

Despite my misgivings about Crazy Omar's Royal Caterers, I was determined to make the ceremony as tasteful and personal as I could. I called Jenny, the bride, and we spoke for a few minutes. I told her I didn't want the ceremony to be an empty recitation of legalisms.

"Yeah, bummer."

I said I wanted the wedding to be very special and memorable for her.

She said "Cool."

When I asked about her groom, she said he was "hot." I left a message for the hot groom, but he never called back.

Over the years, I had attended a fair number of weddings. Some were incredibly moving and beautiful. Others were not. This being my first, I was determined to make it an event the young couple would remember and treasure always. All day Saturday I studied the laws and rituals of the marriage ceremony, but I was at a loss as to how to tailor a wedding to a couple I had never met and barely spoken to; except to elicit three words from the bride-to-be: bummer, cool and hot. I researched some of my favorite love poems from the classics, the Bible, the Romantics and even a verse from one of the Beatles albums. I hoped the transcendent words of love might weave gossamer bonds around them when they pledged themselves to honor and cherish one another for the rest of their lives. If they had their own words, so much the better, but if they didn't, these poems would speak for them.

At the hall, Dorothy Gruber, Omar's sister was curt, cold and reminded me of something out of High Anxiety.

"We run a tight ship. Events begin on time. If the Bride and groom are late, we begin without them. If the corpse is delayed, the wake goes on," she said as we briskly walked through the ornate complex of gilded halls.

"What about circumcisions?" How could I not play with this martinet?

"What about 'em?" she said without breaking her stride.

"If the baby is late, do you cut off someone else's foreskin?"

"What are you, some kind of comedian?" She shot a disdainful look my way and picked up the pace.

"That's Milton," she nodded to the heavy set man who kept a video camera trained on me as we walked through flamboyant halls and extravagant rooms loaded with plaster of Paris gargoyles and cherubs. Mirrors on every wall enlarged the paintings of past presidents whose eyes followed you everywhere.

When we arrived at the bride's Dressing Parlor, Dorothy turned to Milton and snarled. "That's enough for now." Milton turned off his video camera and I suddenly felt relieved that my every expression wasn't being recorded.

"Procession starts at 5:30, with or without," Dorothy said and quickly left.

The bridesmaid who opened the door looked as though she was half asleep, then started to giggle and couldn't stop. A cloud of pungent smoke wafted from the room and judging from the joint she was holding, the bridal party was probably stoned. After introducing myself, the bridesmaid led me to a closed door.

"Some guy's here to see you, Jen," she yelled out. "His name's Robby, I think."

Moments passed and the door remained closed. I knocked several times.

"It's open," a voice called out.

Inside the room the bride was sprawled out on a chaise lounge with her shoes off flipping through a magazine.

Like all brides, Jenny looked pretty. Not unusually so, but not unattractive either. She had good teeth, a nice figure, a stylish hairdo, trimmed nose and a sweet smile.

"Jenny?"

"Who wants to know?"

I told her I was the Rabbi and that I was honored to officiate at her wedding.

She looked at me quizzically for a moment. "I already talked to some Rabbi on the phone, but thanks anyway."

"That was me," I said.

"Oh, cool," she forced a smile and went back to her magazine.

I sat down next to her and waited a few minutes while she continued to flip through pages. She picked up a roach from the ashtray next to the chaise lounge and took a hit. I decided to try and bring a semblance of clear-headedness to the situation by asking if there was something in particular she would like me to say or read.

She thought long and hard, then said brightly, "no."

I asked if she would like to hear some of the poems I had prepared.

"Cool."

"Any author you particularly like?" I was hoping for some clue.

"Pretty much all of 'em."

I took a small notebook from my vest pocket and read. "I carry your heart. I carry it in my heart..." I noticed that she was looking at me strangely. "Do you like this one? It's e.e. cummings."

She leaned towards me, touched my lapel with her forefinger and whispered in my ear "are you hitting on me?"

"No!"

"Just checking, I don't want to miss out on anything just because I'm getting married and stuff."

My instinct was to get out of there right away but she held onto my lapel and smiled. Suddenly a raspy voice called from the doorway and Jenny released her grip.

"Who the hell are you and what you doing there?"

I jumped to my feet. "Uh...I'm Rabbi Zelig." I looked at the woman walking towards us and for a moment, I thought I was seeing double. She wore the exact same dress as the bride, only a slight shade off-white and her hair was full of curls and ribbons, like an elaborately wrapped gift.

"Oh...hi, I'm Caprice Pomeranz, mother of the bride. She shook my hand and whispered "I was about to have a *caniption* when I saw a man on the couch with Jenny. Thank God it's only you. All I need is for her old boyfriends to come sniffing around for one last hump."

She looked at Jenny for a long minute. "Where are your gloves?"

"I took 'em off. They were too hot."

"Well, put 'em back on. It's your wedding day." She picked up a pair of white gloves from the table next to the ashtray. "Here," she said, tossing the gloves to Jenny. Then, she picked up Jenny's roach and lit it. "I'm so glad you're here to do the honors," she said holding her breath, and offered me a hit.

"Thank you, no...I..." What is a Rabbi supposed to say when someone casually offers marijuana?

"Listen, Rabbi, I hope you're not going to make this thing too boring with a lot of prayers and stuff. You don't want to wear out the guests because we've got a great show lined up for the reception."

"I'll keep that in mind," I said as I backed out the door. "Nice to see you both."

I decided to discuss the ceremony with her chosen one. The groom and his buddies weren't smoking grass, but they were in a similarly grandiose room drinking tequila slammers and watching a porno movie on an oversized monitor. I took one look at the groom's party and decided to conduct a wedding that would be straight out of the Rabbi's Manual.

The ceremony began at exactly five-thirty sharp. Under Dorothy's strict supervision, everyone was in their place when the music came up and the processional began without a hitch. The wedding party was attractive, and despite the constant intrusion of Milton's video camera which he stuck into people's faces at the most inappropriate times, I felt we just might have the makings of a respectable ceremony.

After reciting the blessings and the exchange of vows, I began to feel that I had done a pretty good job...that is, until the final benediction. That's when everything came tumbling down. The moment I placed the glass under the groom's foot, Milton instructed me to "hold it" while he changed camera angles. Not knowing what to do, I held the glass and smiled into the camera.

"Okay, now let her rip," he called out and the groom smashed the glass before I had time to remove my hand. Milton moved in for a close-up of my bloody hand and the ceremony came to an abrupt halt. Fortunately, at most Jewish weddings there are doctors in the crowd who can attend to a wounded Rabbi. While he was bandaging my hand, the Bride and Groom remained under the canopy, giggling and groping. The best man surreptitiously handed me a card.

It read: "Let A.M. Schlaffer, Attorney at Law, get angry for you!"

"Hi, Rabbi. I'm Alex Schlaffer, the groom's brother. You and I have some important things to talk about," he spoke through his teeth, like a ventriloquist. "Call me first thing tomorrow morning."

I told him not to worry, that I had no interest in taking any legal action against his brother.

"You don't understand, Rabbi. This goes way beyond family. This place is insured to the hilt. I know because I handled a few cases of E-coli from their kitchen. We're talking deep pockets here."

"It's only a cut. It'll heal. I appreciate the offer, but no thanks."

"Temple Beth Israel in Lake LaSalle, right?" He wrote that down on the back of one of his cards. "I'll be in touch."

Shoving people around and screaming at the top of her hoarse voice, Dorothy got the ceremony back on track after losing just eight minutes, not to mention a significant amount of my blood. I couldn't help wondering if this had ever happened to anyone else. Was it *my* fault?

Shouldn't Milton have warned me that he was going to take a close shot of the glass and give me time to remove my hand before instructing the groom to "let her rip"?

Aside from my throbbing wound, the ceremony proceeded without further incident. I had hoped to leave immediately after the ceremony but Omar said that clergy always stay until the very end of the reception. "What's your hurry? You got to get home to the wife?"

"I'm not married."

"So stick around, have a bite, meet a bridesmaid or two. Maybe you'll get lucky." Milton aimed his camera at us while Omar walked through the crowd with his arm around me and proudly proclaimed, "This handsome young man is Crazy Omar's favorite Rabbi."

Omar and Milton left me to join the guests who were milling around tables, holding drinks and small paper napkins overflowing with deep fried hors d'oeuvres.

"You-hoo!" A striking woman in her forties, bursting with energy and dressed to the "nines", waved to me as she made her way through the crowd. She wasn't that tall, but with spike heels and teased hair, she made a towering impression. She greeted everyone she passed with a familiar smile. When she reached me, she gave me a huge bear hug. I had no idea who she was so I reciprocated, hoping she would give me a clue.

"Hi, I'm Foxy. Foxy Flange, the M.C.?" she said as though we had met before. I, of course, had no recollection. "You're the preacher, am I right?"

Obviously we had not met before, that was just her universal greeting.

"I'm the Rabbi, Ben Zelig is my name."

She grabbed my good hand and shook it vigorously. "It's so good to meet you, finally. I've heard so much about you," she said sincerely.

What could she possibly have heard? Nothing, I guessed, just more freely dispensed flattery. Foxy Flange was attractive in a way, but too heavily made up and flashily attired to be appealing up close. Her thickly drawn eye liner was the kind ballerinas wear and looks better from a distance. Her bountiful breasts, exuberantly revealed in a low cut dress were more interesting than attractive and her short skirt caught every man – and woman's – eye.

"Where did you say your parish was?" She had a way of looking deeply into my eyes for a brief second before spinning around to wave enthusiastically to someone else in the crowd she thought she should know.

"Lake LaSalle," I said.

She continued to hold my hand but her head was on a swivel. She would smile to someone, then wave to someone else, holding up my hand as though I were a trophy.

"Lake...? Oh yeah, I had a gig up there a couple of years ago, remember?"

"I've only been there...around a year."

She didn't react.

"You must have met my predecessor, Rabbi Schulberg," I said.

When she turned back to me, I had the impression she hadn't heard anything I said. I don't know why, but I felt obliged to continue.

"Beth Israel is my first pulpit. In fact, this is my first wedding."

That caught her attention. "Virgin, huh?

Don't worry about it, it only hurts the first time," she laughed. "Why don't you perform more weddings? No catering hall?"

"Oh, the Temple is fully equipped. It's just that ours is more of a retirement community. We do have a school and some young members, but not many of marrying age."

"Well, if you ever *do* need anything, remember Foxy." She squeezed my hand and smiled seductively.

Just then, a voice boomed over the loud speaker announcing last call for dinner accompanied by a loud bell and flickering lights.

"There goes Rocco." Foxy couldn't resist a joke. When I didn't laugh, she pointed to the flickering lights. "You know, the old prison movies? Lights flickering means the electric chair's using all the juice."

I didn't know what she was talking about, but I didn't understand much of anything that was going on.

Foxy took out a card and wrote on it. "This is my home number. I'm available for weddings, bar-mitzvahs, you name it. I do everything except full frontal nudity, but in your case I just might make an exception." She winked and laughed. Her laugh indicated that she was just kidding...but maybe not.

I was definitely a stranger in a strange land as I made my way into the dining hall where Dorothy was waving a large bread knife at me and pointing to her watch. I recited the blessing, cut into the gargantuan loaf of *challah* in front of the bride and groom and plopped down into a chair at the end of the head table.

After several slow dance numbers, the band turned raucous. Each set concluded with a hora, a jitterbug, a Greek line dance or some combination of all of them, after which Foxy would tell a few risqué jokes, then chant: "Sit down, sit down, your dinner is served..." The guests didn't waste a second. When they heard another course was coming, they deserted the dance floor and made for their seats.

I watched with amazement as Foxy waltzed around the room with a mike glued to her mouth. Pointing to the Bride and Groom she feigned awe.

"Are they beautiful, or what?" The guests managed to applaud without skipping a bite. The drummer punctuated Foxy's commentary with rim shots and the tuba broke musical wind in harmony as the guests continued to feast.

"And will you look at the size of the groom's hands? What does that tell you, honey?" Foxy pointed the mike at the bride, who couldn't stop giggling. The comedienne helped out. "What it means is that he has huge feet, isn't that right?"

Foxy turned to the audience who got the joke even if the bride didn't. "I heard what he did to the Rabbi's hand with that big foot of his. All I can say is, it's a good thing it was only his foot."

Snare drum and tuba: Ba-boom.

When the laughter died down a bit, Foxy turned to me.

"Speaking of the Rabbi, I discovered something important about him that you should know."

I froze.

"The Rabbi," she slowly revealed "is a virgin."

The audience cackled. I blushed.

"That's right folks. This is his first wedding. Tell me, how did he do?"

They applauded on cue.

"Stand up Rabbi, take a bow."

I was terrified, but Foxy wouldn't let up.

"Stand up, Rabbi. Come on, show us you're a regular guy." Then she turned to the guests and they all joined her in a loud chorus. "Stand up! Stand up! Stand up!"

I knew this was not going to turn out well but what could I do? I stood up. Now the crowd was animated.

Foxy smiled sweetly. "Now I would like to see a show of hands, women only, please. How many of you ladies think the Rabbi looks better in clothes?"

They howled with laughter as every female from tot to grandmother joined in the joke and raised her hand.

Milton's camera captured it all and I was numb as I sat down.

The speeches that followed were generally predictable, except for the last one. A palpable shudder emerged from the crowd when a portly man in a silk suit stood up.

"For the benefit of all you freeloaders who don't even know who I am, I'll tell you. I'm Gus Pomeranz, father of the bride." The crowd responded with a loud BOO. Gus was unfazed. "I'm spending over fifty thousand dollars on this blessed event and I have a right to speak my piece."

Everyone at the head table looked as though they were about to watch a beheading. Caprice dropped her head onto the remnants of the *Challah* in front of her. Gus broke several glasses with his fork, trying to calm the rising din. One of the broken glasses sent wine flying onto the bridesmaid who had the misfortune of being seated next to him. The crowd wouldn't stop shushing and Gus wouldn't stop breaking glasses. To settle the standoff, Gus turned to me.

"Tell me, Rabbi, is it right? Do these *shnorers* have the right to deny the man who has devoted his entire life to his beautiful daughter, an opportunity to say a few words on the happiest day of her life? Is that just or fair? Please tell me Rabbi, I want to hear it from you. Do I not have a right as a father and a generous contributor to the U.J.A., the Boy Scouts and every other damn chiseler and beggar, to offer my heartfelt wishes to the most important person in my life?"

All eyes turned towards me. Literally hundreds of people waved their napkins and shook their heads at me.

"DO NOT UNDER ANY CIRCUMSTANCES LET HIM SPEAK" was the clear message.

What was I do to? Did I have the authority to silence a father at his daughter's wedding? Even if I did, should I? Even if he is truly as callous and vulgar as it appears he is, would that justify my joining the crowd to stifle him? This is no longer a hypothetical question of tempering justice with mercy, this is real life. Milton's camera was on me and I had to make a decision. My profound ignorance of matters "practical" dictated that I decide in favor of the abstract.

"I can't think of a reason why any father should be prevented from wishing his daughter a life of happiness and joy," I solemnly pronounced.

In hindsight, that was a serious mistake.

A low groan went up from the entire hall of over four hundred people as I sat down.

Satisfied that he would have his day, Gus triumphantly waved a glass of champagne, spattering it on the same poor bridesmaid who bore a swath of red wine on her dress from his last spill.

"I could stay here all night and talk about my little Jennie. Of course, in that pushed up dress her hippy mother picked out, she doesn't look all that little anymore."

Judging from Jennie's pasted smile, it was clear that she was either still high or body snatched. Caprice, her mother, held her napkin over her face as Gus rambled on.

"I love you Jennie. I've always loved you and I've only wanted the best for you. Like any father, I always knew the day would come when you would get married and I wouldn't be the number one man in your life anymore. That was a painful thought in many ways but I was happy to think you might find the perfect boy, fall in love, marry and live happily ever after. That's all I ever wanted for you, dear Jennie. You must believe that." His eyes began to water and he stopped for a moment.

"I love you too, daddykins," Jennie called out.

"Don't encourage him," her mother hissed from behind her napkin.

Gus regained his composure. "Now I've got a few choice words about Robert."

The crowd growled audibly. Foxy signaled the band to ring in with rim shots and tuba blasts.

"I will not be shushed," Gus snarled. He

folded his arms Mussolini-style across his chest and waited. The roar finally abated and Gus continued. His tone became uncharacteristically gentle.

"Robert and Jennie have known each other since they were in kindergarten. At first it was amusing to watch them play together but once they got into high school I became a little concerned. The noises I heard coming from her bedroom were definitely not Latin conjugations and I warned Robert that if he tried to hump my virgin daughter, I'd cut his *shmekel* off and I would have too, if I had been around. But as many of you know, while Jenny was still in school, I was kicked out of my own house by the most vile and corrupt woman who ever lived."

Caprice threw a Kaiser roll at Gus. He ducked. Fortunately, so did the bridesmaid.

"With me out of the house and my profligate ex-wife left to guard my little girl's virtue, who the hell knows what went on, so I prepared for the worst. I hired a private detective to check up on Robert."

The pelting of Kaiser rolls became a veritable assault but even that didn't stop Gus.

"Here's what I found out. Nothing. That is, nothing I didn't already know. That he's no Einstein is not news. He can do some pretty stupid things sometimes but all in all, Robert's not a bad young man. On the plus side, his mother is still a great looking piece of ass and I've always been fond of her. Okay, I've said everything I need to about Robert."

Then Gus turned to the bride and groom at the head table and extended his hand. "Having said all that, I would like to know only one thing,

Jenny." Pointing to the groom, he asked "Why? Why in God's name did you decide to blow off Robert and marry this Jeffrey character? Jeffrey is an idiot. He says he's an actor. I've seen him act and though I may not be a critic, I can tell you one thing. He stinks! How much money can a good actor make, let alone a stinko like him? You'll both starve. Who's going to support you, his parents? A couple of losers and ugly as sin, both of them. And you, Rabbi! You joined my daughter with this *putz* in holy matrimony? They should revoke your license if you even have one."

When bottles began to fly and a food fight broke out, I ran for the door.

"I'm crazy, CRAZY!" I looked around the room that had surreptitiously turned into a soundstage. Omar had placed two more cameras in the middle of the food fight and was exploiting the riot for one of his TV ads! The band played a Dixieland Rag and Foxy got the non-combatants to sing along.

My first wedding had degenerated into a Ritz Brothers farce. What's worse, it's going to be on television promoting Crazy Omar's Royal abomination featuring me as "his favorite Rabbi". How did I let this happen? Help me figure this one out, God. How?

On the long drive home, I fumed and drove faster than I should have. The Taconic State Parkway is badly banked and dark. There wasn't another car in either direction, so there wasn't even the advantage of headlights from passing traffic. Normally, I stay under the fifty mile an hour limit, but that night my thoughts were speeding wildly. Suddenly I lurched forward and heard a loud screech of metal scraping against metal. A shower of sparks jerked me back to the other reality, the one outside my head. I had apparently hit the median barrier and ricocheted across the highway onto the gravel shoulder. Shaken, I got out to assess the damage.

Both headlights were smashed, my bumper was completely detached and the front left fender was bent. So was the median barrier. I threw the bumper into the thick grass on the side of the road and with all my might, pulled back the fender so that it wouldn't rub against the tire.

It took awhile to register how reckless I had allowed myself to become. "I could have killed myself ..."

Driving at a snail's pace and barely able to navigate the dark road on my wobbly tires, I had even more time to wallow in my misery. My thoughts flew all over the place. Did Omar plan this thing from the very beginning? He said he contacted every other Rabbi and no one was available, including one who was in jail. Who was that? I never heard of any Rabbi in the area being arrested. Did he wait until the last minute because every other Rabbi knew what a base, conniving scurrilous bastard he is and turned him down flat? He knew this was my first pulpit and I must have seemed hopelessly naïve. Seemed? Hell, I *was* hopelessly naïve. How easily he duped me. How foolish I was to fall for it. But what else could I do?

By the time I got home, I was completely dejected. The fender was worse than I thought, and so was I. I couldn't fall asleep that night. I had no one to talk to. I was too embarrassed to call anyone. I walked around the house like a zombie, unable to eat. By morning I had not slept a wink and I couldn't drag myself to the Synagogue. When I thought of the meetings, the counseling sessions, the lectures I was scheduled to deliver and the classes I was supposed to teach, I felt paralyzed. I was elected to the pulpit to be a spiritual leader, to initiate, to guide, to confront where necessary and yes, to bring down the entire sanctuary if it became corrupt. What a mockery I had made of my calling. I felt like a worm.

I walked around in my pajamas the entire next day. Over and over again I thought of what I could have done, should have done...but every time I did, I heard Omar's voice pressuring me. "...shoulda, woulda, coulda..." I would never forgive him for what he did to me.

By nightfall, I was still unable to eat. How did I allow him to seduce me into thinking I could control events at Crazy Omar's "...where more sacred events are consecrated – both religious and non – than at any other catering hall in the tri-state area." How could I have been so stupid and so deluded to think that I could make something decent – and even beautiful – happen in that sordid, debased temple of sleaze? I made a terrible mistake in judgment and soon – as long as it takes to edit a TV commercial from all the footage - my shame will be a source of amusement to cable viewers everywhere. I suddenly recalled Milton and his video camera following me all around the damn place. CLOSE-UP: my bleeding hand under the groom's foot. CLOSE-UP: Omar's arm around me making it appear as though I was his friend and ally.

CLOSE-UP: Women voting unanimously that I look better with my clothes ON! I could see how this could be edited in such as way as to make me the chief villain in this well-planned sacrilege. What will the members of my congregation say? Will the board even consider renewing my contract?

I'm ruined!

What to do...what do to? The craziest ideas wafted in and out of my head. Let's see...I could disappear. How? Where would I go? My weary brain wouldn't give me a clue. Suicide? Kill myself? Nothing could be more repugnant to a Jew and no matter what I am or am not, I shall always be a Jew.

On the other hand...there might be a way. I remembered talking to one of the older members of my congregation when I first came to Lake LaSalle. Leib Schumacher was born in the Ukraine. His lineage reached back to Rabbi Levi Yitzhak of Berdichev, the revered scholar and saint who was known as "The Advocate of the Jews in the heavenly court".

Leib studied in the great *Yeshiva* and was about to become ordained as a Rabbi when the Germans invaded. For five years, he wandered through forests and ruins of villages, scavenging for food and sleeping with one eye open. The only thing he carried with him was his prayer shawl and phylacteries, which he donned every single morning.

When the war ended, he returned to what had been his home and discovered that his whole family had perished in the *Shoah*. He wept as he wandered around the remnants of his village and saw the desolation and witnessed the destruction

101

the Nazis had wrought. He listened with a broken heart to stories of torture and wanton, brutal murders. He ambled through desecrated synagogues and cemeteries. He was so distraught, he determined that he could no longer live in a world where God's will had been so completely corrupted and His laws trampled. At that moment, he decided to commit suicide. But how could a Jew violate God's most basic commandment? He pondered the question in all of its ramifications. He argued with himself, skillfully employing his keen knowledge of Talmudic casuistry and finally devised a plan. A Jew could not commit suicide, he reasoned, but what if he brought God into the process and made Him the executioner?

THE PLAN: From the day of his Bar Mitzvah, Leib had obeyed every commandment required of him and even tossed in a few extra for good measure. Each morning when he arose from sleep at the crack of dawn - so as not to miss a moment of the day when a *mitzvah* could be performed - he donned his Prayer shawl and phylacteries and recited every single prayer with devotion. Even during the terrible years when he was hiding out in the forests! The plan he devised was diabolically simple. The next morning, when the sun rose, he would not get up to don the *tallit* and *tefillin*. He would not recite the prayers. He would remain in bed and allow God to smite him for neglecting His commandments. Naturally, he didn't sleep that night. He lay in his bed, sweating and trembling and felt as though his heart was going to burst from the moment the sun rose.

Morning came and went. The sun rose

higher in the sky.

"When, God, when will it come?" He cried.

He was on death row without even the comfort of knowing the hour of his execution.

He lay there the entire day, convulsing, shivering, anticipating the swift painful bolt of lightning that would end his life. Several times he believed death was at hand but those were false alarms. When night finally came, he was still alive but totally confused and distraught. Why? Why didn't God punish him?

If he was not worthy to die, on what basis could he hope to live? He finally concluded that there were two possibilities.

The first: It is God's Will that Leib should live, but in a state of utter confusion and uncertainty, a state in which the customs and laws he was brought up to believe and practice were totally inscrutable and he would *never* comprehend their meaning...*or*...

The second possibility: There is no God and religion is a farce.

Why did I think of that terrible story? I hate that story! I guess I thought it might give me some insight as to how to kill myself but by the time I got to the end I realized how stupid that was. His situation was nothing like mine and it certainly didn't shed any light on my predicament.

When night fell again, I lay in bed, eyes wide open. Now that suicide was ruled out, I had only one option. I must find a way to redeem myself. But how? What can I do? Beating my breast and fasting won't do it. I have to find some tangible act...some way to regain my self esteem *and* my reputation...but what could that be? Ideas raced through my brain but none of them were any good.

Think...think. I was too exhausted. My brain had shut down.

I couldn't go another night without sleep, so I took two Tylenol PM's. I don't know how long I slept, but it was still dark when I was awaken by sounds from my TV.

"I'm crazy! I'm so crazy I'm going to double the size of my catering..."

There, glaring at me from the monitor in my bedroom was my mortal enemy, Crazy Omar! How did that happen? I must have set the timer by mistake. I was horrified and enraged. I looked everywhere for the remote control but I couldn't find the damn thing. I tried to turn it off manually but in my dazed, sensory-deprived state I couldn't figure out how to do that. I pushed every button several times. It didn't turn off but it did switch channels.

There was no going back to sleep. On the screen, an animated angel dressed in a top hat and tails and sporting the requisite wings on his back, tap-danced a la Fred Astaire, on the head of a pin. The advertised product was "Angel food cake, guaranteed to lift your sagging spirits".

Lift my sagging spirits? Angel...angels...of course! This commercial was *meant* to grab my attention...but why? What's the message? My discussion with Brigham Horowitz came flying back. That was the prelude to my first conversation with repulsive Omar!

When the commercial faded out, the late movie that had been playing on that channel came on.

"The Lord your God has instructed you this day..." It was *The Ten Commandments* and Joshua was being anointed to lead the Israelites into the Promised Land. In order to fulfill God's prophecy, the children of Israel would have to utterly destroy the city of Jericho, the center of harlotry and abomination.

When the channel logo appeared on the bottom of my screen, my hunch was validated. The movies on this late-night station were called *The-Never-Too-Late show*.

That's it! It's never too late to redeem yourself.

I was glued to the TV. After a series of more inane and seemingly endless commercials, the movie returned. There was God in a cloud of radiant smoke speaking to Joshua, played by the very handsome John Derek, the perfect incarnation of Moses' successor.

God said, "Have I not commanded you to be strong and resolute? Be not frightened nor distracted from your mission. I, the Lord your God, am with you and your descendents."

Joshua's descendents. That's me!

As I watched the walls of Jericho tumble, I wanted to kick myself. That's what I should have done to Crazy Omar's temple of harlotry and abomination! The Chancellor of the Rabbinical Academy had warned us that our task would always be difficult and sometimes painful, but as Rabbis we had the responsibility to guide our generation to a higher spiritual plane. That meant rooting out injustice, intolerance and

105

sacrilege, no matter what the personal cost. I was excruciatingly aware of my shameful inaction. I let my people down. I refused to confront the banalities and idolatries of Crazy Omar. Instead, I made three-hundred dollars and participated in his blasphemy.

Okay, no point going over that again. I needed to perform some redemptive *ACT.* An action...something tangible...

Through the grogginess of the Tylenol PMs and Cecil B. DeMille's heroic depiction of my ancestors' glories, the cosmic plan revealed itself to me. First, the angel in the earlier commercial commanded my attention. Now Joshua is telling me that I must do what he would have done if he were the Rabbi of Temple Beth Israel of Greater Lake LaSalle. I must utterly destroy Omar's hedonistic temple of Baal in the neighboring town of Canaan, from the face of the earth. "*Canaan...?*" The final clue!

Selecting the method was easy. I went to my closet where I kept my High Holiday vestments and found the perfect weapon, my *shofar* (ram's horn). Joshua brought down the entire city of Jericho by sounding the *shofar.* That power was now channeled to me!

I had no idea what time it was as I drove – slowly, darkly and wobbly because of the bent fender - to Canaan, armed with my *shofar* and prayer shawl. Occasional trucks flashed high beams at me as they passed. At first I assumed they did that because I was driving without headlights, but then it occurred to me that Joshua just might be using those high beams to give me a "thumbs-up" to remind me to be strong and resolute.

The glitzy catering complex was dark when I arrived. It was strange to see a burnt out shell of a car where Omar's gold Rolls-Royce was usually mounted but I didn't grasp the significance of that until much later. I parked across the road to prepare to carry out the mission. I had done all the thinking and hesitating and rethinking about what I had to do. The time for reflection was over. The time for action was at hand. This was the place. My assignment was clear. I would rise to the challenge as John Derek had done so courageously before me, and Joshua, before him.

I trembled as I took my *shofar* and prayer shawl in hand and entered the contaminated grounds of Crazy Omar's Royal Catering Hall. I was weak from lack of sleep and it occurred to me that I hadn't eaten for two days, but I would not be deterred from my sacred duty. I wrapped the *tallit* over my head and pressed my lips to the tiny head of the ram's horn and blew until my ears rang.

No sounds came out, but I felt a surge of darkness rising up to my brain. About to pass out, I leaned against a wall to catch my breath. "*Hazak ve-ematz!* Be strong and resolute," I said to myself in Hebrew and English, over and over. I rested for a few moments and tried again. There were sounds this time, but only of me, wheezing. I needed another few minutes to rest before trying again. When I was ready, I took several deep breaths and blew with all my might. A pathetic, broken little whistle emerged from my *shofar*. I sustained it as long as I could but when I looked around, nothing had tumbled. My head was spinning and I had to catch my breath and rest again. I couldn't recall how long it took for the walls of Jericho to tumble after the *shofar* blasts. Maybe I should give it a few minutes. I did. Still, no tumbling. Then I remembered. It took Joshua six days of warm up and on the seventh day, after circling the city seven times with lots of *shofrot* bellowing, the walls finally collapsed. After a quick reality check, I deduced that I didn't have a chorus of horn blowers to back me up and I wouldn't last the night, let alone seven days, so I had better just give it my best shot.

I straightened my prayer shawl, took several deep breaths and raised my *shofar* high. I blew out a perfect blast and held it as long as I could. I marched around the periphery of the building, continuing to blow. I tripped occasionally, but got back up each time. Exhausted as I was, I found the strength to carry out my mission. I must have gotten a good twenty blasts out of that thing before stumbling back to the road.

When I reached my car, I had to lean against the door to keep from falling on my face. I just stood there, looking at the Hall...still standing.

I watched and waited...and waited...and waited.

Nothing.

Minutes went by. More minutes...and still nothing.

I felt the mark of Cain emblazoned on my forehead as I slid to the ground and stared into the darkness. Before, I felt useless, inadequate and miserable. Now I felt hopeless.

After more minutes – I don't know how many - of self-loathing, I picked myself up, threw my *shofar* onto the front seat, took off my prayer shawl and got into my car. It took the longest time to find my key. When I finally did, I put it into the ignition and...the most amazing thing happened. I heard a mighty EXPLOSION and the entire road lit up. With hot dust flying into my car from the open window, I looked around to see what it was. The catering hall was burning and this was not just a small flare-up! The entire complex was on fire. It was an inferno, a conflagration. Red and yellow swirls danced heavenward like a spectacular light show.

Through ash-encrusted lips, I proclaimed triumphantly, "Vengeance is Mine!" I chanted one of my favorite psalms all the way home. "From the depths of my depravity, I called to you, Lord. You heard my plea and girded my loins with strength. You defeated my enemies and redeemed my soul."

I don't know how long I slept but when I awoke the sun was shining and I was ravenous. The milk was rancid, so I ate frosted flakes with pineapple juice. I went into the bathroom and brushed my teeth, trying to remember my dream. I turned on the small TV next to the sink as I shaved and was astonished to see Crazy Omar, Dorothy and Milton in handcuffs, being led to a police car.

An on-camera reporter surrounded by a crowd of on-lookers announced from the scene. "By the time the police arrived, the whole complex was ablaze. A combination of police, fire fighters and our video team caught Omar, his sister

Dorothy and her husband, Milton Gruber, setting fire to their establishment in an obvious attempt to cash in on an insurance policy. It backfired because some mysterious, other-worldly sounds roused the neighbors from their sleep." He turned to a middle aged man with a barrel stomach. "What do you think those sounds were?"

"Sounded to me like bagpipes. I figured somebody died, 'cause that's the only time you hear those damn things."

The woman next to him said "I believe it was mother nature giving us a wakeup call."

"Maybe it was Jesus," said one young man.

"I don't think so," replied the lady. "It was definitely a woman's voice."

The reporter put the microphone in the face of a familiar looking boy who couldn't be more than twelve.

"What's your name, young man?"

"Brigham...Horowitz."

"Where do you think those sounds came from, Brigham?"

"Well...I know exactly who made those weird noises."

"You do?"

"Yeah...it was an angel."

"You saw an angel?"

"Well, you can't always see 'em. Sometimes angels have arms and wings and stuff but sometimes they're invisible like incorpora borealis."

"You seem to know a lot about angels."

"Yeah, I do. I got this real neat Rabbi who explained it all to me. You see, sometimes regular people decide they got to do stuff they wouldn't normally do but they go ahead and do it anyway because it's important. They don't get credit for the good stuff they do, because most people don't realize how things worked out the way they did, but once you know how angels operate, it's pretty clear."

"So it was an angel who blew the whistle on Omar and his accomplices?"

"No doubt about it," Brigham said confidently.

Tears ran down my cheeks as I watched Brigham and finally understood why I was called.

Eden

Eden

"Pretty...better looking than most of the girls you've dated, but a little young, don't you think?" Peter handed back the snapshot of a smiling co-ed in a cap and gown.

"Yes, she is good looking...and young, but curiously, the woman who answered the door didn't look anything like this photo."

Peter choked on his martini. "They pulled a switch on you?"

"Not exactly, it was the same girl alright, only twenty-five years older. When her mother gave me the snapshot she did say it wasn't recent, but what she didn't tell me was that it was taken at her graduation from Vassar when I was in the second grade!"

Peter Magnussen loved to hear about my failed blind dates almost as much as he loved to dine at the Jewish country club. He was Vicar of St. Bartholomew, one of the oldest Episcopal churches in the county and one of the most affable men I ever met. When I came to Acadia-on-Hudson two years ago, we became best friends. Our professional crises and pulpit experiences were so similar that we found ourselves crying about the same terrors of death and bereavement, laughing at the silliness of domestic squabbles, gossiping about some of our more volatile elders who love us one day and hate us the next and just about everything else from Wittgenstein to Bill Maher.

He thought the attempts to "marry me off" were hilarious and this time he started to howl even before I got into the story. He only stopped when the waitress interrupted to ask if we were ready to order. Peter had finished his third martini and I was still working on my first white wine spritzer.

"Have another," I offered.

"I should have something to eat." Turning to the waitress he said "Bring me another Beefeater martini, but throw in a few olives this time."

She looked at me and pointed to my barely touched spritzer.

"The Rabbi will have another popsicle." Peter loved to taunt me about my inability to drink.

I couldn't understand how anyone can drink three martinis at lunch and not fall on their face. I barely drink one glass of wine and I spend the rest of the day walking up a steep hill. Amazingly, Peter could drink indefinitely without dulling his humor or intelligence one whit. In fact, the more he drank the more cogent he became.

"Make that a tuna fish sandwich on wheat toast for me," I said, "and Father Magnussen will have...?"

The waitress tapped her pencil impatiently on her pad as Peter studied the menu. We both knew what he wanted, but he was never sure it was okay to select the most expensive items on the menu. I ordered for him.

"The Vicar will have the double rib steak," I said, and asked her to also bring every side dish on the menu to be preceded by every appetizer he could take home in doggy bags and three of the five desserts.

Unlike Rabbis, whose remuneration is roughly equal to most professionals, Peter received neither salary nor honoraria for the many rites, rituals and other religious *and* civic duties he performed. He had to provide for his ailing wife and four young children with the sometimes meager offerings in the Sunday wickets.

It was two thirty and we were the only ones left in the dining hall. Everyone else was either out on the golf course, in the gym playing racquet ball or more likely, in the health club, kibitzing and smoking cigars as they watched TV. My congregants were "Jewish gregarious", that is, gentle people who were interested in everyone else's business and ended every argument with a joke. One of their favorite jokes was how they acquired a major portion of real estate in one of the last pristine WASP "Juden-reines" or Jew-free communities in America.

Acadia-on-Hudson is a magical enclave on a promontory overlooking the Hudson River where Manhattan's elite movers and shakers built their country estates in the beginning of the twentieth century. Over the years the town grew, but the pure white Christian town council managed the expansion of their insulated community by maintaining strict standards for ownership of land. Strangers were not welcome and to that end they created a private police force that did not deal kindly with "people who looked like they didn't belong". Until the early nineteen-fifties, there was a huge sign on Highway 46, the only road leading into Acadia that read "This is God-fearing Christian land. No Jews, Niggers or stray dogs allowed".

After World War II, many previously segregated communities within commuting distance of Manhattan were invaded by voracious bands of newly created non-WASP millionaires. Acadia-on-Hudson, one of the last such enclaves was thought to be impervious to such assaults *and* they might have been, had it not been for the determination of Becky Conway, wife of Bernard Conway, né Cohen. Becky was nine when her father was beaten to death by Cossacks led by a Priest who declared that Mother Russia was a Christian land and Jews were a pollutant to be expelled or exterminated. The next day, she and her mother began their two year trek across Russia to Romania and then Turkey to board a boat bound for America. From her mother, she learned to survive by viewing every misfortune as a challenge to be overcome by shrewdness, hard work and a dose of vengeance. When Becky and Bernie married, they didn't have the proverbial "pot", but after five years of skimping, scraping and learning how to befriend powerful men, they acquired a New York City taxi medallion. Bernie worked two shifts, she worked one, and five years later they owned three cabs and were working on a fourth when Bernie was run over by a bus. Becky won a sizable court judgment against the City and bought twenty more cabs. War was looming and on a tip from one of her Wall Street friends, Becky sold her entire fleet to invest in something called nylon.

By the end of the war, Becky Conway was one of the richest women in New York. On a tour of several of her manufacturing plants Upstate, she saw the sign on Route 46 barring entrance to non-Christians, non-whites and stray animals. In that moment, Acadia-on-Hudson became the Village in Russia where her father was murdered and from which she and her mother were expelled.

Becky sent Gentile members of her senior staff to Acadia to befriend the townspeople. Through them, she discovered all she needed to know about the "Jew-free" oil, steel and rail companies controlled by the local power brokers and in ways known only to her closest friends, she secured a significant voting interest in all of them. When the town elders realized that their firms had been infiltrated, they brought lawsuits, which they lost. Becky initiated counter-suits which the landed gentry also lost, collectively and individually and for which they paid dearly. The family fortunes handed down to them by their pure white Christian ancestors were diminishing rapidly and they were left with no alternative but to sell their lavish estates at fair market value - to a *Yid*! As soon as Becky acquired most of the prime river-front property and ruled the town council by proxy, she hired Frank Lloyd Wright to design a magnificent Synagogue to be built on Route 46 right next to the sign barring Jews, Niggers and stray dogs. A year later, half the original residents had fled and were replaced by a large community of affluent Jewish families. Since the old country club excluded them, the "nouveau-riche" built their own, twice the size of the *goyishe* club and provided far better facilities.

The Jews of Acadia were genuinely delighted to see the Episcopal Vicar dine with their Rabbi. It made them feel morally superior to their Gentile neighbors, who never invited any Jew, including the Rabbi, to their *far-kackte* club.

As they passed by during lunch, each had a ritual joke for us. The opening line was always the same: "You're gonna love this one." The joke featured a Priest, a Minister and a Rabbi *or* a Pollock, a Frenchman and a Jew *or* one of several other familiar combinations. The setting could be darkest Africa, an active volcano or a Broadway delicatessen but they were all the same joke. My congregants usually tried to delete the coarsest words. Sometimes when they stumbled, Peter would help them out. "Cunnilingus might be the word you're looking for," he would say. They were more than decent people, they were generous souls who enjoyed making people laugh and Peter loved their openness *and* their generosity. They never allowed either of us to pick up a tab.

"So what does this middle-aged spinster do?" He asked, looking at the out-dated photo of the pretty girl in the cap and gown.

"Not much of anything from what I gathered. Her mother said she's considering several careers but so far she hasn't yet figured out what she wants to do with her life. Fortunately, there's no pressure because daddy set up a generous trust fund so she can explore as long as she likes. I don't know if the mother told me that to throw me off about the age thing or to let me know 'daddy' is well-healed."

"Since when are you interested in P.H.G.'s?"

I have no idea where Peter learned the expression familiar to all Jewish boys but I couldn't help being impressed. Our parents used to say, "it's just as easy to fall in love with a rich girl as a poor one, so keep an eye out for P.H.G.'s," that is, *poppa hut gelt* (rich daddy).

"I have never been interested in P.H.G.'s and I certainly wouldn't consider that a factor in selecting a wife, much less a date. I got roped into this one at my monthly book review-lecture. The women's auxiliary ganged up on me. They were determined to get me to go out with...this woman, I can't even remember her name. The incredibly aggressive mother led the assault but she had plenty of support. It's as though they had rehearsed for weeks. 'This is a girl, Rabbi, *blah, blah, blah*'. When the grandmother got caught up in the frenzy, I knew there was no way out. The old lady grabbed my lapel and stared at me intensely. 'She's *really* good at the sex stuff,' she said in a loud, raspy whisper."

Peter went into a coughing jag and raised his hand for me to stop. I did, he drained his martini glass and I continued.

"I felt like Gulliver trapped by raging Lilliputians. There was no way to put them off. They insisted I call the girl then and there, and I caved."

The waitress brought more drinks and all the food. Peter removed his olives and started to work on his fourth martini. He arranged the food so that it could easily be put into doggy bags. I felt awful that his family feasted only on his leftovers. I tried several times to slip him some money, suggesting it was for parking or gas but he graciously declined.

"*Nu?*" Peter smiled. I couldn't get over his ease with Yiddishisms. "So what happened?"

"There I was in a gilded and glass elevator on Sutton Place South moving up rapidly toward the forty-second floor when I suddenly got that uneasy feeling in my gut. How did I let them nab me again? Over the past two years, I had gotten myself fixed up with a dozen or so blind dates and every one of them turned out to be a disaster."

"What made you think this was going to be any different?" Peter sucked the gin out of the olive then put it back in his glass.

"One of the reasons I buckled was that a cousin of hers is a particularly striking woman and the wife of a Rabbi-turned-lawyer who always sat in the first row of my lectures. She managed to distract me regularly by crossing and uncrossing her long legs to the point where I fantasized that the cousin they were trying to pawn off on me just might be something like her. Obviously, I was wrong because when this girl...this woman opened the door and said, 'Hi, I'm Felice...are you... Ben?' I freaked."

"What did you do?"

"For a long moment, I just stood there. She bore a faint resemblance to the cute girl in the cap and gown but she was older...much older. In fact, she resembled her grandmother more than her mother. From the disappointed look on her face, it was clear that she had expected a much more mature man. I guess the title Rabbi implies graying temples and a white beard. It was a terribly awkward moment. Neither of us knew what to do. Obviously, we had both been sucker-punched and we were both reeling. I had to find a way to get us out of that car wreck as quickly and painlessly as possible so I said the first thing that flew into my head.

'Is this apartment 3902?' I asked sheepishly.

'No, this is 4202.'

'Sorry,' I said and pretended to feel foolish.

She slammed the door and I made a dash for the elevator."

Peter laughed so hard, his martini dribbled down his cheek. "You're going straight to hell, you know that."

"It was a humiliating situation for both of us. What was I to do?"

"What happened after you left? Did you call the woman?"

"Sure. I waited about half an hour, then I phoned to say that an emergency had arisen that required my immediate attention. I apologized for standing her up and told her I'd try again sometime. I called her mother and made the same excuse just to cover my ass."

"Did they buy it?"

"I think so, I hope so...I don't know."

"Why do you let your congregants get into your social life? That's a guaranteed recipe for disaster."

"It's complicated, Peter. You don't remember what it is to be lonely. What do I do? I try to avoid blind dates as best I can, but pressure from my own libido combined with the aggressiveness of the matchmakers becomes overwhelming. You should hear them. 'She's perfect!'...'Call her, what have you got to lose?'...'I'm just asking you to go out on one date. Cupid will do the rest'...'Don't get frightened. I'm not asking you to marry her. Well, maybe I am.' Then, they laugh and say 'I'm kidding' but we all know they're not. Everybody's got 'the perfect girl', it seems, until I meet them and realize it's just another catastrophe in the making."

I expected Peter to roar with laughter.

He didn't.

"What is it?" I asked.

Something was up.

"I repeat the question," I said.

"I can't help it," Peter started on his steak, but it was clear he was saving the best part for his doggy bag. "When you talked about the perfect girl, someone actually came to mind."

"Oh no, not you too."

"Absolutely not and that's why I won't say another word about it." He fell silent again.

"Who is she?"

"Who?"

"Come on, Peter. What's she like, this perfect girl?"

"I'm not going to say."

"Why? Is she not beautiful, is she not brilliant, is her father not a multi-millionaire, is she not 'perfect' for me?"

"Yes and no. She is exquisitely beautiful, smart, spiritual and extremely talented. Her father is very wealthy, but he's disowned her so there won't be any of that coming her way. I must say she is perfect for someone, but not you."

I was hooked. Peter's wife Bridget is an unusually attractive, intelligent woman, so I trusted his taste.

"Why is she not perfect for me?"

"For one thing, she's not Jewish. "

As I drove across the Tri-Borough Bridge toward Broadway and 47th street to meet Peter's idea of "the perfect girl", I tried to visualize what she would be like, this renegade daughter of one of the richest families in Acadia who dropped out of Wellesley in defiance of her parents and took a job first as a bar-tender, then stand-up comic in low-life saloons and soon became a hugely successful Broadway actress. I had not dated a girl who wasn't Jewish since high school but Peter's description hit every one of my buttons. The fact that she was also interested in philosophy and that he had lent her his copy of William James "The Varieties of Religious Experience" definitely rendered her kosher in my horny mind. He mentioned something about a health issue but he didn't know any details so I didn't give it much thought.

This was my first experience meeting a Broadway star backstage and I wanted to look the part. I must say I felt pretty good in my new double breasted cashmere coat as I walked all the way from the parking lot on Tenth Avenue towards the Hitchcock Theater. On the corner of Eighth Avenue, a Black wino wrapped in a combination of cardboard and rags winked at me and pointed to my coat.

"Whooee, check out the bad vines," he grinned.

I couldn't help smiling because that was precisely how I felt about my new coat, but when he started to follow me and imitate my stride, I picked up the pace. When he strutted alongside me as though we were together, I tried not to notice.

"We sho look good tonight!" he said proudly as he waved to passers-by, smiling broadly and pointing to *our* coat.

I finally lost my escort in the crowds spilling out of the theaters along Broadway. At first I breathed a sigh of relief but the truth is I was glad so many eyes were drawn to my beautiful coat, even if they had to be guided there by my weird friend.

The guard let me pass through the throng of autograph hounds pressing against the stage door when I told him I was a guest of MaryAnne Pembroke. There were cast pictures on the walls and it was easy to recognize her. Peter had shown me clippings of her in a variety of poses and shows. Her exuberant expression atop a perfect body in motion was what one hopes to see in a great performer. When she opened her dressing room door she was wearing a short silk gown that barely covered her black pantyhose and bulging bra. She wore heels that weren't too high but very sexy and drew my eye directly to her perfectly shaped legs. For a moment I thought I was looking at a magnificent tall tree transmogrified into the most elegant of women. I had difficulty breathing as I looked at her. She was that stunning.

"I'm Ben..."

"I guessed," she forced a distracted smile. Her long black hair was the perfect frame for her radiant, aristocratic face. She had a small straight nose, thin sensitive lips and piecing dark brown eyes.

"...yes, of course I'm still here..." she said into the phone she was holding.

I couldn't take my eyes off her. She looked something like...I couldn't even think of anyone more beautiful. She was beyond comparison. She waved me in with her free hand and pointed to a chair but her attention was obviously elsewhere so I continued to stand.

"Call me back as soon as you know," she said "...it doesn't matter, anytime...if I'm not here, leave a message...thanks, Alan." She looked distraught and I suddenly felt I was intruding. She put down the phone and let out an involuntary squeal as she sat on a hard chair opposite a huge mirror. She held her stomach as if she were having some sort of spasm and reached for a bottle of pills, downing a couple of them with a long draught from a half filled bottle of white wine.

I waited for a moment not knowing what to say when she turned to me and smiled warmly although her eyes still showed signs of lingering discomfort. "Hi Ben, I'm MaryAnne. Did you see the show?"

"No, I'm sorry...I couldn't make it, but I hear it's great. I'm definitely going to try to get..."

The door flew open and a cute, very short girl with bowers of blonde curls dangling around her unusually large head, big saucer blue eyes and the brightest teeth I had ever seen, popped in.

"Please don't leave," she pleaded. "We need you. I need you." MaryAnne stood up and embraced the munchkin who was attractive in her way but at least a foot shorter.

"You'll be great, Marci. I have no doubt about that."

Marci noticed me. "You look like some kind of power dude. Are you her agent? Would you please convince her to stay? The show will collapse without her."

"This is Ben, Marci. He's not an agent, he's a Rabbi."

She looked me over with a put-on lascivious smile. "Aren't you kind of cute to be a Rabbi?" she pretend-flirted as she ran her hand down my tie.

"Marci, you're gay," MaryAnne gently reminded her.

"Not always," she said, but judging from her immediate loss of interest in me, I assumed she was *always*. She gave MaryAnne a long hug. "Come see me and promise you'll give me notes."

When Marci left, the room became suddenly quiet.

"I didn't know you were leaving the show." I didn't want to pry but I felt I had to say something. "Just tired of it or are there bigger plans in the making?"

She thought for a long moment before deciding just how much she wanted to reveal. "It's time to move on." The phone rang and she picked it up quickly. "What's the story?" Her face screwed up as she listened. "Shit," she said despondently. "Of course...whatever you can do..."

I thought she might be looking my way so I gesticulated: "I'll meet you outside."

She was very much on the phone as I slipped out the door.

MaryAnne was someplace, but nowhere I could reach her.

It was a mild evening and I exited the stage door with my coat draped over my shoulders when I suddenly found myself surrounded by a screaming mob asking me to sign their programs. I tried to tell them I wasn't in the show but they were so busy vying with one another for autographs that they didn't listen, so I picked up one of the programs and signed my name. When the young girl looked at it, her face screwed up. "Ben Zelig?" She shouted above the noise of the throng. "You're not anybody!"

No one else bothered me as I pushed to the periphery of the crowd. "Not anybody?" It occurred to me that I never thought of myself as either "somebody" or "nobody." Do most people? Who makes that distinction...how...and why?

I was mulling over that question as I sat at the uneven table that shook every time I leaned on it in a very dark oyster that MaryAnne took me to bar called "Triton's Tomb". The thick dirty rope nets strewn across the entire room convinced me not to order anything fancy, not that I would anyway. MaryAnne was talking nervously into the phone behind the bar near the restrooms. She had taken her double vodka with her but left her oysters untouched on the table. I had never eaten shellfish and from the looks of those raw, slimy mucousy things floating in flat barnacles, I couldn't imagine why anyone would want to. The tuna sandwich on white bread in front of me was swathed in mayonnaise and tasted particularly *goyish*. The tepid cider in a heavy mug with a stick of cinnamon did seem to be a cool thing to order, but it was hard to believe apple juice could taste so bad.

MaryAnne had called her service as soon as we ordered and there was a message she said she had to deal with right away. I couldn't hear the conversation but from the intense look on her face, it was obviously important. From the bits of her conversation that I picked up in her dressing room, it was obvious that she was agitated about something. I had no idea what it was and she didn't appear to want to share it.

At one point in her phone conversation, she became so animated she spilled most of her drink on the floor.

When she came back, she flopped down in the wooden chair opposite me. She sat silently for several minutes, absorbed in her thoughts. Then, noticing the glass of Vodka I had ordered to replace the one she had spilled, she leaned over and gave me such a big hug I had to hold onto the shaky table to keep it from turning over. She exuded the most heavenly fragrance I had ever inhaled. I couldn't have imagined that anyone so pleasing to the sight could enthrall all my other senses as well. When she sat down, her eyes were moist.

"Bad news?" I didn't want to appear to pry but I wanted very much for her to know I cared.

She clenched her jaw to keep from crying. Then, she shrugged. She took a long sip of vodka and savored it as it went down.

"Talk to me, Rabbi," she said.

"About...?" I didn't know if she was referring to life in Acadia, our mutual friend,

Peter, movies, the theater or if she was just trying to find a subject that was less disturbing than the one that had absorbed her on the phone.

"Life, death, good, evil, love, cruelty, why we're on this planet. Tell me everything you know." She took a yellow pad out of her large bag and set it on the table.

There was so much passion in her voice, I wasn't sure what she wanted me to say. "What I *know*...about...all that? To be perfectly honest, not much."

"But you've studied the holy texts, you've spent years in the company of great men..."

"And women," I thought that would be a salve in case she was a feminist or possibly an opportunity to move away from these very heavy subjects, if that's what she wanted.

"So you must know a lot," she rummaged urgently through her purse and came up with a vial of pills. She took one and swilled it down with the remainder of the vodka. She waived to the waitress to bring refills then turned to me.

"So?" She clicked her pen, ready to write.

"MaryAnne, all I have are my own beliefs. I don't know for a certainty that they are any truer or more valid than anyone else's. I can't scientifically prove anything if that's what you want."

"I'm not asking you for scientific proof. I want you to tell me what you *know*."

"That could take a long time."

"That was my oncologist on the phone, Ben. I may not have a long time."

As the hours passed, she questioned me endlessly about theology, eschatology, mysticism, etc., writing down voluminous notes in the yellow pad that was already bulging with diagrams, sketches, assorted articles and ads for "alternative" cures.

I kept trying to find out exactly what the oncologist said. "What precisely is the diagnosis? Just how serious is your condition? What is the prognosis?"

"When I know you better, I'll tell you," she said, deflecting my questions. Reacting to the anxiety on my face, she said simply. "It's nothing I can't deal with, so don't you worry about it." Then, she emptied her second or third vodka, depending upon when one began to count, and swished her fourth oyster around in some red wine sauce with shallots, garlic and God knows what else. I had never seen anyone eat so slowly. My sandwich, which couldn't have been any worse than her slippery little barnacles, was gone in no time flat. Somehow, amid all the *goyishe* stuff, the liquor and the shellfish, the Protestant upbringing, the alienation from her family and all the rest of it, something called out to me and I found myself desperately wanting to reach her. I couldn't help thinking and worrying about her disease. What was the nature of her cancer? Are there tumors? What stage and size? Would they respond to treatment or was it too late? I didn't ask because I knew she would deflect those questions as she had my earlier ones, and frankly I was afraid the answer might be too terrible so I was relieved in a sense that I never had to hear her say it. In the five years I had been a Rabbi, I witnessed more sickness and death than most people do in a lifetime but I never got used to it. I don't think one can. Every time I held the hand of someone with a terminal condition it was an intensely emotional experience for me. I learned early on that the best way to help is to listen, not talk, but MaryAnne wasn't speaking to me of her illness, her fears, her life, her hopes or dreams. She kept drilling me for answers to abstract questions for which there were none. What made it unbearably poignant was her desperation to find something to cling to as she bravely confronted the worst of all nightmares. I felt I had nothing substantial to give her and that saddened me.

She put her hand on mine and said sweetly "Don't be so glum, Rabbi, you're not the one who's dying."

"Sure I am, MaryAnne. We all are. Life is terminal, you know."

She thought for a minute then wrote that down in the ever-decreasing margin of her yellow pad. Something in her notes caught her eye and she plunged right into the heart of the moment, transfixing me with her powerful gaze.

"The Old Testament. What kind of weasel was Abraham? According to the story in Genesis, he told that petty Egyptian warlord that his wife Sarah was his sister. He must have known that scumbag would hit on her. How could God forgive him so easily for that kind of cowardly behavior?"

"What makes you think Abraham was forgiven?"

"Didn't God bless him and reward him with an unusually long life? Read your Bible, Rabbi."

"I have and from everything I've studied – and experienced - I never found any reason to believe that a long life is necessarily a reward *or* a blessing." I began to go on when she put up her hand to stop me while she scribbled.

When she finished writing, she looked at me and smiled.

"I love smart men. Go on."

"I'd better stop here. I may become stupid and you'll hate me."

"What I hate are cowards." She put her hand on mine and I'm embarrassed to say it was exciting. "Take your best shot, Ben. Tell me why living isn't always better than the alternative."

"It usually is, but not always. There are times when life becomes too excruciatingly painful. I've witnessed that and believe me, it's no blessing. The important point is, if you accept the fact that life is terminal, what difference does it make how long you travel so long as you're on the right path? The only really significant thing about this life, as I see it, is what you do with the time you have."

"You're slipping into a sermon and I hate sermons. Get back to Abraham. He got far more than he deserved considering all the times he screwed up. You have to agree about that."

"No, I don't agree. Nobody gets a pass in the Old Testament. When someone messes up, whether they're patriarchs, prophets or kings, there's a price to pay. Sure, Abraham faltered along the way and made some stupid mistakes, all of which are clearly delineated in the Bible and not glossed over, by the way, but he took a lot of hits, too. Just think of the soul wrenching anguish over Isaac. What goes on in a father's heart when the path he's chosen risks the very life of his child?"

"Strange archetypes you Jews have. The best of them do some awfully reprehensible things at one time or another."

"The question is do they ring true and what can you learn from the choices they made?"

"You've got a point there. I'll take the fiery Old Testament Jews any day over the sanctimonious cherubs of the New Testament who look like they're either faking orgasms or doing disgusting things to other sanctimonious cherubs."

"If you want to understand the Old Testament, think of charts that show the physical evolution of our species from tree swingers to homo erectus. The Bible charts our moral evolution by placing people, real or mythical, in situations everyone can understand. By exposing their weaknesses, recounting their triumphs and tragedies, examining their courage and cowardice and laying it all bare, the Bible can be seen as an ingenious how-to and how-not-to book. Every story..."

"Got it, don't drift." She had no patience for anything that sounded facile or polemical. She wanted something else, something deeper, something transcendent that she could internalize immediately.

"I don't want to hear about allegories. I got all I can handle from the Catholics and the Yogis." She stopped for a moment and sipped her new drink. "I thought of becoming Catholic once, did I tell you that?"

"No, you didn't." I had hoped she would express some interest in me beyond religion and philosophy. She didn't seem to and that was a let-down.

She focused on my mind. "Where did it all happen, Ben? What was it like? Ur of Chaldees? What did it feel like to be there in Abraham's time? I know Jerusalem's a magnificent place and I want desperately to go there. Will you help me?"

"Of course I will. Maybe we'll go together." I was still hopeful.

She brightened up for a brief moment, then became very quiet. "Ben," she said after a long silence, "Where is Eden? Was there a real place called Eden?"

"I have no first-hand knowledge but I can tell you what the *Kabbala* says. The mystics believe there was actually a place called Eden. It was, they say, a paradise like no other. Lush fragrant flowers, colorful plants and an endless variety of trees flourished in every direction as far as the eye could see, but its most dazzling feature was the sparkling river that ran through its heart."

"Where is that river, Ben? How can I find it?"

"Believers say it will find you. That river, the mystics contend, continues to flow through the souls of the Just in every generation."

"The Just? Like in Andre Schwartz Bart's book 'The Last of the Just'? Is that from the *Kabbala*? Tell me about them. I need to know how to become one of the Just."

Her anxiety was so intense she didn't notice that she was totally engulfed in the world of allegory. She needed some idea, some vision, some hope, something strong enough to support her now and it didn't matter what it was made of. Suddenly, she winced and reached into her purse. She seemed to be having another one of those stomach spasms. She dropped a vial on the floor. I picked it up. The label read *M.S. Contin* which I knew to be a powerful pain medication extracted from morphine. I handed the small bottle to her and she quickly downed a pill with vodka. She sat quietly for several minutes, bravely dealing with the throbbing tremors rippling through her body. When the pain passed, she picked up her notes, looked at them and turned to me, confused.

"What was I talking about?"

"The *Kabbala*," I said simply. It was disorienting to look at this magnificent woman whose skin was smooth and vibrant, knowing that underneath the surface was a voracious malignancy gnawing away at her.

"Of course, the thirty-six righteous souls in every generation...that ...that what? What did they do, again?"

I talked about the legend of the thirty-six anonymous saintly people whom no one recognizes but whose deeds convince God to save their entire generation from extinction.

She scribbled as fast as I talked. MaryAnne had chosen to believe that some combination of notes, insights and formulae would provide her with the key she needed to cure herself. It was agonizing to watch her fight so hard through what must have been a heavy fog in her head to find some *truth* she could hold onto as she moved inexorably toward a certain, but hopefully distant end. Of course, neither she nor I wanted to talk about just how distant that end might be.

She touched me deeply and I didn't know what to do. I wanted to comfort her, encourage her, say something that could sustain her, but what could I tell her? I certainly wouldn't give her a bunch of soppy homilies. That would only enrage her and make her contemptuous of me. What she wanted was to circumvent science, to find something outside the physical world to enable her to survive.

"I studied Catholicism. Did I tell you that?"

"You mentioned it."

"Total bust. I liked the pomp, the art, the music, but when you examine what's going on underneath it all..." She suddenly stopped and put her hand on her stomach. "False alarm. What was I talking about?"

"Catholicism."

She reached inward for a moment and then remembered.

"Oh yeah. This cute young Priest tried to explain the Trinity, which by definition is three, but by theological calculation, is one. When I asked him to explain the math, he said 'it's a mystery, like electricity.' I couldn't believe he actually said that. I admit I don't know what goes on in every level of Dante's inferno or the names of all the saints, but I do know something about basic science. Electricity is no mystery. It's a simple form of energy created by an accumulation of electrons that dance around a magnetic field and produces a current. That's it, the secret behind everything from a light bulb to space travel. I looked at that sweet young innocent and it saddened me to think that this 'mystery, like electricity' was the very foundation of his faith. Is that why he goes through life without ever getting laid, because he never learned how a car battery works? Well, that was it for me and Catholicism. The Greeks had a better understanding of electricity twenty-five hundred years ago than this well-meaning simpleton who was supposed to guide my spirit into..." She stopped in mid sentence. She was getting groggy now and the more her consciousness drifted the more anxious she became about finding the answer she believed was somewhere in her notes. She went through them, page after page until she dropped the pad on the table in despair and looked at me pleadingly.

"What exactly did they have to do, those thirty-six people, to convince God not to let us die?"

"What was I talking about?" It was four in the morning and we were in MaryAnne's bedroom on West 79th Street. I had never been thrown out of anyplace before and it would have been a harrowing experience for me if MaryAnne weren't there to kick ass. It was after three when the oily Moroccan manager of Triton's Tomb started to scream at us because MaryAnne refused to leave.

"You get out now or I call police. We closed godammit an hour ago already."

"How long do you have to live?" She said defiantly.

"What you talk crazy? Get out!"

"I know the answer. You've already lived too damn long." MaryAnne didn't budge.

She even turned on me. "Explain this to me, Rabbi. Why do shit-heads like him get to live so long while the good die young? I demand a reasoned theological response, not some allegory. This worm is probably one of the thirty-six vermin who give the rest of us humans a bad name. Can't God see that?"

And so it went. When we arrived at MaryAnne's house, she nearly fell as she got out of my car. I helped her up to her apartment and she asked if I would stay with her. I suppose I should have thought more about what that might entail, but it was late, I was tired, she needed me and the sweet fragrance of her perfume enabled me to skip having to make a decision.

She had an open bottle of vodka near her bed along with a bottle of water and several bottles of pills. She wore a modest white granny nightgown and I was fully dressed as she lay in my arms on her small double bed. Her yellow pad was next to her and after several attempts at reading her scribbled notes, she dropped it on the floor and passed out in my arms. I allowed myself to believe I was somehow protecting her. The comfort I felt with her asleep on my chest dissolved into happiness and I drifted into the most peaceful repose. After a couple of hours, with her eyes still shut, she said.

"Tell me about *The Last of the Just.*"

"You said you read Andre Schwartz-Bart's book."

"Yeah, but I don't get it. There are supposed to be thirty-six righteous people scattered around the earth whose miraculous deeds in each generation prevent God from completely destroying the earth, right?"

"So the legend goes."

"But in the book, this guy is in Auschwitz about to be gassed, so what does he do in his last moments of life? He has sex with his crippled wife. What's miraculous about that? Is that the most significant deed one can perform on earth, sufficient to invoke God's mercy?"

"Solomon tells us that the only thing that can conquer death is love."

She opened her eyes and looked up at me. "Do you believe that?"

"Does it really matter what I believe?"

She rolled back and cradled her head in the crook of my arm. "It's beginning to matter to me."

Semi-awake, MaryAnne had the sweet smell of sleep in her hair. Her body radiated an intoxicating fragrance and I dared not think about what was to come. The only thing I knew for sure was that every breath I took now was Divine and I prayed for it to continue.

The sun was coming up as I reached the Cross Bronx Expressway. Cool air flowed through the car bringing with it the scent of freshly cut grass. What a night! MaryAnne was the most intriguing woman I had ever met. Just lying next to her, fully clothed, breathing in her heady essence filled me with a sense of joy and delight, but I couldn't stop thinking about the impending devastation of her advancing disease.

I arrived at the Synagogue around seven-thirty, just as the old men were coming out of the small chapel.

"What's the matter, Rabbi, you too good for the Hank Sperling Religious Committee *minyan* Service? One morning a month! Is that so hard for you to remember?"

Hank Sperling was only in his sixties but the unmasked hostility on his face made him look like the grim reaper. After his retirement, with nothing to occupy his time, he drove his wife of thirty years crazy. His children deserted him and he had no friends. When he discovered that Synagogues were places a person could go and vilify everyone and criticize everything and not get dragged into court for slander, Hank became devout. When he moved to Acadia, he joined my Temple. His style was to come to every meeting of the board of directors and venomously malign everyone whether he knew them or not. He would have liked to be either the Rabbi or boss of the Temple but those positions weren't available so he satisfied himself with chairmanship of the religious committee, a job nobody else wanted. The primary functions of the religious committee had always been to collect money to feed and clothe the poor, support families who might require a quorum of worshippers when they sat *shiva,* create scholarships for children to go to summer camp, etc. That all changed when Hank became chairman of the committee. Rather than worry about the needy, he saw it as an opportunity to create a legacy for himself. He decided that there should be an early morning prayer service once a month, to be officially known as "The Religious Committee *Minyan,* Hank Sperling, Chairman". He rounded up ten reluctant senior citizens who would rather have remained in bed with their wives, pets or hot water bottles, at six-thirty in the morning, provided transportation to and from the Synagogue and coerced them into attending his "service" each month. "The only temple north of the Bronx where you can find a morning *minyan* the first Monday of every month," was Hank's crowning achievement.

At first, I offered to create a special prayer guide with translations and inspirational readings that might make the event more relevant. Hank refused. "Save that stuff for your *own* service. In my *minyan*, we *doven*." He had found his grandfather's old *siddur* which was entirely in Hebrew and that was going to be the official prayer book of the monthly service. It didn't matter that none of the seniors who made up the quorum – including Hank - understood the Hebrew. This was Hank's domain and not even the Rabbi had the right to interfere.

His question hung in the air. "...you too good for the...Hank Sperling m*inyan*?" What could I say? Prayer is a cornerstone of my life. I approach it joyously, with a sense of awe and an awareness of the ineffable that connects us to one another and to the cosmos, but the mechanical recitation of rote words is worse than meaningless, it's a hollow mockery. It's sex without love or reverence. I thought of what was truly Divine for me, what roused my passion, what was spiritual and transcendent. It was MaryAnne, temporarily free of pain and the terrors of her disease, peacefully sleeping in my arms.

"I was detained," I finally said.

"Detained? Pish, pish! Don't get detained next month. I got *Yortzeit* coming up for my grandmother, *alov ha-shalom.*"

I thought of correcting his Hebrew for a brief moment but I didn't bother. He was just too big a pain in the ass.

When I arrived at my study, I thought only about MaryAnne. Was it too early to call? Was she feeling any better? Did she want to talk to me, see me? I hungered to see her, to be with her, hold her again, sleep alongside her, inhale her fragrance and hopefully, help her find some respite from pain. Over the years, I had enjoyed a variety of sexual experiences but nothing ever meant as much to me as the chaste few hours I spent with MaryAnne lying in my arms.

I spent the better part of the morning answering calls and working on an article for the Temple weekly. I remembered MaryAnne's interest in the legend of the righteous, so I made it a point to review relevant sections of the *Zohar*, the core text of the *Kabbala*, so I would have a pretext to call her. After three rings, her voice came on. It was strong, mellifluous and direct. "This is MaryAnne. You may leave an inspirational message or hang up now. Name and phone number optional." I put the phone down immediately. Even the *Kabbala* might not pass a test like that.

For the rest of the day, I met with congregants and reviewed the Hebrew School curriculum with the teaching staff, but all the while I couldn't get MaryAnne out of my mind. Should I have said something? What passes for "an inspirational message"? I'm in that business and I wouldn't for a moment have the *chutzpah* to think anything I have to say would qualify as an appropriate message. By late afternoon, during one of the most painfully ineffective counseling sessions of my career with a feuding couple who addressed each other in the third person and

142

their twelve year old son who didn't stop playing his portable video game for one second, I couldn't stop thinking about her. As soon as they left, I called again and got the same message. This time I wasn't going to hang up.

"MaryAnne, dear, dear lovely lady," I said. "This is Ben, as in last night. You've been on my mind all day but I haven't left a message because..."

"Hi, Ben," her cheery voice broke in.

"MaryAnne...I...are you alright?"

"Yeah."

I wasn't sure how to continue. "Last night you were in so much discomfort, I didn't know what to think."

"I have good days and bad ones. Last night was one of the worst. Today the sun is shining and the weather is great and I feel wonderful except for a slight hangover. I just took the best walk! I love to watch toddlers race around barefoot in the park, climbing over each other like a litter of puppies and having the most exhilarating time. Kids are fantastic." She paused for a moment. "So were you last night, Ben."

"I loved being with you," I said. "I...I hope I helped in some way. It was terrible to see someone as...lovely as...what I mean is, watching you suffer was just awful!"

"That happens sometimes."

"I'm so sorry."

"Is that a turn-off for you?"

"Me? God no! MaryAnne, I'd love to see you, talk to you, watch you eat slippery creepy-crawlies my people have disdained for millennia, argue with waiters, get thrown out of restaurants, anything so long as you'll let me be with you."

She exploded with laughter. "Oysters are slippery creepy-crawlies? You're hilarious!"

"Will that make up for my inability to come up with an inspirational message?"

There was another pause. "I assume you're up in Acadia?"

"Yeah."

"How soon can you get here?"

When I knocked on her door exactly one hour and thirteen minutes later, a record for the fifty-mile drive, MaryAnne opened the door looking even lovelier than I remembered. She wore a brown jersey, beige pants and a chocolate cap, cocked on her head.

"You're a rhapsody in brown," was the best I could come up with.

"Are you looking for apartment 4202?" she played it so seriously I was thrown for a minute. Then I remembered.

"No ma'am. I'm here to deliver this to the *young beauty* in room 301." I handed MaryAnne the book I brought her.

"The Kabbala!" She was like a little girl, excitedly flipping through the pages. "What a great gift! Thank you, thank you, thank you," She threw her arms around my neck and kissed my face. She felt so good, I would have been happy to stand with her in the doorway all night.

"Now that's a great gift, thank you!" I said as I followed her into her apartment. "How do you know about apartment 4202? Did my Vicar betray a confidence?"

"Peter adores you. He knew I would find it endearing."

"Did you?"

"That depends. How big a louse were you?"

"Fairly sizable, I guess. I should have handled it better. Do you hate me for that?"

"No. I'm actually glad you can be a swine occasionally. It makes you more accessible."

After watching her suffer so much last night, seeing her laugh made my spirits soar.

"Can you be de-Rabbi'd for that kind of thing?" She teased.

"I don't know but Peter can definitely be de-Vicared."

"When I was a kid, we called it dickered, but you wouldn't snitch on the man who led you to me, would you?"

"According to that book I just brought you, bringing us together was nothing less than Godly so I guess I'll have to drop all charges."

I felt we were on a roll and I wanted to go on with it when I noticed suitcases on the floor of the living room and my heart dropped. "Are you going somewhere?"

"Those are my room-mate's. She just flew in from Vegas a couple of hours ago."

"I didn't know you had one," I said, when a door opened and someone who looked like Mike Tyson came out with a towel around his waist.

"Hi", he smiled. "Where's the bathroom?"

"You're...?" from MaryAnne's look, this man was obviously not her room-mate.

"I'm LeMonde, Rita's friend. I really need to get to the bathroom."

"Second door past the kitchen."

Inside her bedroom, with books and notes strewn around her bed, MaryAnne explained that her room-mate was a showgirl who worked in Las

Vegas. She comes to town every couple of weeks and I shouldn't be surprised to find strangers wandering in and out of her room at all hours. MaryAnne plopped down on the bed in the middle of the books and papers, picked up her yellow pad and looked at the scribbling on it.

"A river runs through the Garden...? What were we talking about last night?"

"Life, death, good, evil, friendship, loyalty, why we're on this planet, stuff like that."

"You make it sound like shop talk. Is that what it is for you?"

"Pretty much. What is it for you?"

"Foreplay."

"Bliss" was the word that came out of my deepest dream into my first waking moment. The sun was bursting through the gossamer cloud curtain and the first thing that welcomed me was the delicious scent of her body that was now clinging to mine. I felt serene and full of optimism. I was never happier. MaryAnne was up reading The *Kabbala*. I wonder if she slept at all. After our exhilarating love making, I passed out. "Le petit mort," she laughingly called it. I watched her intensely drinking in the esoteric wisdom of those pages. Delighting in the perfection of her long, slender body lying on her flowered sheets, I allowed myself to believe - no, I made myself believe - that she was really going to be alright. Then I noticed the array of pills on her night table and gloom singed my brain once again.

"Hi," was my way of saying I love you without the complications that accompany that phrase.

"Me too," she smiled knowingly and kissed me with the sweetest breath I had ever inhaled, then, read aloud. "...lovers are a single soul divided at birth. Their mission is to find their other half and when they do, they are rejoined and become one for all eternity. Therein lies their salvation."

She put down the book and rested on her elbow, her face practically touching mine. "So, when the heroes of *The Last of the Just* made love in the face of certain death, that was their salvation?"

"The mystics believe love is the glue that keeps all elements of the cosmos in balance."

"What happens to that balance when one dies and the other doesn't?" MaryAnne was impatient to understand in an instant what others spend a lifetime studying, but the truth is that she comprehended subtleties more thoroughly and more rapidly than anyone I had ever met.

"That, my sweet, brilliant MaryAnne is the question that caused the heavenly Hosts so much consternation. They were fearful that after the death of Eve, Adam would not be able to survive without the love of his pre-ordained 'other half,' and the entire world would collapse around him. They had good reason to be frightened. As it turned out, even God could not console Adam when his mate died. It wasn't only his rib that had been severed; it was his very soul that was withering inside him. Where was the one he could talk to without speaking? Whom could he caress and be delighted by in return? God saw that life without one's lover was a curse every husband or wife after Adam and Eve would have to endure.

147

The *Kabbala* takes some anthropomorphic liberties in describing God's anguish as he watched the inconsolable Adam, broken-hearted with a brain that felt ashen and eyes that took no pleasure in sight. God was so overwhelmed by Adam's grief that He created the River that flowed through the heart of Eden."

"That's the river you told me about last night!" She was like a little girl making important discoveries.

"What a memory. That's precisely what I was talking about. The Rabbis say it is a mystical river that flows directly from Eden into the hearts of all lovers everywhere, binding them for all eternity. The anguished, bereaved and spiritually wounded could bathe in those sparkling waters and literally pierce "the veil" to connect with their *'ba-sherte'* on the other side. That is the balm which heals and enables them to go on."

"Where is that river, Ben? I have to know."

"All will be revealed, but only after one's mate passes through the river alone."

"What happens then?"

"The bereft lover is magically transported to the holy river where their souls are reunited. There, as one, they regain the bliss and rapture they knew when they were alive, together and whole."

"Do you believe that?" Her eyes were moist.

"I've seen enough grieving in my life to want to believe it."

Tears rolled down her face and she buried her head on my chest. I had never before – nor have I since - felt such ecstasy as was coursing through my veins at that moment.

The days blended into weeks, then into
months. In the face of ever increasing demands
from my congregation, the biggest challenge for
me was figuring out what I could get out of so
that I could spend more time with MaryAnne.
Every night I raced into Manhattan to be with her
and every morning I made the long trek back to
Acadia, but I was never so energized, so full of
enthusiasm and optimism and yes, so happy.
MaryAnne was the single focus of my life. I
judged everything by how it measured up to my
growing love for her and her struggle to defeat her
illness and live! I must have given off some kind
of vibration that made me appear impervious to
petty stuff. It's as though everyone who looked at
me saw MaryAnne's face on my forehead. The
women in my book review program stopped trying
to find me dates. Even Hank Sperling avoided
pissing me off.

Maryanne and I were well into the fourth
month of our idyllic romance when Peter threw
me a curve.

"I understand MaryAnne is thinking about
converting to Judaism," he said. We were having
lunch at the "Jewish Club" and he was just
beginning to work on his third martini. The
dining room had emptied out enough for us to
speak freely. MaryAnne and I had been in each
other's hearts and minds for exactly one hundred
days now and I assumed I could read her every
thought. I knew she was receptive to many of the
ideas we discussed and studied but I didn't put it
together that she intended to convert. I wasn't

sure how I felt about that and I was a little resentful she hadn't talked to me about it.

"When did you speak to her?"

"I didn't. I spoke to her father briefly after the service on Sunday, and he told me he had finally been in touch with MaryAnne, after years of silence."

"He called her?"

"No. She called him."

MaryAnne didn't talk to me much about her parents. I got the idea that her mother was an empty shell who was raised to be the wife of a millionaire and be agreeable, no matter what. Her father was far more complicated. She adored him when she was growing up. She loved nothing more than sitting on his shoulders. He used to call her his monkey because she was all over him. If he was reading a book, she'd get her picture book and climb onto his lap. They played baseball and tennis together, they rode horses and water-skied. They were extremely close until puberty hit. Then, for no reason she could understand, he drew away and became distant. She felt like a leper. Once she began to develop into a woman, he wouldn't touch her and what's worse, he didn't allow her to touch him. She remembered the day it started. It was the worst of her entire life. She had just gotten her first period and like all young girls, she was both horrified and jubilant. She asked her mother not to say a word to her father because she didn't know how he would react. Whatever she feared, nothing was as brutal and awful as the icy distance he set between them that very night at dinner. Obviously, her mother had ratted her out. Her father wouldn't give her any explanation. He wouldn't even speak to her.

She was devastated. What had she done to make him fall out of love with her? He was her daddy, the one person in the world she could trust and love without conditions or boundaries, and he jilted her! She begged him to love her and be her daddy like before, but he didn't bend. Over time, she had to accept the truth: Their love affair had ended. As she got older, it got worse. The more reserved he was with her, the more rebellious she became. When she dropped out of Radcliff to become a performer in bars, he cut off her allowance. When she threatened to become a Catholic, he disinherited her. All she told me was that they hadn't spoken in years. MaryAnne was clear and forthright on every subject except one, her relationship to her father.

"What exactly did she say to him?" I tried not to look directly at Peter but he knew what I was asking.

"You have to understand Horace Pembroke. Third generation chief executive officer of one of the most influential Wall Street brokerage firms whose antecedents arrived in Jamestown in the seventeenth century. It was probably on a ship of debtors and criminals but the passage of time and accumulated wealth erased any lingering stigma. Pembrokes have always been patriots allied with great causes like isolationism in World War Two and virulent anti-communism to this very day despite its fall in Russia and the rest of the Soviet Bloc. Some say his great-grandparents were founding members of the Klan but no one knows for sure. What everyone does know is that Horace Pembroke is one of the great outspoken anti-Semites, so when his daughter called to tell him she was considering converting to Judaism, I don't know if he heard anything beyond that."

"Did she talk about anything else?" I had to ask.

"She said she was seeing a really nice guy," Peter said, faux-conspiratorially. "He assumed it was a Hebrew so he didn't want to hear about it and she didn't volunteer any names, if that's what you're asking."

"Did she tell him anything about...her?"

Peter took another long sip of his martini. "She told him she had long since left the show and finally she mentioned that she was taking a battery of tests at Mount Sinai Hospital."

"Did the son of a bitch at least ask what kind of tests?"

"I'm sure he sensed something wasn't kosher, pun intended, and I don't know if it scared him or if he just doesn't like to hear bad news. In any event, he didn't ask for specifics and she didn't offer any. He said he told his daughter to stay clear of hospitals because they're full of sick people and since he didn't trust doctors his advice was to eat right and get plenty of exercise."

I was enraged at this brave girl's stupid father. He had dismissed out of hand the tortures she was enduring without ever trying to find out what was going on with her, how she was feeling, was she optimistic or in despair, how could he help, all the things any normal father would want to know.

"What a *putz!*" was all I could say.

"Yeah..." Peter said, shaking his head, "You can say that again."

"Don't worry about it, Ben," she said in response to the look on my face. I never mentioned Peter or that I knew about her conversation with her father. I didn't have to. She could take one look at me and know everything I was thinking.

"It's not like I will have to undergo circumcision."

"But it is a major step," I said.

"Everything is at this point."

We generally avoided that expression, but when it emerged, those words sent waves of anxiety shooting through my body.

She grabbed my hand and stared into my eyes. "Ben, this is not a desperate last minute attempt to get in good with the God of your patriarchs. I've been thinking about it for awhile. I'm still thinking about it and when I finally make a decision, if I do, you'll be the first to know. The one thing I want you to understand is that it's all about living, not dying, okay?"

"Okay," I said and realized that as long as I had MaryAnne, everything *was* okay.

After months of commuting daily, I became an ace path-finder. I found the best routes and the best hours to avoid the heavy traffic. These were minor triumphs I delighted in sharing with MaryAnne between love-making, studying together, walking and talking. I didn't mention conversion again.

I even met her room-mate, Rita. One day when I arrived early, MaryAnne was out shopping for groceries and Rita and I got to talking. Rita was very tall with long red hair. She said she was a dancer at the Prado in Las Vegas. Essentially, she walked up and down stairs on a large stage wearing wide-brim hats, long gowns and bare breasts. She felt she was more suited to acting than dancing but "...it's so hard to get a tit in the door." She laughed at the joke she had obviously told many times before.

I was never happier to see MaryAnne when she came back. "I don't know how to talk to her," I explained.

"I don't imagine she'd be any more interested in your synagogue business than you are in her career, but she's a good soul and the perfect room-mate. She's not here much so that's good but when she is, she's considerate and she genuinely loves people."

"I know. I counted three of them using the bathroom last night."

When MaryAnne accused me of being a judgmental prig, I promised to try and overcome my prejudices, but as Rita was the first Vegas showgirl I had ever met, it might take some doing. Over time, I did try to engage Rita in conversation, but no matter what topic we started on, we always seemed to work our way back to the same theme, only with different casting directors, producers, etc. I must admit I never really understood the Rita mentality, but the fact that someone as sophisticated and erudite as MaryAnne was able to connect with her showed me once again that she had evolved way beyond my narrow mindset. I once joked that MaryAnne could communicate with animals.

"Doesn't everyone?" she asked innocently.

By the end of our fifth month, it became more and more difficult to ignore what was going on in her body. She felt tired all the time and she had no energy. The slightest exertion exhausted her. I went with her to see her Oncologist, a compassionate man who was about my father's age. He spoke in gentle and encouraging terms but made no attempt to hide the truth. He told us her chances weren't great but some people with her condition do survive and lead fairly normal lives. He emphasized that the odds were not in her favor and we should be prepared for all contingencies. Neither of us was willing to hear that. We were determined to beat this thing and we really believed we had the spiritual determination and a working pact with the Almighty to do just that. MaryAnne deserved to live more than anyone I had ever known and I put my faith in that rather than the emerging "scientific evidence" we kept hearing about her disease. After all, who knew better than God what Adam went through? I could not let myself believe He would do that to me.

The following week she took a turn for the worse. I got a call in my study from Mount Sinai Hospital telling me that MaryAnne had fallen in her bathroom and is now in the intensive care unit. Her room-mate found her and gave them my number. I dropped everything and raced down the Cross Bronx Expressway. I nearly fell on the floor when I saw her hooked up to machines monitoring her vital signs with tubes plugged into her hands, her nose and under the sheets.

"This is all so sudden," I heard myself say, "when...how...what...?" Her eyes were closed and I knelt down beside her and prayed and prayed

155

like I've never prayed in all my life. I felt the air whooshing out of my body and I became light headed. An alert orderly saw me swaying and he quickly carried me out of the ICU and into the hallway where he put me in a hard wooden chair and made me sit with my head between my knees until the fog cleared.

The next three days were the most miserable and desolate of my life. When they opened her they saw that the cancer had invaded her colon and both ovaries and was spreading to her kidneys and liver.

When she regained consciousness, she held onto my hand as tightly as she could. Neither of us could utter a word for the longest time. Finally, she spoke.

"You have to do something for me," she said. She was ready to convert to Judaism and she wanted to do it as quickly as possible. "Will you do that?"

"Of course," I said, fighting as I have never fought before to hold back tears. "But you have to do one for me."

I told her what I wanted and we both wept.

Peter was the only one I thought of calling. A little more than an hour later he entered the room carrying a Rabbi's Manual and soon we were into the ceremony. As difficult as it was, MaryAnne and I managed to hold back tears until Peter read, first in Hebrew, then in English "...we welcome you, our sister, to the faith of Moses and Israel. May you grow in strength and stature alongside Sarah, Rebecca, Rachel and Leah and all the other great daughters of Zion."

The final stage of her conversion required that she immerse herself in the *mikveh*, the ritual bath. That wasn't available so an attending nurse brought her a bowl of water. She put her hand into the bowl.

"I'm afraid I'm going to pee. Is that okay?" She said.

"Sure, Jews do it all the time," Peter said.

We waited for the bag under the bed to fill up.

Then, I asked her.

"Will you marry me, MaryAnne?"

Thirty-six days after we were married, I stood at her gravesite. The plot she had selected was on a high hill with a perfect view of the Hudson River. I stayed there until the sun set. During the entire afternoon I watched the river that ran through our souls and I thought of the question she asked on our first meeting. "Where exactly was Eden?" I didn't know the answer then, but I do now. Wherever MaryAnne was, there was Eden.

For the Love of Bertha

For The Love Of Bertha

"The Kosher Luncheon Club is offering a free trip to Sidneyland! We leave by bus at eight in the morning. They provide a light breakfast with coffee and donuts...who needs their donuts? I have fresh bagels at home. We can go on all the rides free, even the holocauster, then lunch...it will be dairy, but that's alright..."

Seeing my mother so energized and involved in a variety of activities that took her mind off her very real aches and pains validated my bringing her all the way out to California. The transition was more difficult than I expected, but definitely worthwhile – for her as well as for me.

Breaking up is hard to do.

My father died nearly twenty years ago and since then Mom's life in Youngstown had been steadily shrinking. She had a part time job at May's department store as a saleslady in "coats". She had a few friends in the store and she got to talk to shoppers three afternoons a week. She received minimum wage but her needs were minimal and together with her social security checks she was able to maintain the lifestyle she enjoyed, which meant depriving herself of even minor luxuries so she could send generous gifts to her children and grandchildren on their birthdays, holidays, etc. When May's announced that it was going out of business, the prospect of sitting home everyday and staring at the walls in her small apartment sent her blood pressure soaring.

I had become Rabbi of Temple Har Zion, a prestigious Synagogue in Westwood just over a year ago and I thought this would be an opportune time for her to move to Los Angeles and make a new life for herself. Let's be clear about one thing. I never contemplated her moving in with me. The very thought of spending more than a couple of hours at a time with my mother gave me hives. My mother is a lovely, generous woman but she never stops talking! I had acquired a special appreciation for silence and I needed it to maintain my equilibrium. On the other hand, with most of her friends and relatives either dead or dying, I couldn't let her sit alone at home becoming more despondent by the day, so I flew to Youngstown to convince her to make the move.

She was so depressed when I arrived that she barely said a word, which for Mom is a serious symptom. I had hoped she would greet my offer with enthusiasm but she had strong reservations.

"Bennie, I'm not prepared to be a Rabbi's mother. People will ask me to advise about the holidays, the Bible, all kinds things. What do I know? I'll embarrass you darling and that's the last thing in the world I want to do."

"Mom, do you expect your doctor's mother to know how to read an x-ray, or your accountant's mother to file tax returns?"

"Uncle Jake always does my taxes," she said. She wasn't evading the issue. For Mom, "the issue" was whatever popped into her head.

"Honey, I never went to college. I had a couple of years of night school when I came to America but who can remember anything from so long ago? The worst thing is I never even became a naturalized citizen. People will think the Rabbi's mother is a stupid."

"People will not think that Mom and if they do they can *kush mir in tochus*."

"I never liked that expression," she said, "but somehow when you say it, it doesn't sound so bad." She couldn't look at me without *kveling.* "Such a *punim*," she pinched my cheek.

"Move to California and you can pinch to your heart's content."

"Benny, darling, I can't just pick up and leave. Daddy is buried twenty minutes from here by bus. I visit his grave whenever I want to talk out the heart. What will I do when I'm so far away?"

"Mom, daddy's spirit isn't in the ground. He'll be with you wherever you go."

"It's not the same. I don't know how to explain you, Bennele, but when your *ba-sherte* dies, it doesn't mean he disappears from your life altogether. Daddy is here, you understand? He advises me about everything, like last week when I was in the A&P? He liked the one on East Federal. He used to go there after work to pick up fresh fruit. Anyway, I was in the A&P and I was stuck. Should I buy a small can of Del Monte fruit cocktail on sale or a fresh peach not on sale? I didn't even have to think about it. Daddy told me what was good and I went straight for the peach, not on sale! Don't you know it turned out to be the sweetest piece fruit I ever ate? Like sugar. If I was to move away, what would Daddy know from where to buy what in California?"

"Did you ever ask daddy what he thinks about the possibility of you moving in a totally new direction?" I was told that romance often blossoms among senior citizens who meet through various organizations and quite a few of them end up marrying. I thought that would be a great idea for Mom. She's gregarious, craves company and is still attractive enough to snag a friendly widower.

"*Ich farshtey dir nicht.*" She really had no idea what I was talking about.

"Maybe dad would want you to travel, meet new people. Who knows, maybe even meet a nice man?"

Her mouth dropped. "I should cheat on your father? From the day I met daddy, I never thought of another man and I never will. Please God, strike me dead first."

"Okay, Mom. Sorry I brought it up." I should have realized that's a difficult concept to consider in the abstract.

She continued to steam. "What am I, *meshugah* altogether? I should bring a strange man I don't even know into my house?"

"First of all, if you ever decided you want someone to come in, presumably you will have met him."

"They'll want to get married right away so they can boss me around and control my TV remote. I won't even be able to watch my programs!"

"As far as the TV goes, most people discuss their preferences and make compromises."

"I should make compromises with some slop who dirties up my house and leaves laundry on the floor and snores so loud he wakes up the whole neighborhood?"

"Who does that?"

"My nice Italian neighbor's new husband, Nick the bum. You remember I told you about the nice Italian lady who moved in next door? Such an angel! She's living through hell, excuse me. She says her children told her they got a message from their dead father, you know, from the other side that he wanted she should remarry. They found an old friend of the husband who was a widower and looking for a wife. He told her he got the same message so they figured it was meant to be. Everybody said this Nick was a nice guy and she didn't mind him hanging around, but after they got married, no more Mr. Nice Guy. This bum turned into the biggest *stronzo*."

"Do you know what that word means in Italian?"

"Not exactly, but I figure it's plenty bad."

"I guess somebody got the wrong signals from the other side."

"So how do you know which message is real and which one's baloney?"

"You feel it in your *kishkes*, Mom. I'm not sure how the process works but I do think it is sometimes possible to communicate with loved ones in different places and even on different planes."

"Benny, you read the holy books. You know so much about everything. My nice neighbor, Josephine, needs help and I don't know what to advise her. She is so religious, she prays all the time. She's even got a special payroll saint. She talks to that little statue and lights candles and everything. Shouldn't that saint have warned her about Nick the bum?"

"Wrong religion, Mom, I have no experience with saints, patron, payroll or any other kind."

"You know Bennie, I have an idea. Josephine is American born and her Italian isn't too good but her Saint lived in Sicily. Maybe the Saint talks to her in Italian and she don't get it right. Isn't that possible?"

"Anything is possible."

"I can't think of any other reason. She is such a good person, so refined, that saint of hers would have to be a real *stronzo* not to warn her about that bum."

I couldn't think of a thing to say.

"Benny, how would you like to do a big *mitzvah*?"

Dead dogs tell no lies.

I stood next to Mom as she knocked on her neighbor's door. After a few minutes, a frazzled woman dressed in black, opened it slowly. As soon as she saw Mom, they fell into each other's arms and the two of them embraced like long-lost sisters. In fact, they had gone shopping together a couple of hours earlier. When the nice Italian neighbor saw me, she looked me over from head to toe and her smile became radiant.

"This is your son?" Wonder of wonders, splendor of splendors! The look on her face was positively beatific.

Mother preened like a peacock. "Benny, this is my nice neighbor, Mrs. Bevilacqua."

"Please call me Josephine. Such a pleasure to meet you, Father Zelig. I heard so much about you."

I had no doubt. For as long as I can remember, my mother always made me feel like a painting on a museum wall when she introduced me to her friends, neighbors or just someone she sat next to on a bus. They would stare at me as though I were some object of considerable value. What is it with mothers who can look at a kid with teeth missing and a runny nose and marvel at his beauty? And it doesn't change when the kid gets old, grows a paunch, loses his hair and becomes boss ugly. I suppose, as there are "Black things" and "Jewish things" there are "Mother things," not to be understood, just endured.

We entered the dark apartment and were seated on furniture covered with plastic. Crucifixes with red painted droplets of blood hung on every wall. In the center of the room was a small icon, hands clasped, head looking heavenward and surrounded by votive candles. I assumed this was the nice Italian neighbor's "payroll" saint.

"What can I get you, coffee, tea, connoli, gabba-goo?" She asked sweetly.

"Nothing, thank you. We just ate," I said, which somehow sent her directly into the kitchen to make coffee and tea and bring out mounds of pastry and some unspeakable bologna-salami-type thinly sliced things. If anything deserves to be called *glatt traif* (unkosher in the extreme), that meat was it.

I sat on the rocking chair while Mom and Josephine sat on the couch holding hands. They were both looking at me, smiling and commenting to one another about my extraordinary qualities.

"He's so handsome," the nice Italian neighbor said, then, to our surprise, she started to cry uncontrollably. I didn't know what to say.

"Is it that bum, Nick?" Mom was ready to

do battle for her friend. "Did he hit you?"

"No, Bertha...it's your son. He's so gorgeous...I can't help it. I feel like Christ has risen again when I look at him." When she finally stopped crying, she said, "you see, Bertha, your Bennie is so lovely to look at...so beautiful, he reminds me of my dog."

"Your dog?" Mom was stunned.

"You remember I told you about my little friend, Alfredo? I loved him more than life. He died exactly a year ago." She paused to wipe away more tears, then crossed herself. "I named him after my favorite pasta. They say he was a boxer but he wouldn't hurt a flea. I loved that dog so much. I couldn't wait to wake up in the morning to look at my little lover, pet him, feed him and take him out so he could do his business in the yard where nobody would step in it. I wanted him to sleep in our bed but my dead husband Ugo, may God rest his soul, was so mean he wouldn't let Alfredo sleep in our bed. I always hated him for that."

"I'm sorry. I didn't know that about him," Mom said.

"Don't get me started on Ugo, that miserable *somna bitch*, may he rest in peace. I hope he drowns in hell. One time I fell down in the bathroom and hit my head. I was bleeding and I couldn't get up. The bastard was in the backyard playing bocce-ball with his *paesans*. I know he heard me scream but he didn't want to interrupt his game. Alfredo ran out and barked so he would come and help me. Ugo said the barking made him miss his shot so he kicked my Alfredo. Well, when I heard that poor creature squeal, I dragged myself up and went outside, bleeding

166

like a...I don't know what. The-good-for-nothing doesn't even say two words to me. To this day, I don't know where I got the strength to get up off the floor or how I walked all the way downstairs without fainting, but I did." She thought for a moment. "I don't know why I didn't stab the *sumna bitch* right there," she said. "Anyway, there I was in the backyard, all bloody and everything and the minute my Alfredo saw me, he jumped into my arms and licked my face and suddenly everything was okay. I swear to God, I was in heaven."

Mom turned to me. "She's a saint, this woman, a saint! She never before said a bad word about her husband."

"Why would I? Aside from that, he was a wonderful husband, God rest his soul." She crossed herself. "Anyway, after he died, Alfredo slept with me every night. I thanked my Saint Philomena every day for that beautiful dog. I know she sent him to me as a reward for all the shit I took all those years from that *sumna bitch,* Ugo. Anyway, when my dear dog died, it will be exactly a year ago this Saturday...where was I?"

I waited for Mom to jump in but she didn't. Her mind was somewhere else.

"You were talking about your dog and your patron saint," I volunteered.

"Oh, yeah. Well, when my Alfredo died, it will be exactly a year next Saturday, did I tell you that?"

"Yes, you did," Mom said in a strange voice.

"I tell you, I thought I was going to have a mental breakdown. If it wasn't for Saint Philomena telling me my dog's in heaven waiting for me, I would have gone off my mind. Maybe I did. I'm so nervous all the time it's hard to know for sure. So, anyway...why am I telling you this? It's something I'm feeling now that I haven't felt in a whole year and I don't know why I can't stop crying. It's just that when I look into your son's deep gentle eyes, all I can think about is the one thing in this life I loved most" and she started to cry again. "Saint Philomena has been telling me all along Alfredo's at peace with the angels. But now, I'm looking at your son and I feel like she is telling me something different."

"What is it, dear?" Mom was right there holding her hand.

"I feel like she's telling me it's time to go away, to leave Youngstown. Am I going crazy or what?"

Mom moved closer and looked into her neighbor's eyes. "You say your dog died last year, a week from this coming Saturday? What was the date, exactly?"

"April 26th . I'll never forget that day as long as I live."

Mother turned ashen.

Josephine rambled on. "How can I leave Youngstown? Where will I go? My kids are here and I can't leave Nick the bum. I don't understand. Oh, I'm so nervous, Bertha. I don't know what's going on."

My mother sat in uncharacteristic silence.

I sat down next to her. "What's wrong, Mom?"

"April 26th. That's daddy's birthday."

She got the message, loud and clear.

For the Love of Bertha

Sidneyland (Los Angeles)

After the first few weeks of doubt and misgivings, she began to find her way around. She liked her new apartment. It was bigger, sunnier and more cheerful than the one she left behind and it was close enough to the Temple that she could come and *kvell* every Friday night when her brilliant son spoke from the pulpit to an adoring (her perception) congregation of some five to six hundred worshippers.

In Los Angeles, just as in Acadia and Lake LaSalle before that, there were women in the Congregation who saw the single young Rabbi as the perfect match for one of the divorced, widowed or otherwise available single women in the community. When my mother arrived, they thought they had found an ally. What they didn't manage to convey to her was that she should support their recommendations and not go out fishing on her own, but mom was friendly to everyone, so if she met a girl in the supermarket who seemed attractive and personable, she would flash a picture of her son, the single Rabbi. Soon, she was getting calls from dozens of lonely women all over west Los Angeles, Beverly Hills and Santa Monica. At our weekly Sunday morning brunch, she would read off the latest list of possible dates. The look on my face didn't please her.

"It's not normal. A single young man, especially one that's brilliant and gorgeous like you, can't make time to go out with a pretty young girl every so often? I'm not saying you have to get married right away or even go steady, but if that should happen, what would be so terrible?"

"It's complicated, Mom. Rabbis live in fishbowls. Everybody who sees me with a girl will want to know what's going on, why her and not *my* daughter, why her and not me, is she Jewish, what kind of family does she come from, am I serious, is she divorced, a widow, a virgin or what?"

"So you'll never have a date? You'll sit home alone and lock yourself in the bathroom and make noises like a twelve year old?"

"Lock myself in the bathroom? What are you saying?"

"Me? Nothing. My friend Ida from Akron says all young boys lock themselves in the bathroom and do things before they're old enough to go out on dates."

"What kind of things?"

"How would I know? So tell me Benny, what did you eat for lunch yesterday?"

Los Angeles provides a variety of social, cultural and educational opportunities for Seniors, and Mom joined more clubs in her first month here than she had all the years she lived in Youngstown. She went to the Westwood Seniors coffee klatch every Tuesday, the kosher luncheon at the Federation on Wednesday, the YWCA for water aerobics on Thursday and a host of other activities that were available twenty-four-seven.

"The Sunshine Club is offering a bus trip to Las Vegas with a free stay in a fancy hotel. What do you think, should I go?"

"Of course. It will be a totally new experience for you, that I promise, but it's pretty far away."

"That's okay, I like long bus rides. The old men in the group say Las Vegas is where all the hot young girls are. Is that true?"

"I'm sure there are hot young girls everywhere. Is that what you're looking for?"

"Me? No. But if you wanted to come along, maybe you could meet one of them and have yourself a date, for a change."

"Sorry, I can't get away but I see no reason why you shouldn't go. I'm sure you'll have a good time."

Bertha does Vegas

When she came back, she couldn't contain her enthusiasm. "Such a city, bright lights on every street, big fountains and flowers everywhere you look, and the hotel! Don't ask. They were such sports. As soon as the bus pulled up the manager gave each of the seniors a twenty dollar bill so we could gamble. Isn't that something? And the girls! So pretty and sexy *and* friendly. I met one by the elevator, such a pleasant girl. She would go right up to a man and ask him if he wanted a date. Girls would never be so forward in my day. You should go there. I'm telling you, in Las Vegas you'll never be lonely. You'll have all the dates you want, and you don't have to be afraid somebody will see you having a good time. Oh! I didn't tell you. I also made money."

"You gambled?"

"Of course not. What am I, *meshugah*? Everybody who gambled, lost."

"So what did you do, find a date at the elevator and get a tip from some high roller?"

"Don't talk foolish."

I wonder if she had any idea what those women meant when they asked men at the elevators if they wanted a "date"? I don't know why, but I hoped she didn't.

"So how did you make money?"

"I watched some of the high risers in the group play the slots, but I didn't see the sense in that. Why leave the lounge where everybody was so sociable, to go sit alone with a machine that swallows up your money? The pretty cocktail waitresses with the nice long legs brought me plenty of free cokes and seltzer and all kinds snacks and when it was time to come home, since I didn't gamble, I kept the twenty dollar bill."

"Amazing, Mom. You beat the system."

"And I had such a good time! Everybody was so nice. Wherever you go in Las Vegas there are people to talk to. It's important to have somebody to talk out the heart with. You should hear what some of them have been through, especially the pretty young dancers and entertainers, it would break your heart. One has a husband who ran away with her sister and then came back, now all three of them live together in her trailer and she supports everybody including some kids from another marriage. They asked me for advice. What could I tell them? I said respect yourself and be honest with everybody, even people you don't like."

"Sounds like good advice," I said.

"That's what the pretty young girls with the nice legs told me. They all said how much they enjoyed talking to me. Isn't that something? Anyway, I brought you these."

Mom whipped out a stack of snap shots. "They gave us disposable cameras so I took some pictures." She handed me a packet filled with promotional material and advertisements for "Hotel Extravaganza" *and* eighteen four-by-five photographs of Mom's idea of *hot girls.*

"The hotel developed the pictures for us while they served us a huge luncheon. So much food. Who can eat all that? Most of it was terrible *traif* (non-kosher) stuff, but they also had cottage cheese and..." She recited the entire menu, from salads and appetizers all the way to desserts and soft drinks in exhaustive detail as I looked at the pictures. On the back of each photo was a name, a phone number and a few personal words addressed to Bertha. There were showgirls, cocktail waitresses and aspiring actresses. Some of them wrote that in the event Mom knew any agents, they were available for roles with partial nudity. There were also some of the sleaziest hooker-types I had ever seen. I was grateful that there weren't any female impersonators. At least, I didn't think there were and I didn't want to get into that discussion with my mother.

"Nice, huh?"

"Yeah, Mom. I'm glad you made so many new friends."

She was obviously disappointed that I wasn't more enthusiastic.

"You're still young and you're plenty busy right now, Benny, but the years go by so fast you don't even notice. Before you realize it you'll be old and that's when you'll understand how lonely life can be. Bennele, Bennele, you've had enough grief in your young life. It's time you had some *fargeneigen.* Look through the pictures again.

What can it hurt? You might decide you want to call one of them."

At our next Sunday brunch, Mom mentioned that she had been in contact with some of her new "Vegas" friends and one in particular was planning to visit Los Angeles.

"That's great," I said without a trace of sarcasm. Visitors for her meant a respite for me.

She didn't mention it again for several days, then the following Sunday she brought it up again.

"You remember I told you about my friend, Sonia, from Las Vegas? She'll be in town next week-end. Would it be alright to invite her to join us for brunch?"

"Of course." I was always happy to have someone else around with whom she could "talk out the heart". Mom needed to talk. I understood that, but it exceeded my need to listen by a million-fold, so I was delighted to share her with as many friends as she could bring around. "There's a playoff game on TV I'd like to see. You don't think your guest would mind if I watched it, do you?"

"Why should she mind? Of course it would be nice if you would say a few words and don't sit there like a couch tomato."

"Potato Mom, and yes, I will be civil. I'll even try to be charming."

She grabbed my chin and squeezed it. "Such a *punim*! Are you kidding me? My Bennele, when are you not charming? My Bennele, *a brocha auf dine keppele*, the most charming man in America."

America, for Mom, took precedence over the planet or the universe. Mom had her own store of prayers which usually began with thanking God for America, the pinnacle of freedom, justice and hope, but ended with something more personal like, "please God, my darling Benele should be well and find a nice girl, get married and raise a beautiful, healthy family, o-meyn". Mom was convinced I was perfect and on that point, there was not even room for hesitation. Once, when she came to visit me in Lake LaSalle, we drove to the Bronx to see her aging aunt Esther whom she hadn't seen since we both visited her when I was nine or ten. After the usual crying, eating, more crying and dessert, Mom beamed as Aunt Esther looked at me through both pairs of glasses. She wore one right over the other. Finally, she said to my mother in Yiddish and Russian. "I don't remember your son being such a *krasavitz*. When did he get to be so handsome?" I thought Mom would be pleased with the compliment. She wasn't. She took offense. "What do you mean, when? When was he not a *krasavitz*? My Bennele was always the handsomest boy in America!"

The Rabbi and the Scream Queen

The next Sunday morning, when I knocked on Mom's door, I was greeted by an extremely attractive young woman.

"You must be Ben," she said in a mellifluous voice that matched her good looks.

This gorgeous girl couldn't be..."Are you Mom's friend from Las Vegas?" I finally got the words out.

She looked me over and said "I don't know why, but I imagined you were taller."

"You're not what I expected, either."

"What *were* you expecting?"

"Someone thirty or forty years older, for one thing." Wow, this girl is some beauty. With looks like that, she must make a killing in Vegas. Was she a lap-dancer, hooker, showgirl?

Mom came out of the kitchen and gave me her usual warm embrace and cheerful smile. She had obviously imported this Vegas stripper in a desperate attempt to fix me up.

"Did I lie to you, Sonia? Is my Bennele gorgeous or what?"

I was ready to be put up on the wall while these two marveled at my astonishing features...but that isn't what happened.

"Gorgeous isn't the word I'd choose, Bertha. I'd say he's more...respectable, dignified, intellectual-looking."

"I know," Mom beamed. He was always intellectual but who knew he'd grow up to be so brilliant!"

I felt my nose drift a little off kilter. Gorgeous is a perfectly fine word. Respectable, dignified and intellectual-looking are simply not the same. Is Sonia trying to pretend she's not really out to get me? I followed them into the dining area where I usually set the table. To my surprise, it was already set.

Mom proudly announced that her new friend had prepared the table. "Isn't Sonia the sweetest thing? She won't let me lift a finger. She wants me to sit down and relax while she makes brunch. And so pretty! I could just look at her all day."

Mom was right. Sonia was stunning, but I couldn't figure her out. She pretended not to have any interest in me, or at least that was the vibe she was giving off, but why would she come all the way from Los Vegas to visit my mother if not to stake a claim on the available young Rabbi? I turned on the TV. The Forty-niners had just kicked off but I couldn't get into the game. I kept thinking about Sonia. She looked familiar but I couldn't place her. Had I met her somewhere?

I walked into the kitchen and watched for a moment. The two of them seemed to be playing house, babbling and giggling.

"Excuse me for interrupting but do I know you, Sonia?" I asked. "You look very familiar."

"My name isn't Sonia, it's Soji. I didn't correct your mother because it sounds so cute the way she says it."

Soji...Soji. "Are you Soji Mack?" How could I not recognize Soji Mack, the Scream Queen? I have a weakness for gothic horror flicks and I must have seen every one of her films.

"In the flesh."

Her reference to "flesh" recalled the many times I relished watching her lithe body being menaced and ravaged by everything from psychos to aliens.

"I've seen your movies. They're classics. I especially loved Beyond Evil."

"Um," she couldn't have been less interested.

Mother watched with curiosity. "What's behind evil?"

Soji laughed out loud. "Behind Evil! That would have been a much better title. It's equally

177

inane, but it has a comic twist to it. If only my producers had your sense of humor, Bertha." She gave Mom a warm hug.

"So, Behind Evil is a movie?"

"It's a movie Soji starred in that was a huge hit," I explained.

Mom looked at Soji as though her belief in her new friend was now completely validated.

"Sonia, are you a famous actress? Why didn't somebody tell me? Better yet, why didn't I guess a young girl as attractive and as nice as you, why shouldn't you be a movie star? Isn't that exciting, Bennie? I didn't even know my nice friend was a celebrity. How can a person be so beautiful and so modest? Have you ever met anyone like her?"

She looked to me for an answer. "The *emes* (truth), Bennie. Have you ever?"

I didn't answer but I knew Mom well enough to know it didn't matter what anybody else thought. When she liked someone, they were in her club for life.

"Are you still making movies?" I asked.

"No, I gave that up two years ago."

"And moved to Vegas to...?"

"It's a long story."

"Is there a short version?"

"I'm a financial advisor. I deal mainly in overseas investments."

"Sounds exciting."

"That's not the word I'd choose," she said.

"How about respectable, dignified or intellectual?"

"You're funnier than I thought you would be," she said.

"But still not gorgeous," I said.

"No, but funny is good."

"Speaking of funny, is Soji your real name, or is that something a press agent dreamed up?"

"I was named after Sojourner Truth, an early feminist and abolitionist. My parents were devout Trotskyites."

"How do they feel about you laboring in the vineyards of the capitalists?"

"They're both dead, so I don't think they feel too much of anything, or am I wrong about that, Rabbi?"

"Sonia, how many eggs, darling?" Mom called from the kitchen.

"I'll be right in, Bertha." Soji blushed and said quietly "I don't remember my own mother ever calling me darling."

She was gone in a flash.

What was this girl's agenda? I heard them in the kitchen as I sat in the Barcalounger watching the game while Soji showed Mom how to make a puffy omelet stuffed with fruit.

"Ben loves new dishes, don't you Bennele? Remember when I made you the tuna bake? They say it looked like those fish cakes the *Goyim* make from crabs that crawl around like bugs, but mine were kosher and delicious."

I was used to not responding to Mom's ongoing monologues, so I said nothing.

Soji came into the living room, holding a spatula.

"Your mother asked you if you remember her tuna bake."

"I heard her."

"You didn't say anything, so I thought you didn't..."

"Soji, I don't know how well you know my

mother. She's a lovely person but she never stops talking. I care deeply about her but if I have to listen to her endless prattle I will go nuts. I want to continue to spend as much time with her as I can, but in order for me to do that we had to establish certain ground rules."

"Rules? Defining what your mother can talk about and when?"

"It's not as draconian as all that. Anytime she's troubled or has something important she wants to discuss, I'm always there for her. It's just the continuous patter that I can't deal with."

"I see. The fact that your mother tries to engage you in a discussion about dishes she hopes will please you is not important enough to distract you from your football game. Gotcha."

She went back into the kitchen and I felt bad that she so misinterpreted what I meant. I wanted to explain, but then I thought the best way for her to understand my predicament, was to wait until she's had an earful of my mother's nonstop chatter. We'll see how much she can handle before she retreats into her own head.

I continued to watch the game but kept the volume low so I could hear them in the kitchen. I must say I was surprised that so little was said about me. Mom explained why she didn't recognize Soji's name because first of all, she doesn't go to movies much since her husband died and that was over twenty years ago and they don't make movies the way they used to anyway. Then, without stopping to make a connection she continued. "My best friend who was maid of honor at my wedding, we got married in Akron, her name was Sonia!"

I expected Soji to run for the door after

that characteristic dose of Mom's free association. Instead, she laughed and said "Bertha, you are the most precious person on God's earth."

I was pretty sure she said that loud enough for me to hear.

At the table, Mom was outraged to hear how much Soji paid for a hotel room the previous night. "It's silly to throw away money on a hotel when you can sleep here. After brunch, let's go get your things and you can move in with me. Please Sonia, that would make me so happy."

I nearly choked on my omelet. An ex-B-movie queen from Vegas staying with my mother? The Temple Sisterhood would burn her house down.

"That's so sweet, Bertha, but I have to drive back to Vegas tonight. I've got tons of work to do. I came in to see you and to attend a party for my biggest client."

"A party?" mother brightened up. "Benny, how long has it been since you went to a party?"

Soji turned to me. "Would you like to come, Ben?"

"Sorry, I've got a funeral in about two hours and a wedding this evening. What kind of party is it?"

"It's Ernie Fryberg's birthday. Do you know him?"

Ernie Fryberg, the billionaire junk bond king! "No I don't, but I certainly know who he is." This scream queen-turned-investment- broker was in town to attend a party for the most notorious white collar criminal of the decade.

"I read somewhere that he was serving time in a European jail," I said, trying not to sound supercilious.

"He was at a Swiss government restricted facility for ten months, but he's back now and his friends are throwing him a bash this afternoon at the Playboy mansion. Sure you wouldn't like to come?"

Would I *like* to come to a party at the Playboy mansion? Are you kidding me? Put yourself in my place. I haven't been with a woman in nearly four months. I've been working my ass off and given the choice between an afternoon at Hef's, surrounded by the sexiest women on the planet or performing a funeral, which would *you* pick?

"I really wish I could, but unfortunately..."

"What about you, Bertha? Would you like to come?"

"Me? I haven't been to a party in years. I don't have what to wear."

"It's very casual. Most of the action will be around the pool. What you're wearing is fine. Just take off the apron. Or, leave it on if you like. This is Hollywood, anything goes." Soji shot a teasing smile in my direction. "Sure you don't want to stop by for a quick dip, Ben?"

"You have no idea how much I would love to do that. Unfortunately I can't, but why don't you go, Mom?"

"You think I should?"

"Go, you'll enjoy."

Mom was thrilled. She ran into the bedroom to find something appropriate to wear to a Hollywood party, whatever that is.

"That was nice of you Ben and don't worry, I promise to bring Mom home before eleven and I won't let her drink or do drugs."

This woman was bewitching me! What's

with this "Mom" business?

"How well do you know Ernie Fryberg?" I asked. This time I didn't mind sounding supercilious.

"You mean, did we do it?"

She trumped me again! "I didn't ask you that."

"But you'd like to know."

"Not really," I lied. I read stories of how fat, bald Ernie always travels with at least a dozen gorgeous girls. He buys them thousands of dollars worth of clothes and jewelry, but that gives him the right to enter their unlocked rooms at any hour of the day or night. I wonder if he has the same arrangement with his female investment counselor and I suddenly felt jealous.

Just then, Mom came out of her bedroom dressed in a simple white jump suit with yellow embroidery.

"You look lovely, Bertha," Soji said.

"I was just going to say that! You look great, Mom."

Bertha at the Playboy Mansion

I left the wedding immediately after the ceremony so I could get home and call Mom. I told myself I just wanted to find out how her party at the Playboy mansion turned out. I was concerned that she might be exposing herself – and me – to ridicule by going to a party where girls allegedly swim nude and who knows what else?

No answer. It's ten o'clock! Where the hell could she be? She never stays out this late unless she's with me. I started to work on an article for the Temple weekly that was due the next day but I couldn't concentrate. I called a few more times and finally, after eleven, she picked up. She was so excited.

"What a lovely party" and she immediately went into a detailed list of every dish that was served.

"Did you meet Ernie's Fryberg's mother? I heard she goes everywhere with him."

"I did. What a nice little old woman. Thelma's her name"

I knew they were about the same age and probably the same height, but I wasn't going to get into that.

"We sat by the swimming pool and talked out the heart."

I have seen that duel often enough to know the protocol. Two mothers of similar age with sons they adore talking at one another without any pauses, whatsoever. Neither listens to what the other one says. They wait until one of them needs to catch their breath then they jump in. They don't really compete. Each has won in her own mind before they even begin. If you were to ask either of them about the other's son, their answer would be: "He's nice, but where does he come to my..."

"And Sonia, what a doll! She took me all around the house. A regular mansion, I'm telling you. What a big place, so interesting with all the paintings and statues and tapestries, *Gottenyu!* Must be worth a fortune. Sonia didn't want to leave me alone for a minute, but I finally convinced her to go swimming with the young people. Boy oh boy, you should see what she looks like in a bathing suit. She is some beauty!"

I know Mom, I wanted to say, but didn't. Several million other people who go to movies have also seen that and much more. No doubt about it, Soji Mack is one sexy girl.

"Anyway, it was a wonderful party. Did I tell you Sonia introduced me to everyone as her second mother? Isn't she something? I'm sorry she has to work in Las Vegas, otherwise I could see her every day. She called me her second mother, did I tell you that?"

"Yes you did, Mom."

"I only wish she was my daughter."

I found myself feeling terribly conflicted. Mom thinks of Soji as a daughter and I can't stop thinking of her in a bathing suit or better yet, topless. The bottom line is that I was jealous, resentful and immensely attracted to Soji at the same time.

All during the next week, Mom raved about her new friend who calls her long distance.

"How much do you know about her?" I asked.

"I know she's Jewish. I know she's had a hard life. Her own mother never showed her any affection. She was treated like a soldier and made to go on protest marches where people threw garbage at her. Her first husband was cruel and spiteful. She had to work night and day to get rid of the louse. She ended up paying him off plenty just to leave her alone. Did you ever hear such a thing? It's a crying shame. Such a sweet girl and so much *tzores* (troubles). Did you talk to her? She's got such a good *neshoma* (soul), she deserves better. Maybe, with God's help, she'll find a good man to take care on her."

"Mom?"

"Yes darling, what is it?"

"This man you hope will look after Soji. You're not thinking of anyone in particular, are you?"

"Who would I...you mean you? You think I'm trying to fix Soji up with you?"

"The thought had occurred to me."

"Please Benny, don't make me out to be some kind of schemer. When I first came out here I tried to find you a date. I didn't want people should say because your mother's in town and you'll have somebody to make you meals, you won't think anymore about getting married. You said no so I stopped looking. I brought you pictures of some of the nice girls I met in Las Vegas, just for a date not even anything serious. You said no again. I finally learned, no is no. You're a perfect man Bennele and any girl you end up with will be the luckiest person in America, but who am I to say who that person should be? Soji is my friend. I love her and she loves me but that has nothing to do with you, my gorgeous prince."

I was glad that we cleared that up. Soji has no plans to ensnare me. Good...that should have given me a sigh of relief.

It didn't.

It saddened me. I wish it didn't but it did.

The phone suddenly went quiet.

"Are you alright?" I asked her after a couple of moments of silence. She couldn't read my disappointment over losing Soji...whom I never had, let's face it...could she?

"I'm alright, dear. It's just that I got

distracted thinking about Sonia. There is something I should talk to her about."

"Call her." Maybe you'll get to talking about me, I thought, in spite of myself.

"She said she'd be out late tonight. I'll call her tomorrow."

Out? With whom? Why did she have to tell me that?

A Conspiracy?

When I arrived for brunch the next Sunday, there was a note attached to the screen. When I saw Soji's handwriting, my heart started to beat faster. "Stop it!" I waited a few moments for the flutter to abate before reading the note.

"Ben, please enter quietly. I'm guiding Mom through a meditation."

I reread the note. "*Mom!*" That suggests joint possession as though we're part of a triangle. Are we? I wish she'd be a little more forthcoming, at least give me some clue as to whether she has any interest in me at all. I mean, where do we stand? Mom doesn't think she's trying to nab me but this girl is some smart cookie. I wouldn't put it past her to exploit Mom's naiveté to make her way to me. If that's what she's thinking, it would be truly reprehensible. Tracking a man through his mother smacks of a devious nature and I would resent that mightily. On the other hand, let's not kid ourselves. Soji is incredible and I would be thrilled if she would ...but that's beside the point. I'm talking about character now.

I stood at the door studying her note.

"Guiding Mom through a meditation?" Excuse me! There already is a spiritual guide in this family and we're not looking to expand our faith. Besides, what comes to mind when I think about Soji is not entirely spiritual. Why doesn't she lead *me* through a meditation? Why doesn't she ask me to lead *her* through one?

All this flashed through my mind as I entered the house. Mom and Soji were sitting cross-legged opposite one another. Mom's eyes were closed. When Soji saw me, she raised her finger to her lips. I will admit that Mom looked more relaxed than I had seen her in years, but then, relaxation wasn't one of Mom's defining traits. She always seemed to be in a state of heightened anxiety. I can't remember seeing her sit in one place very long. She was either popping up to bring another dish to the table or rummaging through letters to show me the latest pictures of my nieces and nephew, or shuffling through a pile of papers to find the one that was dunning her for a bill she forgot to pay.

Guiding her through a meditation? There is nothing wrong with relaxing but does it have to be disguised in some mystical, quasi-religious, oriental formula for reaching the no-state of no-thingness?

"You are now moving from the lustrous color orange to the golden *chakra* at the center of your being," Soji's gentle voice filled the void.

I waited. I looked at my watch. I'm always on a tight schedule on Sunday but today was particularly jammed. She's only on the navel *chakra*? How many more of those damn things are there? I couldn't remember.

188

"Feel the inner harmony between your lower, base *chakras* and the luminous rays of celestial light emanating from your third eye."

Soji knew I was there. She was purposely torturing me to see long she could make me wait. Dammit! This sadomasochistic tease could go on forever. Sorry, I don't play those games. I've had it! I'm leaving...but I can't leave without letting Mom know I was here. On the other hand, I don't want to interrupt her meditation...since when is she doing meditations? I've got a bear of a schedule today, but like a good son I set aside an hour to spend with my mother. I deserve some credit for that! If she's busy, fine, but I can't rearrange my life to accommodate her every whim.

"The last time I checked, Mom had only two eyes," I said. Okay, that wasn't the cleverest thing I could have come up with, but dammit, I had to assert myself.

Mom's eyes popped open. "Bennele, I didn't hear you come in." She picked herself up, not without some considerable difficulty.

That was the first time I noticed how bad the osteoporosis in her bent back had gotten.

"Was that supposed to be funny?" Soji was not laughing.

"We started your brunch but then we got distracted somehow," Mom said as she hobbled into the kitchen, favoring one side. "I told Sonia how much pain I get from my back and she figured out how to help me. We were marinating when you came in. It felt so good, like a nice nap. I don't sleep so good anymore. Anyway, I'll finish your brunch in no time, *dollele*," she said from the kitchen.

189

"Don't let me interfere, Mom. I'm really glad Soji is helping you with your back. Please continue. It's just that I'm running late this morning. I can pick up something at the Deli."

"God forbid!" she called out from the kitchen. "Pick up something at the Deli? They charge you an arm and a leg, those *ganovim*. Besides, Sunday is our day, Bennele. I look forward to it all week. I should miss out because of a little back-ache? Only when they put me in my grave, not before."

Mom was in the kitchen banging pots and pans as Soji got up off the floor. "Let me help you, Bertha," Soji called out.

"No, darling, rest. It's almost ready. All I have to do is heat up the coffee and make the eggs the way Benny likes."

Soji looked at me for a long moment.

I felt like such a *shmuck*. "I really am sorry, but I didn't know she was going to be busy this morning. If I did, I would have cancelled. I've got..."

Before I could finish, Soji turned away and walked to the kitchen.

I flopped down on the couch, took out the draft of a speech I was going to deliver at the interfaith meeting that afternoon and tried to concentrate.

"How do *you* like *your* eggs, Mom?" Soji said loud enough for me to hear.

"Me? I like everything," Mom was smart enough to see where the question was going and she deflected it.

"What about that, Ben?" Soji came into the living room. "You know your mother. Does she really have no preferences at all, except for what

190

she thinks will please you?"

"I honestly don't know but I'd be deliriously happy if she made something *she* liked. I just don't want to spend the whole day talking about it." Of course, I never liked what Mom made for herself, like cottage cheese and rotten tomatoes that she buys at a discount and "cuts around nice," but I didn't want to get into that argument, ever.

"Whatever she makes is fine," I said. "Believe me, I won't go away hungry. There are always bagels and blintzes in the freezer."

"Do you like I should defrost some strawberry blintzes?" Mom heard me and called out from the kitchen.

"Sure, anything!" What I really meant was please don't bother me for the next ten minutes so I can stop feeling like an insensitive *putz* and proofread this damn speech.

Soji shook her head and went back into the kitchen.

"Okay, Bennele. Strawberry blintzes coming up...oh, my God!" Mom shrieked.

"What's wrong?" Soji and I called out together.

Mom stood next to the open freezer compartment holding a baggie. "The blintzes are all moldy. I must have left the door open by mistake. What a stupid I am." She looked at me in utter desolation. "I can run out to the Kosher market on the corner and get some fresh..."

"Please don't bother. Eggs are fine," I said.

Soji put her arm around Mom and gently rubbed her bent back. I felt miserable. The tranquility I saw in her face when she was "marinating" cross-legged on the floor had totally disappeared.

"I feel so terrible," she agonized. "I know how much you like strawberry blintzes and I ruined it for you."

"It's not a problem Mom, believe me. It's fine," I said and kissed her on the forehead.

"Five minutes, that's all it will take. Please, Bennele, I can get you..."

"What I really need now are a few minutes to look over my speech. Please believe me mom, eggs are perfectly fine. What would really help me is if we could please talk about it later while we eat."

Completely forlorn, Mom shut up and immediately started on the eggs. Soji steamed silently and I returned to the living room.

A few minutes later, Soji came into the living room and sat down next to me. She looked towards the kitchen. "Can Bertha hear us?" she whispered.

"I doubt it. Her left eardrum is pierced and she doesn't hear too well in the right one. Soji, I want you to know how sorry I am about disrupting your meditation..."

"I've got to talk to you," she said simply.

"I'd like to talk to you too, but I just don't have time this morning. Can we chat later?"

"I'm going to talk right now. I don't observe your rules."

"...Okay." Did I have a choice?

"You have to explain something to me. How can you not answer your mother when she asks you a question? How can you not listen to her when she talks to you? Aside from being rude, doesn't that violate one of the Ten Commandments?"

"If you're suggesting that I don't honor my mother, neither she nor I would agree with you. She's never complained..."

"Just how insensitive are you, Ben? Your mother would never complain to you, no matter how much pain or humiliation you caused her. You're her sun in the morning and her stars at night. *She* would never confront you about your appalling behavior but that doesn't mean *I* won't."

"Appalling? There's nothing I wouldn't do for my mother. I see her every single week, sometimes twice. I take her to every Yiddish or Russian show that comes to town and believe me, that's not how I prefer to spend my free evenings. Whenever I go to a restaurant I think she'd like, especially if there's music like the Greek or Romanian places where she can get up and dance, I always..."

"You do lots of nice things for her, Ben. That's not what I'm talking about. She's alone all day, every day and when she sees you she wants to talk. That's natural, that's human. You don't say more than two words to her so rather than sit in silence she tries to talk to you but you won't let her. That's unnatural and it's inhuman."

"She talks all the time," I said, still whispering. "I know she has some important things to say but everything is woven into some Byzantine labyrinth that comes out sounding so trivial I simply don't know when to listen."

"So you shut her up."

"I call her every day!"

"You call her? You dial the phone and as soon as she picks up, you probably read a magazine or watch TV. Do you think she doesn't know you never listen to her?"

"My mother is a very smart woman. I'm not surprised she knows what I'm doing and why, but I also know that's okay with her."

"How do you know that? Sure, she puts up with your crap but you have no idea what your mother thinks or feels or what *she* really wants."

"I certainly do. She wants me to get married, raise a family, be successful..."

"No, you're not listening, Ben. I'm not asking if you know what she wants for you or for your brother and his kids or for your father when he was alive or for her "nice" neighbors. Think about her, just *her* for a moment. Do you have any idea what *she* wants for *herself*?"

What *does* she want? I had no answer. I don't remember my mother ever asking anything *for herself*. What could she want that she wouldn't share with me and...why didn't I ever ask that question?

I suddenly flashed back to the year my dad lost his bread business. I was in grade school; the steel workers at the mill were on a long strike and nobody had money. Families would come to dad's bakery and beg for bread but they had no money to pay for it. It broke dad's heart to see kids go hungry, so he gave them whatever he had and put it on a tab he knew would never be paid. Within a couple of months he ran out of flour and money and he had to close up the bakery. Ultimately, he found a job from a competitor who wasn't as soft-hearted as he was and prospered during those tough times by gouging the poor. But for nearly a year before he got that job we had to get by on whatever dad found to bring home a dollar, whether it was delivering coal in the winter or ice in the summer or hauling junk. During those months, my mother made the most delicious meals seemingly out of air. She worked hard to keep everyone's spirits high and every Sunday after Hebrew School, she brought home an ice cream cake the size of a small dixie cup, more like an ice cream cookie. It was so tiny she was barely able to cut it into three pieces, one for dad, one for Art and one for me. She said she didn't like ice cream, so it worked out just fine for all of us.

I didn't think of that all these years, until now. When dad got a full time job at Schwebel's bakery, we celebrated by going to the ice cream parlor where we all ordered huge chocolate sundaes. Not only the three of us, but Mom too.

"I thought you don't like ice cream." I remembered saying.

"I didn't used to," she said. "I guess I developed a taste."

It was crushing to recall all those years of sacrifice coupled with my ingratitude. Soji watched me without saying a word. Then, she put her hand on mine and held it. Her presence was so comforting, I wanted to...I don't know what, but whatever it was, the moment passed quickly when Mom dropped a pot in the kitchen and muttered "darn, I'm so clumsy!"

Soji instinctively got up to help Mom but I stopped her. "Soji, I have to ask you...how it is that you and Mom formed such a strong bond so quickly? I mean, you're as different as two people can be."

"You think I have some ulterior motive,

like getting to the single Rabbi through his mother?"

"That's ridiculous," I lied. How did she know that was exactly what I had hoped?

"There's nothing ulterior about it," she said. "You remember I told you where my name came from? What I didn't tell you was that I was raised by martinets, not parents. For unrepentant communists, motherly love was bourgeois. I was suckled on party-line propaganda. What I wanted from my mother was love. All I got were lectures. At boarding school, my friends got letters from home talking about the family, the neighborhood, the parties, who's going out with whom, who's wearing what and all the stuff a teenage girl wants to hear. My mother's letters were marching orders to rise up against the fascist imperialist corporate bosses and fight for the rights of the oppressed workers.

When I first met Bertha at the Extravaganza in Vegas, we talked a little, exchanged some niceties, then somehow, I'm still not sure how it happened, I found myself pouring my guts out to her. I thought she would run away from me as fast as her little legs could carry her. She didn't. I shook my fists and bellowed. I must have looked like some nut going through primal scream therapy. When I finished, she took my hands in hers and looked into my eyes. 'I understand, dear,' she said. 'Believe me, I know from heartache. I see the anger in your eyes but I know that comes from deep wounds inside. Talk to me angel, let me help you.' I fell into her arms and sobbed. She held me tight and gently kissed my forehead.

In her embrace, I realized what I had

hungered for all my life: A mother to listen to me and love me. Someone to let me cry or laugh or dream out loud.

Well, I was a mess. We both cried and talked....and laughed, and talked...and talked. No one had ever expressed such a genuine personal interest in me. Me, just me, not for any ulterior purpose, not to make me do yet another soul-eroding movie, not to use or try to influence me. This woman just wanted me to know that I was worth being listened to and yes, loved. Then she asked me the sixty-four thousand dollar question.

'Tell me, sweetheart,' she said so lovingly, 'what is it? I mean deep in your heart, what do you really want?'

'What I really wanted,' I told her, 'was my childhood. It was stolen from me and I want it back!' It was hard to believe she could understand what I meant but she did and she held me while I bawled my heart out. I've had occasion to scream and howl in my life but this went way beyond any of that. It was uncontrollable. There were all kinds of people around and Bertha, who is a fraction of my size, half-carried me to the ladies room and let me sob until I was all blubbered out.

I don't know what it was Ben, but there was something in her; a radiance, a simplicity, a purity that touched my very core. I knew that I needed this woman in my life. And the most miraculous part of it was that she felt the same way about me. As I've come to know her better, I love her even more. I'm sorry I stepped on your toes by asking you to think of her differently from the way you always have but I had to do that. You watch out for her most of the time but when you falter I am going to be there for her."

"It's almost one o'clock, Bennie. What time do you have to give your speech?" Mom came running out of the kitchen and I could see that she had been listening and shed a few tears of her own.

"I didn't realize it was so late."

"Come darling, better eat so you'll have strength to talk."

"Where are you speaking?" Soji asked.

"It's an interfaith service at Saint Sophia, the glass cathedral on Sepulveda. I'm delivering the sermon, but every other clergyman in West Los Angeles will be 'saying a few words' so it may be a very long, drawn-out affair. I'd ask you to drop by but I'm sure it would bore the daylights out of you," I said, half-joking and half-wishing Soji could see me do what I do. Maybe she would forgive...maybe she would understand or even appreciate...maybe...

The heart of the matter

About an hour into the interfaith meeting, I was finally called upon to deliver the sermon. The audience was fidgeting from all the pompous invocations and benedictions and people were looking at their watches when I stepped forward to the podium.

I was surprised to see Mom and Soji enter from the main entrance at the rear of the nave just as I began to speak. Soji wanted to sit in the back of the church but Mom led her to the first row, where she sat and waved to me. I waited for them to get comfortable.

"Hi Mom," I said, knowing how much pleasure that kind of recognition gave her. Soji loved seeing Mom *kvel*. I was going to begin my sermon with a joke about John Bulova, creator of the wristwatch. When his wife asked him why he was wearing a bracelet, he explained to her that it wasn't about jewelry, "it's about time!"

I thought that after wading through an hour of stuffy, pro-forma bullshit, that play on words - it's about time - would be a good ice breaker but when I looked at Mom and Soji something came over me.

I looked up a passage in the Bible that was left on the altar and when I found it, I read aloud.

"Whither thou goest, I shall go and whither thou lodgest, there I too will lodge...and where you die, there will I be buried..."

It took a moment to collect my thoughts, then, it flowed.

"The Book of Ruth is a powerful testament to love and loyalty...," I said, "...to friendship and devotion to one another. It's about two amazing women and how they turned each other's grief into triumph and misery into redemption." I told the Biblical story faithfully, but the sub-text was clearly about Mom and Soji. There could be no doubt in their minds that I was talking directly to them. Through the allegory of a Biblical narrative I was asking my mother for forgiveness and thanking Soji for opening my heart.

When I finished, Mom and Soji were holding each other's hands so tightly I could see their white knuckles all the way from the pulpit. Tears were streaming down both their faces.

After the ceremony, Mom gave me a bear hug and held on.

"Hey, mama Zelig, don't hog the Rabbi." The President of my Temple and the Bishop of St. Sophia had their arms around each other. "Oops, did I say hog?" They both laughed as they edged in.

I watched as Soji and Mom moved through the well dressed upscale West-end crowd. Lots of people wanted to talk to Soji, but no one in this group seemed to have any interest in the small woman in the inexpensive plain dress who smiled sweetly but didn't have any prepared witticisms. Mom tried to appear positive but I couldn't bear the look of rejection on her rapidly aging face.

Soji was waiting for Mom outside the ladies room when I caught up with her.

"You did good, Ben."

"Respectful, dignified or intellectual?"

"You bordered on gorgeous." Soji's eyes were still red.

"So what *does* mom really want?" I asked. "I need to know."

What she told me was something I had been aware of but never thought much about. Mom had never become naturalized and it was always her dream to become an American citizen.

I had heard the stories of how she and her sister watched as the Cossacks stormed her village in Czarist Russia on Easter Sunday and slaughtered as many "Christ-Killers" (Jews) as they could, including her mother – right before her eyes - and how the two teen-age girls trekked across Europe, barefoot much of the time. They went from one *Shtetle* (small Jewish village) to another where the local Jews, poor as they were, gave them enough to get to a port city where they could board a ship to America. They were in transit for two years until they made it to Akron, Ohio, where a distant relative took them in.

Mom talked often of her love for America. "In Europe," she used to say, "in the spring after the snow melted, the streets would get all mucky. If a person fell down in the mud, the peasants would stand around and laugh. In America, if a person falls down in the street, everybody rushes to help them up. You want to know what is America? That's America."

Citizen Bertha.

If becoming a naturalized citizen was what she wanted, I promised Soji I would do everything I possibly could to help her. She said the best thing I could do was to build Mom's confidence and she would do the rest.

Ernie Fryberg put Soji in touch with a friendly immigration judge whose campaign he had financed. He made a couple of calls and Bertha was scheduled for a private naturalization processing session that was to include a quiz (wink, wink, elbow nudge) followed by a swearing-in ceremony in the Judge's private chambers at the Federal Court House. The judge assured Ernie that the quiz was strictly a formality. Bertha need not worry about it because there was no way she could fail.

Naturally, Mom was a nervous wreck. Soji and I both tried to alleviate her anxieties but she worried anyway. It is fair to say that she spent most of her life worrying, even about the most insignificant things, so agonizing about a test that could enable her to realize the dream of a lifetime was uncharacteristically normal. Bertha insisted on studying for the "quiz" all day, everyday. Soji was in Las Vegas during the week but they talked at length every evening, and on weekends she spent endless hours trying to allay Mom's fears by giving her positive reinforcement every time she got something right.

As it turned out, Mom learned a great deal. Memorizing dates wasn't her strong suit, but she managed to connect names with events, even though she altered them slightly. Her contextual arrangement turned out to be a valid system of mnemonics. Theodore Roosevelt became Theda because she had a friend at May's department store in lingerie named Theda who also had bad handwriting like the "rough writers". The federalist papers became the "federal papers" because that was the name of the main thoroughfare in Youngstown and they never picked up the newspapers that littered the street, and on and on.

I was amazed and impressed by Soji's patience. When she quizzed Mom about Abraham Lincoln, Mom would go into a confused story about how her father's name was Abraham and he died when she was two or three, maybe even four or five. She couldn't be sure because nobody had birth certificates in Russia at that time. If it were me, I'd have gone bonkers with all that rambling but Soji patiently listened and when Mom finished, she brought her back to the question.

For the Love of Bertha

The Sunday before her interview, I told Mom I would quiz her to see how well prepared she was. I knew the "test" was merely a formality, but becoming a citizen was a great honor and one to be cherished, so I was not going to deprive her of the satisfaction that would come with actually knowing American history. Mom must have been really nervous because she let Soji and I make brunch. She had never done that before. After we cleared the table, Soji asked questions at random from the Department of Naturalization manual. I was astonished to see how much information Mom had committed to memory. Lousiana Purchase? She knew the answer but couldn't understand why anybody would name their state "Lousy-Anna." The ship on which Francis Scott Key wrote the Star Spangled Banner? She knew everything except what was meant by the "rockets red clay". Clearly, Mom was as ready as she would ever be. The only thing left was to shop for a new dress so she would look nice when she finally realized her dream of becoming a citizen of The United States of America.

Downtown Los Angeles is a bizarre architectural mélange of New York's Fifth Avenue and Tijuana. When we arrived at the Federal Court House, we were ushered into the plush chambers of Judge Enrico Hernandez, an aristocratic looking man with a mane of white hair and an avuncular demeanor. He looked through a file on his desk then turned to Soji.

"I see we have friends in common." He took an official-looking document out of the file and looked at Mom over his pince-nez.

"Mrs. Zelig, welcome to my chambers."

"Thank you judge, I can tell already you're a nice person. Maybe your Honor will give me the pleasure of stopping by my house sometime so I can repay your hospitality with some strawberry blintzes. I just bought fresh."

Caught by surprise, Hernandez let out a loud chortle. "That's the best offer I've received all day. I will definitely do that." The judge laughed as he rolled up the document and placed a red ribbon around it. It took him a moment to make himself stop smiling so he could get on with the "serious" business at hand.

"Now, Mrs. Zelig," he postured, "I understand you desire to become a naturalized citizen. Is that correct?"

"Yes it is, your Honor."

"May I ask you a few questions?"

"It would be my honor, your Honor," Mom was nervous but ready.

He held up the Department of Naturalization Manual and said "I trust you've studied this?"

"I did."

"And you know the answers to all the questions at the end of the pamphlet?"

"You bet your boots, your Honor," Mom was definitely prepared.

"Good, that saves us all a lot of time." He smiled and put away the manual.

Mother was confused. She turned red and her hands began to shake.

Soji put her arm around her and smiled. "It's okay Bertha, nothing to be nervous about, everything's going to be alright. Judge Hernandez believes you know all the answers so he isn't even going to ask you any of those questions."

"But the only answers I know are the ones in the book. What if he asks me something I didn't study up on?"

The judge looked at the application forms on his desk.

"I see you've filled out all the appropriate papers. That's good, that's good." He took off his glasses and said in an authoritative but gentle voice.

"Mrs. Bertha Criden Zelig, would you stand and raise your right hand, please."

Mother stood and now she was trembling as the judge intoned.

"Mrs. Zelig, you have requested that the government bestow upon you its highest honor, that of citizenship in our great Republic. Is that correct?"

Mom looked confused. "Republic? Uh...the first Republican president was Abraham Lincoln," Mom was desperate to answer correctly.

"I know," the judge said. "Very good, and now let us complete the swearing in." He continued. "Do you, Bertha Criden Zelig, plan to overthrow the government of the United States by force, violence or subversion?"

Silence.

Judge Hernandez assumed she didn't hear him. "Mrs. Zelig, I asked if you plan to overthrow the government of the United States by force, violence or subversion?"

Then, with her hand still raised, shaking like a leaf, mother said...

"I think...violence."

Soji and I were stunned.

Judge Hernandez, who was experienced in keeping witnesses on track said, "what you really meant to say was none of the above, isn't that right, Mrs. Zelig?"

Both Soji and I were now screaming at Mom.

"JUST SAY YES!"

She got the message.

"You're absolutely right, your Honor," she said. "Yes, none from above."

Judge Hernandez said in all his years on the bench he had never before kissed anyone after performing the swearing in ritual but he couldn't resist Bertha. Nor could he resist her strawberry blintzes. He ate three helpings! Mother was obviously thrilled that the Judge agreed to come to her house for lunch with Soji and me, and she was beside herself watching the official representative of the United States of America enjoying her blintzes. She expressed her delight in her own unique way. "Look how nice the Judge eats," she said to me. "Why don't you ever have seconds when I make blintzes the way you like?"

"I just did, Mom."

"Never mind, there's plenty more."

After he left, Mom wrapped the remaining blintzes in saran wrap, aluminum foil and zip-lock baggies, then stuffed them into her packed freezer.

Soji cleared away the dishes while Mom emptied a large box of family photographs looking for a suitable frame to display her new certificate of citizenship.

Mom went to the bedroom closet to look for more frames while I perused the snapshots. I was amazed to see how my brother's kids had grown.

When was the last time I saw them? I couldn't remember. Obviously, I've been much too self-involved.

I suddenly felt a hand on my thigh. I hadn't been aware that Soji was sitting next to me. She squeezed gently.

A delicious tremor shot through my body.

"*Mazel Tov,*" she said.

"What for?"

"On the occasion of your *Bar Mitzvah,* Ben. Congratulations, today you became a man."

I couldn't believe how much I ached for her at that moment. Everything turned soft and hazy. I didn't know what to do. Does she want me to kiss her? Will that offend her? Will it disrupt...? While I was trying to figure out what to do, she leaned in and kissed me full on the mouth. Her fragrance dazzled my senses and I thought my head was going to burst.

She kissed me again. I kissed her...I don't know how much time passed before I looked across the table. Mom was sitting there with her certificate of citizenship in a gold frame and looking at us. I suddenly felt embarrassed but Soji didn't seem to mind.

When I finally engaged Mom's eyes, she smiled sweetly. I smiled back, still feeling a little uneasy.

She turned from me to Soji and did something I had never seen her do before.

She winked.

Blood

Blood

I came back to the Rabbinical Academy where I was ordained thirteen years ago to see my personal Rabbi, Professor Jacob Rothstein, in a desperate attempt to recapture my lost faith.

Downward spiral

For me, faith had always been a rapturous fire in my bosom. It connected my heart to my brain and both of them to the cosmos.

Now that the fire was out, there was no clarity, no joy, nor purpose left. Nothing was certain anymore. My inner lenses were hopelessly blurred and nothing I saw made any sense. It was terrifying to flick the same switches I had always depended on and not see any light. My most intimate and passionate prayers went unanswered. Meditation was a blank screen. I was speaking into a phone with no one on the other end and the cosmic operator was clearly saying "the number you are calling is not in service at this time."

How could it have vanished? It's as though I was metamorphosed into a beetle. I just awoke one morning to discover that I no longer had a voice or heart. The difference between Kafka's Gregor Samsa and me is that in my case it didn't happen overnight. I felt mine coming on for the past year. Every morning when I looked into the mirror I saw the slow, progressive dying of the light. My soul was eroding and I was turning into a hollow shell. I didn't understand it and I didn't know how to stop it. I only know that the moribund smell of my inner decay was stifling and I was scared stiff. My belief in God, the very core of my being, was evaporating and with it everything that I had built my life on. I was sinking in quicksand.

Nothing like this had ever happened to me before. Even as a child, I was driven by an inner fire. It didn't take much to ignite my passions. Long before I read the Psalms, I saw the glory of God in nature. The advent of spring got me singing and hopping as I raced home from school with a bunch of freshly picked lilacs for my mother. In High School, I was made to believe that skipping and leaping into the air wasn't cool. Some of my classmates thought I was a little light on my feet so I joined the football team to prove that my jockstrap was as big as anyone's, but when I threw a touchdown pass, I jumped all over everyone, to the embarrassment of the whole team. I was a jumper, a dancer, manic. I loved school and learning new things made me even more hyper.

When I entered the Rabbinical Academy, my studies were so exciting, I could barely contain myself. I memorized whole portions of the Bible, the Talmud, Hebrew literature, ancient as well as modern and won the approbation and affection of my professors, all of whom I revered. When I found young Zionists who sang and danced to the words of the prophets, the fire intensified.

"The torch of faith burns brightly within you, Ben," Rabbi Rothstein said to me just before I was ordained, "and that is why you will make a fine Rabbi. You are one of the lucky few. You are a true believer, a bearer of the light and a messenger of the Holy One, Blessed Be He."

I can't pinpoint the exact moment when the light went out but I know it started about a year ago, shortly after my brother Art died.

"How fortunate is the match," he used to say, quoting a Hebrew poet. "It creates a luminous glow and lights the way for many, even as its brief life is extinguished in its own glory." He looked splendid in his smart blue Air Force uniform with the double gold bars on the collar and wings over his heart. Art, my older brother who feared nothing, chucked a promising legal career together with all the other social and economic goals our parents had set for him and entered the Air Force Academy. "A lot of guys go through life without passion or zeal. Not me, little Ben," he said when he hugged me for the first time after all our years of intense sibling-rivalry, "and I pray, not you."

His prayer was answered, because my life had been filled with passion *and* zeal *and* ecstasy.

That is, until the phone call from his wife, Marge, informing me that the plane he was flying had disintegrated in mid-air. I pictured his wife and Sandra, his six year old daughter who was always hanging onto some part of him whether he was sitting, walking or driving. I thought about Justin, his four year-old who wore a superman cape and believed he was invincible and Tess, who was only three months old. He'll never see them grow up. He'll never...

"THERE IS NO JUSTICE AND NO JUDGE!" I proclaimed from the depths of my grief. Those words were first spoken two thousand years ago by Elisha ben Abuya, a famous Talmudic scholar, when he renounced his faith and became an apostate. Hearing myself actually say it troubled me deeply.

At Arlington, I remember feeling my knees buckle as I returned the long shovel to the mound of earth above his grave. When I looked up at the gray clouds, I recalled my first class in philosophy with Professor Rothstein twenty years earlier.

"According to Archimedes," he said, in his uniquely measured Polish accented speech, "all you need is to place a large enough lever at the earth's fulcrum and you can lift the planet out of its orbit."

I don't know why, but that idea always haunted me. With modern technology, isn't it conceivable that someone could make a large enough lever and with laser penetration, find the earth's fulcrum? What was preventing Al Queda or Islamic Jihad from performing the ultimate act of terror? Pluck the earth out of its orbit and send us all reeling into space. That vision of being thrust into airless nothingness became my recurring nightmare.

Jumping, leaping, defying gravity had always made my spirits soar. It never occurred to me that I could get so far off the ground that my faith, like booster rockets, would collapse to earth and leave me flailing in an intergalactic void.

The Honor Guard fired several shots into the air. What I heard were the gates of earth slamming shut behind me.

I made a conscious decision to immerse myself in work. That was the only thing I could think of to distract myself and hopefully find some solace. Maybe, if I were somehow blessed or lucky enough, I just might discover some way to reignite my dormant fire.

It didn't happen. In addition to all the other duties required of a pulpit Rabbi, he is called upon daily to ease the burdens and allay the fears of the troubled, the broken hearted, the sick and the bereaved. Under the best of circumstances that is a tough assignment, but it becomes an impossible one when the soul is inert and belief is called into question. I had nothing to offer, no wisdom, no faith, no life-urge, no survival instinct, nothing. I sank deeper and deeper into despair.

A voice cries out in the wilderness

When I realized I had hit bottom, I reached out to Professor Rothstein, my former teacher, Rabbi and friend; the only person who could fully probe the depths of my desolation. He had been an inspiration to me all the years I was his student. He also became a confidant and my personal guru. In my early years as a novice Rabbi, I came to him with a constant stream of questions about how to deal with the endless tragedies a Rabbi has to face on a regular basis. I called him at all hours with urgent requests for help. He was always there for me, not only with a clear solution to the problems of my congregants, but also with a rich anecdote to soothe my soul. Whenever I was in New York, I made a pilgrimage to his study in the tower of the Rabbinical Academy. I learned more from his gestures, the look in his twinkling eyes, the way he lit his pipe as the match burned precariously close to his fingers, than from years of studying texts. He had a way of smiling as he reflected on a problem that put even the most complex quandaries into a clear context which enabled me to grow with each encounter. He was the only person I knew who had the wisdom and understanding to help me cope with the enormous burdens I had taken upon myself when I became a Rabbi.

Now that I was being torn apart from within, my life was becoming more meaningless and hollow with each passing day and I needed Rabbi Rothstein's guidance more than ever.

"I submitted my resignation to the Temple Board," I said looking at the familiar cluster of books climbing out of the shelves lining Professor Rothstein's office. We had embraced warmly when I entered and as long as he could busy himself preparing tea and cookies, he was his usual charming self, but the moment I broached the subject that was eating me alive he sank into uncharacteristic silence.

He took a small block of sugar from the bowl on the table next to his leather chair and placed it between his teeth. He sipped hot tea for a long moment then put down his cup.

"I see," he said absent-mindedly.

I was surprised by his tepid response. He certainly knew about my brother's death and the lingering effect it had on me. I expected him to find some illuminating insight to address my dilemma and somehow convince me not to act precipitously with regard to leaving the Rabbinate. In the past, he might start with a Hasidic parable or literary allusion.

This time, he said nothing. Instead, he sat for a long time, staring into space. Then to my shock and amazement, I saw tears forming in the corners of his eyes.

"The Board didn't accept my resignation," I said, thinking that I might have been overly dramatic saying that I was planning to quit.

"They asked me to take some time off and think about it so I came to New York and moved into the dorm here at the Academy to do just that."

He still said nothing. How much coaxing does he need?

Professor Rothstein reached for the tea cup and raised it to his lips but his hand began to tremble. I took his cup and placed it on the table.

"What's the matter, Professor?"

A tear rolled down his bearded cheek and he bit his lip so as not to weep aloud.

I was stunned to see this display of emotion. In the twenty years that I have known him he never once exposed his personal feelings in this way. What have I done to him? Was this too great a burden to lay on the man who had already done so much for me? I searched for a way to reach him and tell him not to be so distressed...

"You have a serious problem, Ben..." he said.

"I know," I said, "but I never intended to upset you so...I'm so sorry..."

He interrupted me and said "...you have a

problem...but...so do I. Also...a serious problem
...a *very* serious one."

It took me a moment to realize he hadn't
heard anything I said. He was struggling with his
own demons and his anguish had nothing to do
with me! How blind was I not to have seen that?

He wiped his eyes and tried to pretend it
was nothing.

"More tea?" He rose from his chair and
tried to lift the pot, but it shook in his hand. I
took it from him and led him back to his chair,
where he sat in silent torment.

"What is it, Rebbe?"

His face was ashen.

"I can't trouble you with my..." he couldn't
go on. More tears filled his eyes.

"Please talk to me, Rebbe. You've been
there for me all these years. Now you need help
and I am here for you."

He stopped and looked at me for a long
moment. "You're...here for me...?"

Silence.

He studied me for a long time.

More silence.

"You're here...for me?"

Suddenly his face became rapturous.
"You're here...you're the one!" He raised his
hands to heaven and proclaimed "Hallelujah!"

His behavior was freaking me out but I
didn't know what to say. I just stood there bent
over him while he gazed into my eyes for a long
time as though he were reading a crystal ball. His
face took on a beatific radiance. He stood up,
adjusted the *Yarmulka* on his head, closed his
eyes and sang aloud in Hebrew.

"Lord, You alone have seen the anguish of my soul. You heard my call from the depths of despair. I thank Thee, Master of the Universe, for answering my prayer and..."

He opened his eyes and stared at me. He put his arms on my shoulders and continued.

"...sending me...my Deliverer!"

He embraced me and I felt his tears of joy on my cheek. "You will find her," he said to me. "You will return my sweet pure child to me before it is too late because you are the bearer of the light, the messenger of the Holy One, Blessed Be He."

Now I was really shaken. Has he gone completely bonkers, I asked myself? Professor Rothstein thinks *I* was sent to *him* on some Divine mission to be *his* deliverer!

Reluctant Deliverer

"Naomi, you don't know me," I said when I called, minutes after I left her father's office.

She put me on hold. I waited for about five minutes. When I was about to hang up, she came back on the line.

"Sorry about that. That was 911 and I had to take the call."

"911! Are you serious?"

"No, but since I don't know you I don't see why I should assign you any priorities."

I proceeded to tell her that I had been a student, a friend and an ardent admirer of Professor Rothstein for many years.

"How well do you know him?"

"He is the closest I have ever come to meeting a genuine saint," I said.

"Really," she said, after a brief silence. "That's not the word that comes to my mind when I think of him, which isn't often."

I didn't know how to continue the conversation without falling into her trap. "What word would you choose?"

"There are quite a few. *Shmuck* is probably the closest."

Under other circumstances I would have told her to go to hell and hung up, but I couldn't. I had made a promise.

"I gather you're not very fond of your father," I said. I wasn't trying to be snide or cute, I just couldn't think of anything to say. She was attacking one of the great men of our time and one I truly loved and respected.

"I hate the son of a bitch," she said simply, without emotion. "Excuse me, 911 is calling back," and the line went dead.

I called again and told her I had to see her. "Five minutes is all I'm asking. Just tell me where I can meet you and you can start counting the minute I arrive. Please, five minutes. I can't tell you how important it is."

There was a pause. "Is he dying or something?"

"Or something," I said. "Quickly, tell me where you live. I've got 911 on *my* other line now."

"You've got...?" She chuckled briefly and told me to meet her on the northeast corner of one hundred and twenty-fifth street and Lexington Avenue.

"How will I recognize you?"

"I have big boobs and a small butt, every Jewish boy's fantasy."

"Will you be covering them with clothes I might recognize?"

"Wear a black turtleneck. I'll recognize you."

"You think I'll be the only one wearing a black turtleneck?"

"I'm sure of it. Turtlenecks have been out for years. Only Geeks and Nerds are still wearing them. That includes Rabbis, by the way."

"What time?"

"Six twenty-five. That will give you exactly five minutes before I start work."

"Can we make it earlier?"

"Why?"

"It's Friday evening and the Sabbath begins..."

"Screw you and screw the Sabbath," she said and hung up.

I called again. "This is 911 again. Please don't hang up."

"Give me one reason, five words or less."

"I'm out of quarters. That's four words if you don't take off for apostrophes."

"You sure you're a Rabbi?"

"Why do you ask?"

"Because you don't sound like a complete nerd."

"You don't know me. I assure you I can be as big a nerd as anybody."

"Come by my apartment at six."

When I arrived at the tenement in the entrails of Harlem, I thought I must have the wrong address. The front door was broken and loosely attached. Bare wires hung out of what was once a buzzer. I entered and prepared to climb the six flights to her apartment when I heard a terrible commotion coming from one of the intermediate floors.

"You been cheatin' on me, you bitch," an angry man with a thick Puerto Rican accent screamed.

"No, I ain't neither," a woman cried. "I been true to you, baby."

The sound of a fist punching a face was followed by a loud "owwww" and someone went tumbling down a flight of stairs.

What was I to do? Before I could move, I heard the steps creaking. That must be her, I thought, trying to climb back up.

"Don't lie to me, *puta*. I know what you been doin'. Admit it! You don't love me no more. Admit it or I'll kill you!"

Another punch, another groan and another tumble down a flight of stairs. Now the woman was really crying. "I swear to God I been true to you. I love you, baby, I ain't lyin'. Please stop this."

I couldn't stand by and do nothing while a woman was being beaten to death. I started up the stairs. The wooden banister was broken but I held onto the wall until I touched something slimy, then decided it was better to just walk slowly and maintain my balance. The sounds of the brutal beating filled the hallway. I couldn't understand why nobody else came out to stop the vicious assault. When I reached the third story, I finally understood what was going on.

A very large black woman stood at the top of the third floor staircase as a small Puerto

Rican man, bloody and bruised, climbed up to her from where he had obviously fallen.

"You lousy bitch, You hate me, don't you? Say it, you lyin' *puta*. I want to hear it from you. Say it or I'll kill you." Now he was screaming in her face.

Tears streamed down her face as she pleaded.

"Please believe me, baby. I always loved you. I always will." Then, she reached back and punched him in the face again. He groaned loudly as he fell back down the stairs. She wept as he climbed back for more.

"You better...quit lyin'...or I'll..."

I waited until he could no longer get up, then I climbed past the dueling lovers who didn't bother to acknowledge me.

Out of breath, I finally reached the top floor where two railroad apartments straddled the stairwell. An attractive young woman with a dynamite body and take-charge attitude opened the door. She wore a thin black sweater that emphasized her full bosom and black tights that left no doubt about her small waist and firm bottom. Her reddish-brown hair was pulled back into a tight pony-tail.

"...Naomi...?" I was winded.

"I have two questions," she said as she waited for me to catch my breath. "Are you alive and if so, are you Ben?"

"Yes...Ben Zelig...Sorry," I wheezed.

"You're late."

"There was some commotion on the third floor."

"Oh, yeah. Second Friday of the month."

She explained that every time the couple on the third floor gets their welfare check, they get drunk and fight.

"But she nearly killed him," I said, breathing again.

Naomi shrugged. "The last guy did die but so far this one seems to be holding up."

As the pain in my lungs receded, I checked out the place. There was a ratty upholstered chair next to a small futon on the floor and posters on the window. The sink was brown and brimming with plates of unwashed terrible-looking-stuff.

She slung her backpack over her shoulder. "I'm late for work. You can walk with me."

I practically had to run to keep up as she raced briskly down one hundred and twenty-fifth street.

"He must be pretty sick, huh?" She asked simply.

"Why do you say that?

"I haven't spoken to my father in over five years and you're the first emissary he's sent. Why now? Why you?"

I told her that I had known her father for twenty years and in all that time, though I had bared my soul to him a thousand times, he never exposed anything about himself until this morning. He didn't even tell me why it was so urgent that I see Naomi immediately, he just said it was and I accepted that.

"I've come to doubt a great many things over the past year," I told her, "but one thing I never questioned was your father's sixth sense."

"You love him, don't you?"

"I worship him. Jacob Rothstein is

everything I admire. Many years ago, as a young student, I found myself imitating his style of greeting people by bowing slightly. I even affected his Polish-Yiddish accent until I realized how stupid I sounded."

I couldn't stop.

"To me, he is the epitome of Rabbinic Judaism. The most important thing in his life is being kind to people. I remember walking down West End Avenue one Shabbat afternoon when a woman staggered out of a bar. It was a bright day and seeing how she shielded her eyes from the harsh sun, it was clear that she had been inside the bar for some time. Most people snickered at her as she stumbled along the crowded street. Your father smiled to her and extended his hand. He looked into her eyes with the warmth and compassion of a saint. He told her she looked like a charming woman and he hoped she was enjoying the beautiful weather. The woman held onto his hand for the longest time. At first she looked at him suspiciously trying to figure his angle, but the gentle look in his compassionate eyes relaxed her and the words flowed. 'My hair could look a lot better,' she said, 'but I can't sit in a beauty parlor all day 'cause I got to go to work.' Your father assured her that he understood, but she should know that her hair was fine and she looked perfectly charming. I'll never forget the expression on her face when he said that. At first she blushed, then, tears rolled down her cheek. He raised her hand to his lips and kissed it. When we left, she walked toward the subway, erect and proud. She didn't stumble or falter like some self-loathing derelict, but joined the crowd, feeling like a person worthy of being on this planet."

I suddenly realized I had been carrying on incessantly. "I don't mean to bore you, but I don't know if you've heard those stories about your father."

"All my life."

"And...you still hate him?"

"I used to love my father more than anyone in the world, but he did a terrible thing to me."

I didn't know how much she would reveal, and judging from the intensity of her tone, I wasn't sure I was ready to hear it. Still, I asked.

"Do you want to tell me about it?"

"Are you asking as a Psychiatrist, a Rabbi, or just a nosey *shnook*?"

"I'm not a Psychiatrist, but that still leaves you with a couple of options."

The Gates of Hell.

She stopped at the entrance to a seedy club with a blinking sign that read *ALL GIRLS, ALL LIVE, ALL NUDE.*

"This is where I work," she said defiantly.

I had a bad feeling about this meeting from the moment I heard her say "screw the Sabbath", but this was worse than anything I could have imagined. Am I to believe she is a stripper?

She opened the door and turned to me.

"Coming in or what?"

"Is this a joke?"

"Do I look like I'm joking?"

"But I want to talk to you."

"A lot of lonely nerds do, but they pay for

it, even with my clothes on."

"That's not why I came to see you..."

She laughed. "Okay, I am playing with you now. I know everything I need to know about you but you don't have a clue about me. Come in, you might learn something."

What was I supposed to do? So far, I had done nothing to help her father...or her. I had put the most important crisis of my life on hold and I had no idea what to do next, so I followed her.

We entered the sleazy club and were hit by a blast of music from the huge stage speakers. We walked across sticky floors to a booth next to the bar where a fat man with seven greasy hairs stretched across a bald head dined on a huge plate of something orange and lumpy. Naomi introduced me as her Rabbi. I didn't get the gentleman's name but it was something like Chooch or Cheech. He looked at me and snarled.

"A Rabbi? A Jewish Rabbi? No shit!"

"No shit," Naomi answered for me.

He looked her over and smiled broadly.

"Whatta you, some kinda Jew? I thought you was Puerto Rican. Hey, this is big news. We got to get you a Jew cross to wear around your snatch. Half the *bakalas* that come in here are Jews. Why didn't you tell me this before? This is big!" He called to an even fatter man at the bar who was actually sitting on two barstools.

"Hey, Scungile! Go pick up some Jew stuff for Naomi, stuff she can wear in her act."

Scungile looked confused. Cheech screamed several times. Scungile grunted and repeated select words suggesting that he was getting part of the message if not all of it. Cheech continued to scream hints and clues until Scungile shrugged, meaning he more or less understood the order, slid off both barstools and left.

Naomi went into her dressing room and I was seated at a small table directly in front of a long pole that was being straddled by a heavy-set black stripper.

I couldn't be more miserable. I had started the day with the razor thin hope that somehow I could resolve the spiritual crisis that was strangling me. Instead, here I was in this cesspool of depravity on an impossible mission, and the one person I put my faith in has deluded himself into thinking that *I* am the messenger of *his* salvation!

At first I thought the loud crash I heard was the cosmos laughing but I soon realized that it came from the next table.

"You're sorry? What's that supposed to mean, you're sorry? You piss on my date and you're sorry?" A small middle-aged white man, whose "date" was a young, but large black transvestite in a red wig, screamed at the drunk across the table.

As if sitting through a depressing strip "act" in a slimy club in Harlem on the first Friday night in thirteen years that I didn't conduct a Sabbath service wasn't enough, people around me were pissing on one another!

A fist fight broke out and bottles crashed to the floor. A few shards landed inches from my feet. Every instinct told me to leave, but that was out of the question.

The fight at the next table was over the minute the bouncer, a seven foot tall muscular black man with a shaved head, arrived.

"Who's the jive-ass motha who pissed?"

The small white man was trying to dry his "date's" spotted dress with several soiled paper napkins. *She* was hysterical and he was fuming.

"Him!" He hissed and pointed to the drunk across the table.

"I got a prostate problem..." the drunk began to explain.

With one hand, the Bouncer picked up the drunk whose pants were still unzipped, and tossed him onto the floor like a rag doll.

"Promise me you'll never piss on customers again," the bouncer grunted.

"I promise," the man squealed."

"Now you gonna clean up the whole floor, right?"

"But I didn't piss on the *whole* floor."

The bouncer looked menacingly at him.

"Okay, I'll clean...I won't piss..." He tried to stand up but his legs buckled. He tried again several times and finally was able to stand, but barely. The bouncer handed him a mop which he took, first to lean on, then to swab.

I got out of my seat to allow him more room to mop.

"Sit down," the bouncer commanded.

I sat down.

The other patrons didn't even notice the commotion. They were totally focused on the stripper. From where I sat she looked attractive enough both from the front and the rear except that her balloon-shaped breasts, two bowling balls covered with skin, were planted too far down her chest and the elongated, protruding nipples looked like they were transplanted from something with four legs.

When the music ended, she picked up the strewn pieces of her costume and left the stage as though she were taking a stroll down Main Street.

"Ooooo-ieeee!" The large speakers screeched as the M.C., wearing a beige and green suit and a head oozing Dixie Peach pomade, came center stage holding a mike.

"Take your hands out of your pants and put them together for our next internationally famous dancer, Miss Poon Tang, who comes to us all the way from Vietnam."

A pretty Asian girl walked out in a pair of platform shoes that looked like stilts and a diaphanous robe, barely covering two enormously bloated breasts that were also planted a little lower than they should have been. They must all go to the same plastic surgeon, I thought, who is either too short to know where breasts should be or simply prefers udders.

"So baby, is Poon Tang a popular name in Vietnam?" The M.C., whose head glistened like a ball mirror under the stage lights, stuck his mike in the girl's heavily painted face. She snickered and looked from side to side. She was obviously unprepared to do lines or shtick, or maybe she didn't understand much English, but there was an admirable dignity about this girl who did not accept that she was being ridiculed.

"I not Vietnam. I Micronesia."

"Say what?"

"Micronesia is country. I not Vietman, I born Micronesia."

"That's great news, baby. Ooooo-ieee," he howled then put his arm around the confused young girl and turned to the audience. "Any of you muthas even know Milk of Magnesia is a country?"

The crowd grumbled impatiently.

The M.C. smiled broadly. "Oooo-ieee," he howled again. "They love you, baby. Now show 'em what you got."

As the girl on stage began to gyrate, I found myself unable to watch her humiliation.

"How much longer was I going to have to remain in this sewer?"

It wasn't at all clear to me why I was here. Did I have to see Professor Rothstein's daughter naked in order to convince her to return to her father's home and live a chaste life? What were the chances of that happening? I had seen so much heartbreak in families where submissive parents tried desperately to reconcile with adolescent children. Sometimes, these *adolescents* were in their thirties, forties and beyond, but their tantrums were still juvenile, and the results were always the same: Tragically disappointing. Rabbi Rothstein fully believed that he and his wayward daughter would fare better. I simply could not share that belief, but then, my faith in miracles was tattered. His, apparently, was in tact.

"Find her...talk to my sweet, pure Naomi...," he said. "She *will* return to me. She must! It's a matter of life and death!" That's all he said. When I pressed him for specifics he said "...with patience all will be revealed."

Okay, I counseled myself. I'll be patient...I'm patient...I am patient...so where's my revelation?

"O000-ieeee," the M.C. screamed. "And now I want all you sleaze balls out there to give a big Harlem *shalom* to Miss Tel Aviv, Israel's secret weapon."

I assumed that was going to be her.

It was. Naomi Rothstein danced onto the floor wearing very little. A long black wig sat on her head obscuring much of her face but the black eye-make up and glossy lip-paint peeped through every time she spun around and the long straight fake hair circled her face. A strange looking piece of metal hung from her waist. I assumed it was supposed to be a *mezuzah*, but it wasn't. It was just a vertical piece of metal on a chain. Obviously Scungile couldn't find a *mezuzah* or didn't know what a "Jew cross" was, so he simply broke off the horizontal bar from a crucifix. The armless Jesus on a piece of chrome now swung in front of Naomi's crotch as she twirled around the pole.

The first time I saw Naomi Rothstein was during my early years at the Academy when she was two and a half years old. It was also on a Shabbat. She had decided to climb onto the table in the foyer of the Academy Synagogue to sit atop a pile of prayer shawls. It was heart rending to watch Professor Rothstein plead with his precious child to climb off the *talitot* so the students could each don one and begin the prayer service. Little Naomi adamantly shook her red curls and wouldn't budge. None of the students said a word. We just stood silently and watched as our beloved teacher patiently tried to convince the pride of his life who had obviously learned to say "no", to move. Now, after all these years, I am convinced that had he picked her up by the seat of her pants and given her a good swat, she might not be stripping in Harlem on Shabbat eve twenty years later.

It was hard to watch the drooling row of lusty men depositing dollar bills in her G-string. I couldn't help but believe that her soul was in torment as she straddled the pole and gyrated lasciviously on the Holy Sabbath, naked except for her thong, her wig and her "Jew cross". As I watched her gracefully glide across the stage, I wondered if Professor Rothstein had any idea to what extent his "sweet, pure Naomi" had debased herself.

Why? Why was she doing this? Why would she purposely defile her God-given beauty for the pleasure of lonely men whose only sexual outlet was gawking anonymously at women pretending to perform lusty erotic rituals? I found nothing lusty *or* erotic in her "dance". To the contrary, I was getting dizzy and sick to my stomach.

As I turned away, I found myself staring at the oversized speakers. The reverberation was powerful enough to bring down the walls of Jericho. A strange arrangement of a popular Righteous Brothers song blasted into my face. "You've lost that lovin' feeling, *oi vey*, that lovin' feeling. You've lost that lovin' feeling, now it's gone, gone, gone, *oi, vey, vey, oi, oi, oi, oi...*"

"*oi, vey, vey, oi, oi, oi, oi...*"??? Where did that come from? I listened closely to the refrain again...and again. This is obviously a cosmic message. "The Righteous Brothers" singing *"oi, vey, vey, oi, oi, oi, oi."* But...what does it mean?

The *oi vey* refrain mysteriously ended when Naomi came out front, wearing jeans and a sweater, her backpack slung over her shoulder, still made up but without the wig.

"I'm out of here," she said, barely slowing down as she passed my table.

"Where are you going?" I asked.

"My next gig."

Strippers apparently rotated to different clubs, owned by the same "group".

Running after her down Lennox Avenue, I had to try again.

"Listen," I said as we walked briskly past the dealers and addicts. "Your perception of your father..."

"My *perception*? You sound like the telephone company telling me, after *they've* screwed up my phone lines, that they're sorry *I'm* unhappy. You want to know my *perception* of your beloved Rabbi who lives to perform *mitzvot* and bolster other people's self esteem?"

She unleashed a torrent of invective about what it was like to grow up without a mother (hers died in childbirth) the daughter of a man recognized by the great and the near-great as a genius with the temperament of a saint and the following of a rock star.

"He took up all the oxygen. I couldn't breathe. Oh, he made all the right moves to show how much he valued my "considerable gifts". He liked to pretend people came to the house to see me instead of him and he humiliated me by making me tell stupid stories about some inane thing that happened in school. He forced our guests - world leaders, artists, scholars - to acknowledge that my banal exploits as a girl scout were as significant as their monumental achievements. I remember when a whole flock of celebrities, including Jesse Jackson and Barbra Streisand came to our apartment. My father asked everyone for their unqualified attention so that he could make a spectacular announcement. His unbelievably talented daughter had made the soccer team. Everyone looked at me as though I were a monkey who had learned to pull a lever. Can you imagine what was going on inside me? Sure, my father has boundless compassion for some derelict on the street he'll never see again, but how is it that he never gave any thought to understanding ME?"

She was building up a head of steam. "He framed my first grade finger-paint scrawls and placed them between his Chagalls and Matisses."

It occurred to me that Naomi was actually happy to have someone to dump on. Judging from her apartment, I guessed she didn't have many visitors and with her hostile attitude, probably not many friends.

"My school chums thought it was so glamorous to be Professor Rothstein's daughter, but it wasn't, it was thoroughly wretched. If I could have figured out a way to kill him, I would have. Tell my father that."

I had to stop her. The assault on the most important person in my adult life made me physically nauseous.

"What do *you* know?" She was frothing at the mouth. "You probably grew up with nobodies. How could you possibly understand what it was like to constantly be in the middle of a celebrity bubble? People paid my father a fortune for a lecture they had heard dozens of times. Everything he said was directly from his books. Anyone could have read them but they paid him all that money just to hear that weird Polish accent! Can you believe it? Everywhere we went there were red carpets and limousines. I longed for anonymity, but no matter where I went I was in the limelight; not a person in my own right but the daughter of the messiah. Can't you see how that cripples a child? Where could I go from there?"

I wanted to tell her I had met children in Israel who had survived school-bus bombings and massacres. In several of my congregations, I was involved in out-reach programs where I met kids who were born into drug addicted families and some into no families at all. I spent years following the progress of many of these deprived children into adulthood and I never saw any of the genuinely crippled moan or bitch nearly as much as this girl who grew up in luxury and appeared to be in perfect health.

Her tirade became hopelessly tiresome as she venomously recounted one grievance after another.

"How could I not be totally screwed up growing up with a father like that?"

Finally, I had heard enough. I told her she sounded like spokespeople for Hamas blaming their suicide bombings of innocents in restaurants and Synagogues on the Jews. "If they didn't exist, the Arabs wouldn't have to send freedom fighters out to murder them."

"Don't get me started on the Israelis. They're a country full of egomaniacal sadists, exactly like my father..." She stopped only because we had arrived at the door of her next "gig."

She looked at me contemptuously. "I'd like to throw a small dose of reality your way, Rabbi *Shmuckhead*. My father is no fool, but you are. He is perfectly aware of what he did to me so he sends a *shnook* like you to make nice, like nothing ever happened. You know nothing about anything but you think you can heal all wounds with your *shnookiness*. You are pathetic beyond words. You want a message from me to my father? Okay, I want you to tell him tell him you saw me strip. For ten bucks he can come and watch too, same as any other drooling loser, and if he wants to stuff some bills in my G-string, he can kiss my ass. As for you, Rabbi Ben-whatever-the-hell-your-last-name-is, you can go f.... yourself!"

I suddenly felt faint. I was on overload and this was too much to process. I just stood there as her anger filtered down into my consciousness. "Go f.... myself?" No one had ever said that to me before. I don't know what came over me as I stood there looking at her young face puckered with rage, but I began to laugh. Go f.... myself? If you're not a hermaphrodite, how does one do that? And if you are, that's not much of a taunt. I couldn't stop laughing.

"That was not meant to be amusing," she said.

I could not stop laughing! This was my greatest release in over a year.

She looked at me strangely, unable to decide if I was crazy or just stupid.

"What's so funny?"

My laughter vanished as suddenly as it appeared. "I still don't understand why you do this," I said, trying to return to my mission. "You can't possibly enjoy it."

"God, you are dense beyond belief. Why do I strip in sleazy bars in front of horrible, disgusting men? Why? Why the hell do you think?" She slung her backpack full of G-strings, platform shoes, wigs and unspeakables over her shoulder and walked toward the entrance to the *All Nude, All Girls, All Live, All the Time EXCLUSIVE CLUB.*

Before she went in, she said "You really did believe you could sweet-talk me into forgiving my father, didn't you?" She shook her head. "Either you think I'm very shallow or you're irresistible. Wrong on both counts, Rabbi."

"I'm wrong on one count," I said. "I am eminently resistible, I agree, *but* you are unbelievably shallow."

The door slammed behind her as she marched defiantly into yet another pit of depravity.

I stood in front of the flashing *All Nude, All Girls, All Live* for several minutes, trying to figure out what to do next. I walked back and forth down the block. If this was indeed part of some cosmic plan, it was clear that I wasn't following it very well.

Try again, I told myself. I went back to the club, opened the door and went in.

The entrance way was dark except for intermittent flashes of light in the distance. The cacophonous sounds from inside were deafening. At the end of the corridor, a humorless, muscular black man sat on a high stool. Silhouetted by the swirling lights from the interior of the club, he looked like a psychedelic Mr. Clean.

"Ten dollars," he said.

I had never seen such a blank stare. His eyes weren't connected to anything. A robot or serial killer, I thought.

I knew it might be difficult to explain the circumstances that brought me here, but I tried.

"I don't carry money on the Sabbath," I stuttered. "...I'm a Rabbi and I'm here because I'm a friend of Naomi...that is, Miss Tel Aviv...well, not a friend, exactly..."

"No money? What's wrong with you? You think this is the Salvation Army?" His blank eyes flared and his lip snarled as he pointed to the door.

For a brief nanosecond, I thought of continuing to explain my situation, but instinctively I knew that wasn't a healthy idea, so I left without a word.

I stood outside for several minutes wondering how to get past Mr. Clean when I remembered that Naomi and I had left the first club through a side door. I went down an alley to look for another entrance. In the distance, I saw two hunched figures holding a cigarette lighter under a spoon. I knew I shouldn't be there and I turned to leave, but blocking my path was Mr. Clean. He waited until I sheepishly approached him then he grabbed me by my neck and the seat of my pants and flung me out of the alley. I scrambled to my feet but he was right there to pick me up again. This time he carried me for half a block before he threw me for another ten or fifteen yards. My nightmare was becoming a reality. I was literally being flung into space. I felt heady and totally disoriented. I began to run. I ran and ran, fighting the forces pulling me upward.

Light-headed and out of breath, I stopped to rest at a corner. I looked for street signs to see where I was but the few that weren't broken were entirely covered with graffiti. All I knew was that I was somewhere in Harlem, the sun had set and the Sabbath had descended.

Rabbi Zelig in night town.

Cars and trucks didn't seem to pay much attention to stoplights or pedestrians. I crossed a busy thoroughfare and suddenly felt a violent shock down my back. Everything went dark. Moments later when my eyes opened, I realized I was lying in the middle of a busy cross-section with cars whizzing by on all sides. The Taxi that hit me from behind stopped momentarily. The driver, a man with a cap and a large cigar, stuck his head out the window and called out.

"Watch where you're goin', jerko." He revved his engine and drove off.

Flickering lights from the clubs, restaurants and theaters triggered violent contrasting flashes in my brain. My eyes twitched nervously. The world around me was fading in, fading out, fading in and fading out. I dragged myself to the other side of the street. My legs felt wobbly and I hurt everywhere. "Jerko?" I thought of the name the cab driver had called me. I hadn't heard that word since high school. Who talks like that anymore?

I walked aimlessly, trying to get my bearings. I noticed the tears in my trousers where my knees scraped the pavement and I felt like a poor relative compared to the exquisitely dressed men and women promenading on the main drag. I don't know if I was the only White person on the street, but it felt like it.

I was exhausted and I needed to find a place to rest. Near Columbus Avenue I saw a sign that read, "JOB, a special production of The Theater of Revelation. Admission, free."

Theater of Revelation

The only available seat was on the aisle in the last row. The stage was elevated and a canopied podium stood off to the side. When the house lights dimmed, a tall handsome Black man in clerical robes approached the podium and declaimed in a deep, resonant voice.

"There was a man in the land of Uz named Job. His faith in his God was unshakable and he was mightily blessed."

As he spoke, the lights came up to reveal a highly stylized contemporary setting. There was the hint of an upscale suburban house, a hospital room, a golf course and an elegantly appointed office. A man wearing a black turtleneck sweater and a *yarmulka* leapt onto the stage. He was a powerful dancer and his jumps and twirls were sublime.

"Job served his people with dedication. He tended the sick and dying and inspired them to put their trust in the Lord."

The small stage was soon filled with dancers of all ages, all African-Americans and in a variety of costumes. The choreography was innovative and dazzling. Each dancer played a distinct character, some afflicted with illness and clearly troubled, some limped, while others lurked dejectedly in the shadows. The lead dancer wove through the entire entourage, lifting every one of them into the air. As they landed, they were transformed by the encounter. From crouching invalids, they turned into a robust chorus of joyous, exuberant dancers.

"Job attended to the needs of the poor and the afflicted, feeding the hungry and clothing the naked. He restored the spirit of the desolate and the heart-broken and every act bore witness to his reverence for the living God."

I knew the story of Job and I saw what was coming. But what's with the *yarmulka* and black turtleneck?

"Then Satan revealed his plan," the preacher intoned. "Standing before God, the Prince of the Netherworld threw down the gauntlet. 'Take away the blessings You have lavished upon your servant Job and he will reject You. His precious *faith* will become a millstone around his neck and he will cast it upon the dung heap. He will perform abominations and curse You to Your very face!' Satan hissed."

Suddenly the stage began to shake. The front risers collapsed on cue and the players slid down to the pit below. Only Job was left, stunned and hobbling aimlessly among the ruins.

"And so, God tested Job..." the light on the preacher faded out.

The shaking became more violent and the actor was buffeted from side to side by falling debris. He fell to his knees, looked heavenward, spread his hands in a desperate quest to understand what was happening and screamed as the lights dimmed.

"What happened to my life? Where is my God? Why am I bereft and alone? Why?"

I don't know what made me say it, but the words rolled out of my mouth. *"There is no justice... "*

Out of the darkness, another preacher appeared, this time in the center of the stage. Reading from the Book of Job in Hebrew, he thundered *"Ezor na ca-gever halatze-cha..."* Then, he closed his Bible and pointed directly at me. With fire in his eyes, he said in a deep bass voice that ricocheted off the walls:

"You puny little twerp," he said. *"Ezor na ca-gever halatze-cha,"* then translated: "Get yourself together, man, you're losing it!" His hypnotic gaze was fixed on me. "No justice!' Who the hell are you to question My judgment? Where were you when I created the heavens and the earth? What do you understand about the succession of seasons, let alone the cycles of life? Let's not kid Ourselves. The reason you threaten to abandon Me is because your brother's measure of days wasn't what you expected. Well, where do *you* get off expecting? What if I had called him to Me as an infant or never allowed him to be conceived? How little have you learned since I called you to my service? Don't you know that I drew you out of the womb to guide and enlighten my people? Is this how you repay Me, by turning off *your* lights? Where do you get the *chutzpah* to deny Me your faith? That's the one tiny thing I ask of you in exchange for every blessing I've bestowed. And you, you stingy bastard, you won't even give Me that?" The Preacher's eyes were glazed as he channeled. "So now you're stumbling in darkness and whining that your soul is in torment. What did you expect, jerko?"

Why did he call me that name?

"You think I'm going to edit My entire celestial software program to save your ungrateful ass? Fagetaboutit."

Fade out, fade in.

I ran out of the theater in a cold sweat. I don't know exactly what a concussion feels like, but I think I was having one.

My head was a complete jumble when I stopped for a light at the corner. The light changed three or four times and I still wasn't sure whether or not I should cross. The lady behind me made the decision for me. She pushed me as though I were a shopping cart.

"Make up your mind, jerko. Don't go blocking the whole street."

"Jerko?" Am I wearing a sign? How does everybody know me?

"Please help me, ma'am," I said. "I'm lost."

"Tell me somethin' I *don't* know," she said as she crossed the street without looking at me. "Check out the sign, fool."

Fade out, fade in, fade out, fade in.

Something drew my eye to a one-way arrow, the only street sign still standing. A word had been scrawled over it with spray paint. It was a Hebrew word and I strained to read it.

The arrow read *Emunah*, meaning faith.

As I followed the sign, my mind raced from

Rabbi Rothstein to Naomi, then to my brother Art, then to Job. I must have been talking to myself because an old Black man with a white beard, wearing a square black *yarmulka*, stopped in front of me.

"Did I hear you say Rabbi Rothstein? Would that be Rabbi Jacob Rothstein?"

"Yes, yes," I said. Who the hell are you, I wanted to say, and why is everybody in Harlem suddenly wearing *yarmulkas*?

"He's my Rabbi," I said. "Do you know him?"

"Of course I know him. He's my Rabbi, too," the old man smiled, extending his hand. "I'm Brother Clarence, Sexton of B'Nai Sheba."

I shook his hand. "Zelig's my name. Ben Zelig."

"*Shalom aleiychem a Yid*," he said in a thickly accented Polish Yiddish. "You and me must be *Landsmen*," he chuckled. Then, he looked at me for a long moment and his expression changed. "You are Jewish, right?"

"I'm a Rabbi!" I said, pleading for recognition.

"Really?"

"You look surprised. Why is that?"

"I don't know...you just don't have that...Rabbi look."

The cosmic noose was tightening. Is that the message? Am I no longer worthy of that title, now that I've lost my faith? "What should a Rabbi look like?" I had to know.

"Hard to say, you either have it or you don't."

What does that mean, that I had it once, but I don't anymore? Or, did I never have it?

Sensing my distress, he said "Pay no attention to me." He adjusted his hearing aid and said "I just talk sometimes to see if I can still hear." He asked if I was planning to attend *Shabbes* services (Polish pronunciation) at Rabbi Rothstein's *Sheel* (yet another Polish-Yiddishism!)

I didn't know what to ask first. Why do you speak Yiddish with a Polish accent? How do you come to speak Yiddish at all? Why is there a street sign in Hebrew in Harlem? Why would Professor Jacob Rothstein want to take on the burdens of serving a congregation anywhere, but especially in this neighborhood? And more than anything, what don't I have and why don't I have "it"?

I couldn't summon the courage to ask anything. Instead, I said in Hebrew. "Lead and I shall follow."

He didn't understand so I repeated it in Yiddish. That, he understood.

"Your Yiddish has a strong Haitian flavor," He said. "Is that where you're from?"

"No. I'm from Ohio."

"That must be it."

Since *he* asked, why couldn't I? "Where are you from?"

"I was born right here in Harlem but I learned my Yiddish from Rabbi Rothstein. We all did. He's quite a linguist, you know. He speaks fluent Hebrew and Polish, translated Shakespeare into German and Italian, but Yiddish is his *mama lushon* (mother tongue). His great-great-great grandfather was Moses Rothstein, the greatest commentator on the Bible since the first Moses. Amazing man, our Rabbi." He looked at his watch. "Come along. You're going to love the service and I guarantee you, Rabbi Rothstein's sermon will be one of the great experiences of your life."

He put his arm in mine and I tried my best to keep up, but my legs were still wobbly as we walked through the gaudily lit streets of Harlem.

Fade out, fade in.

Along the way I stopped several times to rest. I asked a few more questions. He answered none of them. I couldn't imagine for the life of me how Professor Jacob Rothstein came to be the Rabbi of a Black Synagogue in Harlem.

"Please try to keep up," was all he said.

Temple B'Nai Sheba

Temple B'Nai Sheba on the corner of one hundred and Twenty-Fifth Street and Lennox Avenue was one of the oldest Synagogues in New York. The carved stones were transported from quarries in the hills surrounding Jerusalem. The glass enclosed roster on the large oak door read "Senior Rabbi, Doctor Jacob Rothstein." The second line read "Sexton, Brother Clarence."

The interior of B'nai Sheba was huge and cavernous. A dome-shaped ceiling hovered over a packed room. An ornate Ark was covered with a royal blue velvet drape that featured a purple and gold Star of David. There must have been a thousand people in attendance, all of them Black and ranging in age from youngsters who ran up and down the aisles to young marrieds, middle-aged couples and seniors. Several young men wore baggy green, yellow and black woolen caps that looked like they might be harboring large manes of dreadlocks. The men wore traditional prayer shawls and *yarmulkas*. Women of all ages were resplendent in their best *Shabbes* attire. Brother Clarence offered me a *talit* and *yarmulka* when we entered the Sanctuary. Although it was not my practice to wear a prayer shawl for evening services, I didn't want to stand out anymore than I already did. On the right side of the Ark was an empty throne-like chair topped with a wooden carving of the Lion of Judah. I presumed that was the seat of honor reserved for the Rabbi. A choir composed of men in royal blue satin robes and women in purple, all with matching *yarmulkas*, flanked the Ark.

Brother Clarence made room for me in the first row among several fashionably dressed attractive young people who smiled and bade me "A *Geeten Shabbes*". Again with the Polish accent! The choir had just begun to sing a rousing rendition of *Adon Olam* I had never heard before. The music was a combination of gospel, Negro spiritual and Hasidic melodies, but the lyrics were Yiddish instead of the traditional Hebrew. The choir was composed of a superb blend of voices and every one of them was clearly moved by the *The Spirit* as they sang and clapped their hands. After a few bars, the entire congregation got up and joined in, clapping and swaying from side to side. The joy on their faces was contagious and I began to feel their enthusiasm as I sang along. I had never heard the Yiddish lyrics before, but they were excellent and moving.

After a long rendition of *Adon Olam*, the Congregation remained standing and the choir segued into a slow, melodic Hasidic chant. Instead of words, they sang *"bim-ba-da-bim-bam"* softly and turned to the main door at the rear as the Rabbi entered, greeting his flock as he walked slowly toward the pulpit. It was difficult to see him from afar, but when he finally arrived at my row, he extended his hand to me. I was shocked to discover that the Rabbi, an elderly man in a purple and gold robe and matching *yarmulka*, bore an amazing resemblance to Professor Rothstein, except for one thing. He was Black. The same bags under familiar soulful eyes, the same curly white hair sticking up around the *Yarmulka*, even the same pained, but dignified gait.

So there are two Rabbi Rothsteins! One White and one Black.

"A *geeten Shabbes*" he said in a thickly accented Polish-Yiddish.

"A *guten Shabbos*," I said, betraying my family's Russian background. I was utterly fascinated by my discovery and I had to ask. "Is it true that you were born in Poland?"

"Yes, indeed," he said, "and many, many generations of my family before me." He smiled broadly. "Many, *many* generations."

"Your accent is very familiar," I said. His accent was exactly the same as Rabbi Rothstein's. *My* Rabbi Rothstein, that is. "Where in Poland are you from?"

"A small village not far from Cracow. Smoloviczi, to be precise. Are you familiar with the history of the Jews in Poland?"

Obviously not, I said to myself. I have three advanced degrees in Hebraic studies. I had read of Jewish communities in every corner of the globe, including all of Europe, Asia, Africa, the Indian Peninsula, Marranos in Central and South America who fled the Inquisition and even traces of the lost tribe of Manasseh in the Far East, but Black Jews in Poland? How did I miss that?

I finally realized that I had not responded to his question. "Not familiar enough, I'm afraid." I couldn't help but blurt out, "Have Black Jews lived in Poland very long?"

"Since the early middle ages. Jews have strong roots there, you know. The Vikings came and went, as did the Russians, the Germans, the French and even the Turks, but our people remained; essentially because we had nowhere else to go. Not until America opened its golden doors, that is. Ah, America," he said, "and now...Israel!" He glowed as he said *"Am Yisroel Chai!"*

I couldn't take my eyes off him. His speech had the exact cadence, and his face, the same radiant smile as *my* Rabbi Rothstein. I had to ask.

"Are you aware that there is another Doctor Jacob Rothstein?"

His eyes twinkled. "Of course, who isn't? Fine man, great scholar, a gift to our people."

"Are you...are you, related?"

"Kol Yisroel arey-vin zeh ba-zeh," He responded in Polish accented Hebrew. "The same blood courses through our veins," he said. "Brother Clarence told me you were a Rabbi. Do you have a congregation?"

"Temple Har Zion in Los Angeles."

"Oh? I heard that pulpit was vacant."

What does he know? I was desperate to find out.

248

"I thought I read in the Rabbinic newsletter that they were looking for a replacement." Seeing the panic on my face, he quickly changed course. "I must be mistaken," he said, "but if you are looking for a change, I'm thinking seriously about retiring."

As he moved on, he smiled and said "a *geeten shabbes* to you once again and welcome to B'Nai Sheba."

I was completely thrown by all that was happening. What was *my* place in this congregation of Black Jews who spoke Yiddish? When I entered, I was a complete stranger, but as I looked around at the worshippers swaying and singing as my people have done for centuries, I began to feel like a member of the family.

After a few moments, the congregation settled back and Rabbi Rothstein rose to the podium. He smiled warmly and nodded to his flock. "A *geeten Shabbes*," he said.

A thousand voices thundered like a celestial chorus "A *geeten Shabbes, Rebbe.*"

The congregation sat down and total silence filled the huge sanctuary.

Slowly, the Rabbi put on his reading glasses, opened his Bible and declaimed.

"In the thirteenth month of our exile, the hand of the Lord was upon Ezekiel, the son of Buzi and he said unto him..."

To my astonishment, his Polish accent was gone and he sounded like John Gielgud.

"Son of man, look heavenward and see the vision I have revealed unto you."

He removed his glasses, shook his head, then walked across the pulpit and stopped several times to look at the ceiling. He turned to the assembled and said, "Ezekiel looked, but saw naught. Now, Ezekiel was sorely troubled. The Lord told him He had just revealed a vision, but the prophet doesn't see a thing. Sheepishly, Ezekiel asks '...what vision is that, Lord?'

'The one I'm revealing to you right now!"

The Rabbi became animated and his demeanor changed again. He was now a fire-breathing Evangelical, possessed of *The Spirit*. "What's wrong with you, son of man? It's plain as day!"

His stylized movements and charismatic presentation gripped me like no other preacher I had ever heard. Gone was the Anglo-Saxon deference, no more smiling Hasid, the Rabbinical veneer faded and the thunderous voice of an Old Testament prophet rang out.

"Ezekiel cried out. 'Help me Lord, HELP ME, for I see naught."

The Rabbi looked out at the congregation. "What's up with the man? The Lord reveals a vision and his servant Ezekiel can't see it? What's the problem? Doesn't God know how to transmit a clear image?"

"Yes he do!" The response was unanimous.

"So why couldn't the man see what God was showing him? He's a prophet, isn't he?"

"That's right! The impassioned response was unanimous.

The Rabbi walked across the pulpit, smiling to himself. "It's really simple, if you think about it. You know, you can have the finest TV set money can buy."

The sermon became contra-puntal as the congregation got into the Rabbi's rhythm.

"It can be top of the line, ah," his voice developed a deep tremolo.

"HDTV, ah..."

"... I know...I got one..."

"...surround-sound, 3-D..." the words rolled out of him. Then, he paused and studied his flock for a long moment.

The prophecy was now at hand.

"But...I say, but..." Rabbi Rothstein's eyes twinkled. "I say but...if your set isn't plugged in, you won't see nothin'."

The enthusiasm was intoxicating.

"The problem wasn't with the Lord. He was transmitting just fine. Ezekiel was the problem. His faith wasn't plugged in and that's why he didn't see anything."

The faithful burst into applause. The Rabbi paused until the congregation fell silent. "So, Ezekiel reached deep into his heart of hearts, then into his soul of souls until he found the right chord, the one called *Emunah* (faith). He took the initiative, he made the plunge, he leapt the leap of faith and plugged his soul into the living God and behold...the heavens opened up and *all* God's glory was revealed to him in *all* its splendor."

"Praise God," the congregation was right there.

Rabbi Rothstein smiled. "Now that's what I call good reception!"

They applauded.

The Rabbi looked from the congregation to the dome-ceiling. He studied it for several moments, then said "...now, Ezekiel was connected. As soon as he was tuned in, he looked up and what did the man see? He saw a wheel!"

"That's right...that's what he saw. Hallelujah," the congregation chimed in.

"I say the man looked up and he *saw* a wheel a-turnin'. I'm not talkin' about a dream, here."

"Ain't no dream."

"Ezekiel looked up and *saw* a wheel a-turnin', way up in the middle of the air. This was no fantasy. It wasn't animation. It certainly wasn't a movie."

"It's for real!" Someone yelled loudly.

"That's right! Oops, wait a minute! There's somethin' in that wheel," he said, looking at the ceiling as though he were narrating an event taking place right there in front of all of us. "...it's a-turnin, I tell you...Good God, is that thing a-turnin'," he paused to get a closer look. "I see it now. There's a wheel *within* a wheel. That's it. A little wheel inside a big one."

"Praise God!"

"Now...the little wheel's run by faith, ah, and the big wheel, ah, the big wheel's run by the grace of GOD, ah!" He spoke as though the image he was watching was growing larger by the moment. He spread his arms as if to grab the wheel and pull it into his bosom.

The congregation was on their feet, singing. "Ezekiel saw the wheel, way up in the middle of the air, a wheel in a wheel, way in the middle of the air."

Rabbi Rothstein took the solo. "The little wheel's run by faith and the big wheel's run by the grace of God..."

After an ecstatic rendition of the song, resung and resung I don't know how many times, the audience sat down amid "praise God,

Hallelujah and a few Polish-Yiddish *o-meyns*."

When the congregation settled, the Rabbi continued. "God is offering us the deal of a lifetime," he said with a sly smile. "It's the best investment you'll ever make. He will give you all the grace you can handle provided...ah provided, I say, you plug yourself in *and* contribute a little faith."

"O-meyn," the crowd was right with him.

"A dollar's worth of grace for a nickel's worth of faith. Nobody can beat that deal, I guarantee it. I say, a dollar's worth of grace for a nickel's worth of faith. Do I hear a witness?"

"I'M A WITNESS!" The spirit within me called out. I stood up and shouted with all my might. Soon I was joined by an ecstatic throng.

The Choir burst into a Yiddish rendition of a popular Gospel song.

"He walks with me and He talks with me *und er zogt mir ich bein zein alein*." Rabbi Rothstein swayed and danced across the pulpit with his arms raised, his face aglow.

Yes, indeed, I said to myself. God does walk with Rabbi Rothstein and He talks with him. No doubt about it! Watching his lustrous eyes and radiant face, I *knew* that *the light within him shineth*, yes that very fire of faith that I once had is now less than ten yards away from me.

I joined in. "Yes, He walks with me and He talks with me..." I sang out with all my heart. I closed my eyes and...I felt a distant echo of the rapture that was once mine.

When I opened my eyes, the Rabbi beckoned me to join him. I leapt up onto the pulpit, we clasped arms and danced and danced!

The movements came from some secret place in my soul and I felt my heart bursting open.

"He walks with me and He talks with me...*und er zogt mir ich bein zein alein.*" The heavy depression drained off me like so much sludge. The choir began to hum and I stood before the podium and said in a loud voice

"THE LIGHT WITHIN *ME* SHINETH!"

"Yes, it do," a thousand voices joyfully affirmed.

Deliverance

"He restoreth my soul," I repeated the Psalm over and over as I walked from Harlem to Morningside Heights, truly understanding it for the first time in my life. I had been granted life's greatest gift. My inner spark had been re-ignited and my faith was restored. Truly, God works in wondrous ways.

The gates of the Academy were locked. When I called for the watchman, he asked me to identify myself.

"You're Rabbi Zelig? There's an urgent message for you," he said.

I walked the ten blocks to St. Marks hospital as quickly as I could. The Resident on the floor explained that Professor Rothstein had been in the Intensive Care Unit, but was released to a private room when they discovered there was little they could do for him. He had an "event", which is to say, something like a stroke but they couldn't be sure. He fell in his office and lay unconscious for hours before the security guard found him. He had bled profusely and was desperately in need of a transfusion but there was a devastating complication.

Inside the small dark room, my Rabbi, Professor Rothstein, lay dying. As I approached, I saw Naomi on the floor beside his bed, holding his hand and sobbing uncontrollably. He was pale as a cadaver. Tubes and wires monitoring his vital signs ran from his nose, mouth and under the sheets, to beeping machines.

I stood behind Naomi for several minutes before she turned to look at me. Without her make-up and salacious wardrobe she looked like a frightened child. Her face was red and her eyes were swollen from crying.

"I killed him...I did this...it's all my fault. I killed the only one who ever loved me..." She tried to muffle her cries but there was too much emotion to be stifled.

I couldn't hold back my tears, either.

A nurse came in and asked us to wait in the hall while she performed a "procedure". A Doctor in a white smock followed her into the room. He introduced himself as Dr. Alan Scheins, a specialist in immunology and hematology.

"Hematology?" Naomi asked. "Does he have some kind of blood disorder?"

Dr. Schiens was a middle-aged man who looked much older. He had the demeanor of a research scientist who was more comfortable with microbes and microscopes than he was trying to explain complicated medical diagnoses to patients' relatives.

"Please wait outside. I'll be with you presently," he said in a tone that didn't sound encouraging.

In the corridor outside his room, Naomi rocked silently in my arms. When Doctor Scheins emerged, she ran to him. "Is he going to be alright?"

The look on his face gave the answer we didn't want to hear.

Naomi burst into tears.

Dr. Scheins explained why he was called in. Apparently, Professor Rothstein developed a rare blood disease that only appears in certain *Ashkenazi* (European Jewish) men. Aside from Dr. Scheins, scientists at the Weitzman Institute in Rehovot, Israel, are the only ones studying the strange affliction, but they're a long way from fully understanding it. The only thing that has emerged from their research is that the problem is related to a vestigial gene that became corrupted during the Black Plague that devastated much of Europe in the fourteenth century. Twenty five million people are said to have died from the deadly bacterium in the first five years of the plague. The best physicians of the time were Arabs and the Jews who lived among them in Spain and North Africa. Judah Ha-Levi, who introduced revolutionary cures and surgical methodology as the Sultan's personal physician, created courses in physiology and pathology to be taught in Rabbinical Academies throughout the Moslem world. When the plague struck in Europe, Rabbi-Physicians from the East sent epistles to the far-flung communities of the Jewish Diaspora detailing the methods they had discovered to ward off the deadly contagion. They gave precise instructions on how to concoct a potion that would make them immune to the disease.

It worked amazingly well. So well, in fact, that the relative health of the Jews convinced the Christians that the plague was a creation of the Hebrew nation, and they inaugurated a wave of bloody pogroms that resulted in the deaths of tens of thousands of Jews.

"Rabbi Rothstein has the Plague?" I asked incredulously.

"No. I wish that were all we were dealing with here," the Doctor said. "We can treat that easily today with streptomycin. The problem is that the powerful medication created by the Rabbi-Physicians of the time involved the alteration of the gene that made one susceptible to the plague. A lingering side-effect is an enzyme released by the corrupted gene that creates anti-bodies in the blood. Over the years, that enzyme became recessive so it's extremely rare to find it manifest so long after it was first introduced, but your people..." he looked around "*our* people...have carried that recessive gene in the collective pool for the past six centuries. Unfortunately, Rabbi Rothstein inherited a dominant strain of that corrupted gene and that's why he's dying. Not from the residual effects of the plague, but from a severe loss of blood related to his fall."

"All he needs is a simple transfusion?" Naomi and I asked, almost in unison.

"A transfusion, yes. Simple, no. The anti-bodies created by the corrupted gene are called anti-krell anti-bodies and they're very potent. Their function is to prevent unfamiliar cells from entering the blood stream. The upside is that Rabbi Rothstein has a powerful immune system. Unfortunately, the downside is that these anti-bodies are equally vigilant in preventing infusions except from a *precisely* matching source. In other words, the only transfusion his system can accept would have to come from a donor with not only the appropriate blood type and cellular structure, but also a history and constellation of matching anti-bodies. Anything short of that would cause his system to convulse and shut down."

Naomi was hysterical. "Give him my blood, for God's sake. Please don't let my daddy die!"

"If we could, we would, but for whatever reason, that gene appears only in males, which by definition renders you unsuitable. We need an XY marker... a male donor of Jewish descent, who comes from the exact area of Eastern Europe he came from and whose ancestors date back to the fourteenth century making them literally extended family. Unfortunately..." he looked at Naomi. "...from what I understand, his entire family perished in the Holocaust."

Naomi nodded.

Dr. Scheins' eyes rendered the verdict.

"But there's got to be someone, somewhere with a matching set of genes and...anti-bodies...and whatever. With all your sophisticated data banks and satellite hook-ups, can't you...?" I said, wishing...wishing I knew what to say, what to do...wishing I had listened to my mother and studied medicine.

"We're trying, but it's very complicated and we don't have months and probably, not even...days."

"No!" Naomi cried.

"I'm sorry, but short of a miracle, the prognosis is not very good at all. I'm afraid you'll have to prepare for the worst."

Dr. Scheins dictated into a pocket recorder as he walked down the long antiseptic corridor.

"Naomi...?" I wasn't sure what I was asking...or why. I could barely see her eyes, they were awash in tears.

"Where did your father come from?"

"A small village near Cracow nobody ever heard of."

"Smoloviczi?"

Harlem was asleep. The boisterous crowds that had filled the streets the night before were gone. I sat on the cold stone steps and stared at the locked doors of Temple B'Nai Sheba.

I must have sat there for quite a long time because I dozed off. A bright light woke me and I looked up to see the sun rising. Watching the sky, I beheld the most amazing sight. The sun appeared to be turning, like a...wheel. My eyes burned but I couldn't stop gazing at the sun.

"The little wheel's run by faith and the big wheel's run by the grace of God," someone said.

When my eyes adjusted to the light, I recognized the handsome face of Rabbi Rothstein – the Temple B'Nai Sheba Rabbi Rothstein – standing in front of me, wearing a beautifully embroidered *yarmulka*. He smiled and extended his hand. I stood up quickly and took his hand.

"Why have you have come back?" He asked.

I looked into his eyes and for a moment, I wasn't sure which Rabbi Rothstein I was looking at.

"Because I need...I need a dollar's worth of grace."

Several hours later, I sat in the hospital waiting room holding Naomi's hand as Doctor Scheins came towards us. Naomi jumped to her feet. The Doctor was silent for a long, agonizing moment, then he said "it's a miracle!"

Naomi practically fainted. "He's alright? He's going to live?"

"The transfusion took?" I asked. Seeing the look on his face, the words of the Psalmist flooded my brain. *"Ka-vey el Adonai..."* I said to myself. "Be not afraid to trust in the Lord..."

"So far, it appears to have worked. His vital signs are improving rapidly. We're not entirely out of the woods yet, but I'd say his chances of pulling through are pretty good."

"Oh, thank God," Naomi said, throwing her arms around the Doctor, who seemed pleased but a little uncomfortable with Naomi's spontaneous intimacy.

"Thank God, indeed," I said.

Naomi hugged me and thanked me repeatedly, tears streaming down her cheeks. She turned to the Doctor. "Can I see him?"

"He's resting in his room. You can go in but tone it down. He needs to preserve every drop of energy."

She wiped away her tears and left quickly.

"What do you mean we're not out of the woods yet?" I asked.

"So far, we've only – you've only - found one donor. At most, he can provide two transfusions in a seven day period. Depending upon how quickly Rabbi Rothstein's blood – that is, Rabbi Rothstein, the patient – can replenish itself, he may not require more than that. If he does, that's going to be a tremendous burden on Rabbi Rothstein, the donor."

The cosmic plan was now completely revealed. I couldn't restrain my joy.

"You seem very sanguine," The Doctor said. "Do you know something I don't?"

How could I explain it?

We watched from the door as Naomi entered her father' s room.

Rabbi Rothstein sat up in bed, without tubes or monitoring devices. "Naomi, Naomi, light of my life," he cried and extended his arms.

"Papa, papa, papa" was all she could say. She ran to him and they embraced, weeping for joy.

"Where is Rabbi Rothstein?" I asked. "The other Rabbi Rothstein, that is, the donor."

"He left shortly after the transfusion," Dr. Scheins said. "He apologized for leaving so abruptly, but he said he was late for his *Shabbos* morning service. Amazing stamina for a man his age. Oh, he did ask me to convey a message. He said congratulations, your investment paid off."

I couldn't help grinning.

"Got any tips?" The Doctor asked. "I'm in the market, myself."

"I've got the inside track. A dollar's worth of grace for a nickel's worth of faith. It works miracles."

GLOSSARY

**Loosely translated from the Yiddish
(not literal)**

a brocha auf dine keppele
   a blessing on your (little) head
adon olam
   a Sabbath hymn
alov ha-shalom
   may he rest in peace
aluv ha-shulum
   Galitzianer pronunciation of the
   Hebrew "May he rest in peace";
   the Galiatzianer accent is as annoying to a
   Jew as Cockney is to an Englishman.
am Yisroel chai
   Viva Israel! We're still here!
bakala
   (Italian) literally, dried cod fish; slang for
   sucker; stiff
baale-batim
   members of the congregation, usually the
   movers and shakers; sometimes laudatory,
   sometimes derogatory
ba-kacked
   crappy. Also, *far-kacked*
ba-sherte
   pre-ordained
bim-ba-da-bim-bam
   onomatopoeic non-words sung to hymns
bobkes
   absolute form of "nothing"
caniption
   unknown origin, meaning: to blow a
   gasket
chakra
   yoga: One of the body's centers of
   spiritual energy

challah
> egg twist bread; the centerpiece for
> Sabbath and Holiday meals

cheder
> primary Hebrew school (literally "room")

chutzpah
> outrageous nerve (Jewish variety)

dine mama challisht avek.
> Your mother is so sick!

dollele, Bennele... "ele"
> diminutive but affectionate suffix as in
> John-ele, Scott-ele or Christin-ele

doven
> the recitation of prescribed prayers

el maleh rachmim
> a prayer offered by a Rabbi or
> Cantor to honor the dead

emes
> truth, as in "the whole and nothing but"

emunah
> faith; belief

er zogt mir ich bein zein alien
> and He tells me I am His own

ezor na ca-gever halatze-cha
> gird your loins like a warrior (be a man!)

fargeneigen
> pleasure

far-kackteh
> see *ba-kacked.*

farshteys du noch nicht
> Literally: Can't you understand?
> Properly intoned: Why can't you get it
> through that thick head of yours?

galiztianer
>one who hails from Galicia (Poland or Russia, depending upon who was occupying it at the time)

ganovim
>thieves (plural); can refer to anyone who sells retail

guten Shabbos
>good Sabbath (to you) – Russian, Litvak, pronunciation

geeten Shabbos
>good Sabbath (to you) – Polish, Galiztianer (barbaric sounding to any other Jew.)

glatt traif
>un-kosher in the extreme

gottenyu
>my God! (usually uttered with a shriek)

goyim
>gentiles, non-Jews; or in the eyes of the orthodox, other Jews who are less observant

goyish or goyishe
>gentile-*like*; generally refers to activities Jews do not normally engage in, like hunting, Nascar racing or female boxing

halutzim
>first Pioneers to settle in the malaria infested marshes and barren desert that became Israel in 1948

ich farshtey dir nicht
>I don't understand you *or* you're not making any sense!

ich gay nicht mit-on dir.
>I won't go without you.

ich vais?
> what do I know? Usually accompanied by a shrug

ivreh
> the Hebrew learned from age six through thirteen; generally, not much

kabbala
> mystical lore

kaddish
> the prayer recited by mourners to honor the dead

kak
> (euphemistically) Dump

kibitz
> idle chatter; unsolicited advice

kichelach
> crispy, sugar-coated hollow cookies

kiddush
> the blessing over wine; also, a modest repast after a religious service

kishkes
> guts

kol Yisroel arey-vin zeh ba-zeh
> all Jews are related to one another

koogles, latkes
> European Jewish dishes: Puddings, casseroles, pancakes (potato or matza)

krasavitz
> (Russian) beautiful

kreplach
> dumplings; Jewish won-ton (without pork)

kum aheim, tay-ere
> come home, my dearest

kush mir in tochus
> kiss my ass

kvel
> the ineffable joy a mother experiences when her son is potty trained or becomes President of the United States

landsmen
> countryman; paesan

le-hav-dil
> Let there be a distinction between the living and dead, and may the curse of the latter not be visited upon the former

macher
> big shot

maricon
> Spanish slang – not flattering

mazel tov
> congratulations

mench
> an honorable person

meshugah
> crazy!

mezuzah
> a small parchment encased in metal or wood containing verses from the Bible; It is placed on the doorpost or worn by some Jews as a sign of their faith.

mikveh
> ritual bath, meant to purify the soul more than simply cleanse the body

minyan
> quorum of ten people required for public prayer

mitzvah
> a good deed; one of the many Jews are expected to fulfill daily

mitzvoth
> plural; generic; many or all good deeds

mudras
> an Indian form of dance emphasizing
> graceful hand gestures

nachas
> the joy that comes to a parent when a son
> becomes a doctor or a daughter marries
> one.

nafka
> a girl of easy virtue

neshoma
> soul

nisht du ge-dacht
> may it never happen here, generally
> followed by "poo-poo"

nu
> so...? (usually intoned)

nudnik
> a pain in the ass.

oy
> Trouble !

oi, oi, oi, oi...
> lots of troubles

oi, vey, vey
> You shouldn't know from my troubles!

oy, va-a-voy
> Why me?

omeyn
> Amen, so be it.

paesan
> (Italian) *landsman* or countryman

pink-farkert
> ass backwards

poo–poo

an onomatopoeic expression known for its efficacy in deflecting the evil eye; spitting permitted, but not required

punim

face, usually an unbearably adorable one

putz

non-clinical term for genitalia; *or,* one's worst enemy

rebbe

term for a particularly revered Rabbi; chief Rabbi

schvarzes

African Americans

shabbos

the Jewish Sabbath (the one that occurs on Saturday)

shalom aleiychem a Yid

Hi, ho! Welcome, co-religionist

shavuot

a major Jewish Holiday celebrating both the handing down of the Torah on Mt. Sinai and the first harvest, seven weeks after Passover

sheel

Synagogue (Galitzianer – read barbaric – pronunciation)

shep

glean

shiva

seven day mourning period

shmata

literally rag; shabby treatment; the clothing industry in general

shmekel
  penis – diminutive
shmutz
  filth
shmuck
  unknown origin, probably related to
  shmekel; idiot; cuckold
shnook
  simpleton
shnookiness
  actions of a shnook
shnorer
  beggar
shoah
  Holocaust
shofar
  ram's horn, sounded in Synagogues
  during the High Holidays
shtetle
  small Jewish village in the Pale of
  Settlement (Eastern Europe)
siddur
  prayer book
stronzo
  Italian – not nice word for fecal matter;
  also, a loathsome person
shul
  Synagogue (Russian – read civilized –
  pronunciation as opposed to **sheel**)
talit
  prayer shawl
talitot
  plural – more than one prayer shawl

tefillin.
> phylacteries

tegelach
> honey coated nut cookies

torah
> literally, the first five books of the Bible;
> also refers to the whole of Jewish law and
> lore, including the Bible and the Talmud

traif
> non-kosher food

tzores
> troubles

yarmulka
> skull cap, worn at all times by religious
> Jews and on religious occasions by most
> others

yeshiva
> Rabbinical Academy

yid
> Jew; an expression of contempt or pride,
> depending upon how it's used and who
> uses it

yiddishkeit
> general term for Jewish culture or the
> Jewish way of life

yortzeit
> anniversary of a death

Ordering Information

Rabbi, Have I Got a Girl for You!

Herb Freed

<u>call toll free</u> **1(800)247-6553**

see our website
www.atlasbooks.com
search: *atlasbooks-rabbi*

or

Google™

search: *rabbi have I got a girl for you*

Price: $14.95
Shipping: $3.50

For bulk orders, email us at
order@bookmasters.com

Meet the Author
readings, interviews, book signings, book fairs
contact: bellrockpress@aol.com